Under the Summer Sky

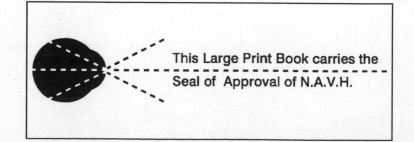

This Large Print Book carries the
Seal of Approval of N.A.V.H.

UNDER THE SUMMER SKY

LORI COPELAND

THORNDIKE PRESS
A part of Gale, Cengage Learning

GALE
CENGAGE Learning·

Detroit • New York • San Francisco • New Haven, Conn • Waterville, Maine • London

GALE
CENGAGE Learning®

LIBRARY OF CONGRESS CATALOGING-IN-PUBLICATION DATA

Copeland, Lori.
  Under the summer sky / by Lori Copeland.
    pages ; cm. — (Thorndike Press large print Christian romance) (The Dakota diaries series ; #2)
  ISBN-13: 978-1-4104-5468-3 (hardcover)
  ISBN-10: 1-4104-5468-1 (hardcover)
    1. North Dakota—History—19th century—Fiction. 2. Large type books.
  I. Title.
PS3553.O6336U53 2013
813'.54—dc23   2012047401

Published in 2013 by arrangement with Lori Copeland

To Ella Parker Copeland
The newest light of our lives

One

Near Piedmont, South Dakota, 1893
"Don't put me in that barrel!"

"Do you want to die, woman?"

"No! That's why you can't put me in the barrel — I can't swim!" She had gone to the river for a simple bucket of water when this beast had swept in and captured her. She loved the good Lord, but she wasn't ready to meet Him face-to-face. The sound of rushing water overwhelmed her senses as iron hands gripped her waist. War whoops filled the air as three riders poured over the hillside. She pounded the solid wall of flesh that enveloped her. "Let me *go!*"

"I'm trying to save your life, lady."

The stranger heaved her over to the barrel and unceremoniously dumped her inside, stuffing her head between her knees before he slammed the lid down on top.

"I can't swim!" Her muffled voice echoed in her ears. Was he deaf? Mad? What kind

of man would put a woman in a barrel and send her over the rapids when she couldn't swim? She banged on the wooden sides. "Let me out!"

All bedlam broke out, and even through the barrel Trinity could hear grunts, shouts, and the sound of bare fists meeting flesh. Her heart hammered in her chest. She willed herself to be still, but she could feel the barrel shifting underneath her, teetering at the water's edge. "Don't let me fall in, don't let me fall in," she whispered. A flour mill sat downstream, but if she reached it she would be too late. A few minutes in the turgid waters and she would drown.

Grunts. More fists.

Please, God. Please, God.

She swallowed back the urge to shout. Calling out would mean certain death. Her brother, Rob, had written tales of rebels, both Indian and white, banding together to plunder and commit unspeakable acts, but never in her wildest dreams would she have thought to encounter one of the lowlifes. A gunshot — then another. Trinity's heart crowded her throat as the fighting grew fiercer. The barrel shifted again.

Don't let me fall in. Don't let me fall in.

A deep rumble. A shove. Trinity's heart sputtered. She was close — too close. She

8

could almost smell the cold, rushing water. She heard the shuffle of men's boots — though now it sounded as though there were fewer of them. Maybe two? Against overwhelming odds, the stranger appeared to be winning.

Rapids rushed in the distance. *Relax. That beast of a man is strong.* He still faced formidable odds, but it sounded as if he were besting the enemy. Trinity felt the tension draining away from her. The ruckus would be over soon and he would release her from her wooden prison.

And then she would demand to know who he was and how he'd had the audacity to risk her life!

Locked in a duel, the men's groans filled the air as they strained against one another. The sheer force in their tones made her cringe. Then — the unthinkable. A boot caught the edge of the barrel and sent it toppling into the churning water.

Trinity screamed as the current caught the barrel and bounced it downstream. Terror-stricken, she watched the water seeping through the cracks in the wood. The rapids were only two hundred yards downstream — she had to be getting close.

She was going to die. Rob had perished far too young, and now she was going to join him. And it was all her fault. She should never have left her nice, safe café job in Sioux City and come to this rugged land. She had refused to accompany Rob a year earlier when he'd pleaded with her to join him and help him settle Wilson's Falls, the plot of land their family had owned for generations. She should have held to her belief that no good would come of her visiting this remote country for even a short time. No amount of money on earth could keep her safe now — not even the handsome sum the railroad was likely to offer for the family's parcel of land.

The trip was supposed to be brief. Never once had she thought her journey would end at the Pearly Gates.

Jones whirled when he heard the barrel hit the water. The man locked in his grip took advantage of the distraction and landed a blow that took Jones to his knees. He swung wildly, landing a punch that momentarily staggered his opponent.

His eyes swung back to the barrel. Only a few moments before it went over the rapids. The other thug came at him and he managed a hard right and then his signature left, the knock-out blow. His opponent slumped to the ground and Jones took off running down the bank. His boots thrashed through a heavy thicket as his eyes followed the bobbing container. When he reached a wide spot, he dove in and surfaced just within reach of the barrel.

"Hold on! I'm here!" he yelled.

The girl's reedy voice came back. "I can't swim! Get me out of here!"

"I'm trying!" He lunged, his hand brushing the barrel in vain. Charging again, he only managed to hurry the barrel along. It flew over the rapids and he heard her screams until the roar of rushing water snatched them away.

Shoot. She was going to be mad as a wet hen.

"Are you still there? I can't hear you!"

He couldn't imagine why not. She was yelling loud enough for them to hear her all the way to Canada.

"I'm *here*! Just hang on!"

"I can't swim!"

Like he hadn't heard her the first eight times. Closing his eyes, he dove under the swift current.

The thin wood split as the water and rocks smashed the barrel into kindling. Trinity gasped for air, her breath lodged in her throat. The wind and water whipped wildly

11

about her. Where *was* he?

Anger churned with panic as she bumped along. Objects blurred as she choked, struggling to right herself. She went down, down, down, thumping and bumping over rocks. This was it. This was the end. She'd never done anything worthwhile in her nineteen years. Nothing but wait tables and serve others — but that was good. To her knowledge she'd never caused anyone an ounce of trouble, so she could meet her Maker in good faith.

Now she would draw her last breath — gurgle it, more like — but . . . she broke the waterline, choking. A strong hand latched onto her hair as she went under again.

Pain blinded her — pain the likes of which she'd never experienced. Her very roots were being ripped out. She struggled to break the fierce hold, and did, momentarily, but then something snared her and yanked her back to the surface.

"Stop fighting me!" a male voice demanded.

She saw him then — the man who'd stuffed her in the barrel. At the moment it didn't matter what he'd stuffed her in; he was an anchor in the storm. Her efforts ceased. She wrapped her arms around his neck and held on tight.

12

He was a strong swimmer, but she was dead weight. Dragging her through the water, he reached a ledge and paused to catch his breath. Paralyzed with fear, her heart threatened to pound out of her chest, and for the first time in her life she couldn't find the words she wanted. His arms around her were powerful, and the feel of his prickly dark beard against her cheek brought a blush to her face. She'd never been this close to a man before — except Rob, of course. When she poured coffee at the café she bent close, but never this close. She could smell him, hear his ragged breath in her ear.

"Sorry I scared you," he said, swiping his face to clear the water out of his eyes. "I didn't mean for the barrel to go over."

She nodded, still not able to find her voice. She was in the middle of a rushing rapid, standing in the arms of a stranger, finding her brush with death very difficult to comprehend.

"Hold on." He hitched her up and swam the remaining distance to shore. Throwing her on the bank like a landed carp, he crawled out and collapsed beside her. For a moment they lay in the warm sun, gasping for breath. In a novel the moment might have been romantic, Trinity thought. Instead it was wet and cold and ghastly.

"Who are you?" she asked, finally finding her breath. Since she could speak she should probably thank him — it was only polite — though at the moment she wanted to throttle him for putting her life in danger in the first place.

"Doesn't matter. I'm just passing through."

"What's your name?" She had the right to know who'd almost killed her, didn't she?

"Jones."

"Jones what?"

"Just Jones." Rolling to his back, he stuck out his hand. "Are you all right?"

Trinity stared at the proffered hand, stultified. "Why did you stick me in that barrel?"

"I saved your life."

"You could easily have taken it. I don't . . ."

"Swim. So you've said." Struggling to his feet, he removed his left boot and dumped out a stream of water. "Sorry I upset you, but those men would have distressed you more."

Her gaze fixed on the tall stranger. She knew she should feel nothing but gratitude, but he'd scared the wadding out of her. "Well, before you stick a lady in a barrel and send her downstream, you might want

14

to make certain you can save her."

Jones dumped the water out of his right boot. "Don't figure there's any reason for me to apologize for saving your neck." He glanced up. "What are you doing out here alone, anyway?"

"I was doing my wash." She pushed to her feet and brushed the wet hair out of her eyes.

"You live around here?"

"Not live. I'm staying here for a while. I'm in the process of selling my land, and once I do I'm going back to Sioux Falls."

"Nice town."

"You've been there?"

He nodded, shoving his foot, wet sock and all, back into his boot. "Couple of times. Do you want me to walk you back to your place?"

"No, thank you." She'd had quite enough of him for one day.

Nodding, he set his Stetson on his head and adjusted the band. "You might want to keep a close eye out for the others. The men scattered, but they'll meet up again."

Trinity swallowed, trying to retain her composure. She'd get home, and then she wouldn't rest until she'd sold the land and left this godforsaken place behind her forever. "Thank you. I'll be careful."

15

"You think you can handle these wilds?"

She lifted her chin. "Of course I can handle myself." Granted, he had caught her in a bad circumstance, but chances were that the men were only passing through and she'd have no more trouble with them.

"Do you have a gun?"

"My brother left one."

"Do you know how to use it?"

The chin rose higher. "I do — if necessary."

He paused, a slow grin starting at the corners of his mouth. Dark curly hair, penetrating brown eyes, and skin browned by the long hours in the sun. He was handsome, no denying it, but Trinity had more important things on her mind. "I see you've got things well in hand."

She nodded coolly. He had every right to suspect that she was one of those helpless simpering females, but she was far from vulnerable. She'd been on her own since Rob had left to work this land, and she'd learned to care for herself nicely.

He started off and then turned back. "By the way . . ."

She pushed another lock of soggy hair out of her eyes. "Yes?"

His gaze drifted down. "You lost your skirt in the water."

16

Gasping, she looked down. She was wearing nothing but her bloomers! And he hadn't said a word until now.

When she looked up, he was gone. Drawing herself up straight, she sniffed. And a good riddance it was.

Two

Aghast, Trinity stood back and took stock of the smoking house. The front door hung on a single hinge, and even from this distance she could see that the place had been ransacked. Smoke poured from the open doorway. Embers glowed in the interior and the strong stench of kerosene suggested that flames had failed to ignite the interior of the two-story stone house. Rob's goats had managed to escape, but little else.

Disgruntled, she marched inside and stomped out two hot coals. Every stick of furniture was broken. The lamps had been overturned and shattered. She didn't care to explore the upstairs. Rob had closed off those rooms, but the thieves wouldn't have overlooked the bounty.

She wandered into her bedroom. The clothing was missing, and the mattress had been ripped to shreds. Not much left there. And the kitchen was worse — flour spilled all over the floor, a few broken cans, and the rest of the food gone — just gone.

Her bag! She'd left her money in her bag. Maybe, just maybe, the thieves had overlooked it? She hunted through the ruins of her home, finally locating it behind a parlor chair. Her heart sank as she picked it up. It had been turned inside-out. Empty.

She was homeless and she was broke.

And she had just informed that stranger that she was perfectly capable of taking care of herself! She almost burst out laughing. What a fool he must have taken her for. What a fool she was.

She plunked down on the floor and put her head in her hands. What now? She didn't know a soul here in Piedmont. She wracked her brain. This land was all she had — this land that had been settled by her great-great aunt Pauline in '32 and passed down through the family ever since. That much she had heard from stories that had sifted down over the years. The aunt had had a younger sister, Priss, who had disappeared when their mother died. Undoubtedly both she and Pauline had passed on — they would be well into their nineties now. A good thing, perhaps — they hadn't lived to see Rob gone, the homestead gone, the money gone, gone, gone. Trinity lifted her eyes and whispered the only prayer she could muster. "Show me what to do."

Her answer was a soft whippoorwill's call that sounded as bereft as she felt.

She couldn't just sit here and feel sorry for herself. She had been on her own before she came here and now she was alone again. But without family or funds, who would she turn to for help? Rob had written little about the closest town, Piedmont, saying only that he occasionally went there for social purposes on Saturday nights — a friendly hand of cards with the banker. He'd never mentioned other friends.

Lifting her eyes, Trinity pleaded. "There's only me now, God. Show me what to do."

If the Lord was answering, she couldn't hear Him.

Hot sun heated the tin roof overhang and made it crackle as though raindrops were falling from the clear blue sky. Trinity's gaze strayed to Rob's garden, burnt up from a lack of moisture. Cornstalks bent in the intense heat and pole beans shriveled on the vine. Shading her eyes with her hand, she focused on the far distance where a dark cloud formed. Rain? She'd welcome a good soaker, but the windows were broken and the house would be drenched. For the better part of a half hour she watched the dark cloud inching closer. The blazing sun sank lower, casting a ray of golden reds and pinks across the west.

Trinity listened for thunder as the storm grew closer. When she was a child she'd enjoyed a good thunderstorm with lightning forking the sky and wind stripping leaves from towering oaks. Her gaze trained on the approaching sight, she listened for the thunderous clap. She sat up straighter when she caught sight of a lone rider coming toward her. So few folks ever passed by the remote homestead. She slowly rose to her feet and reached for the shotgun she kept handy. Thank goodness the thugs had failed to find the weapon. She squinted. Could be a prospector. Folks were still panning gold in these areas.

No lightning. No thunder. Just the dark, ominous cloud and that rider, both coming closer by the minute. Her heart skipped a beat. It was one of the marauders, of course — coming back to finish the job.

A grasshopper landed on the front step and she hurriedly scooted the insect aside with the tip of her boot. The pesky creatures made her flesh crawl. Rising, she carried the gun inside. The door squeaked when she heaved it closed on its broken hinge.

Don't let it be anyone looking for shelter from the storm. Let him ride past.

The sun dipped behind a cloud and the cabin interior darkened. Raindrops — big fat ones — hit the tin roof overhead. *Thump. Splat. Thumpsplat.* Trinity's finger tightened around the trigger as she watched the door. The rider had to be getting close — so close he was sitting outside the doorway, speculating? *Go on past . . .*

The heavens opened and the thumps became a thunderous roar on the roof. Stepping to a shattered window, Trinity peered out. And she could hardly believe what she saw.

No lightning. No rain. Instead, swarms of grasshoppers dropped from the sky. The insects blocked out the sun. Rob's sheep were in a panic, the insects eating the wool off their hides. Terror rose in her throat and she raced to find the remains of a blanket to tack over a broken window. But grasshoppers already covered the floor, crawling over one another. The world tilted as she teetered on a broken chair and pounded a nail, securing the blanket in place. It did nothing to dull the constant beating of wings as Rob's failing garden was eaten to the ground. The insects were everywhere, whirring, the sound so loud her confused

22

thoughts screamed.

A sudden pounding at the front door caught her breath. The rider.

Pressing herself against the wall, she prayed he wouldn't try the latch. It was locked, but the splintered wood couldn't stop him. The door flew open and Trinity shrieked as a man stumbled in covered in grasshoppers. The insects were eating the shirt off his back.

He stumbled to his knees. He wasn't going to make it.

Trinity leaped from the chair and began whipping the insects off him with a piece of torn calico. Fighting until exhausted, she dropped to her knees. Insects still covered the front of his faded shirt, but they were manageable now.

Had she rescued a man who was here to ravage her?

Rolling the stranger onto his back she noted a thatch of snow-white hair and a face lined by wind and weather. He was old — older than most men around these parts. A prospector, no doubt. He didn't look threatening, just spent.

Springing to her feet, Trinity went to wet a cloth and returned to tend to his wounds. The man was dazed, and obviously in pain.

"The hoppers . . ."

"Shhh. You're safe now." Trinity looked back over her shoulder. The thin blanket nailed to the window appeared to be holding against the angry swarm. For now. "What's happening?"

"Hoppers . . . had 'em back in '89. Ate every crop, hides off the cattle . . ."

"Hides off the cattle?" She shivered. "Will they leave?"

"Pray God they will."

She could still hear the critters hitting the sides of the house, their wings beating a loud cadence. "We're safe," she whispered. "We're just fine." Though she didn't believe a word of it. They weren't fine. They were about to be eaten alive.

The man's eyes drifted shut and she sat down on the floor beside him, removing the rest of the insects from his ragged clothing. Shuddering, she dropped the bugs into a pillowcase and knotted it tightly. Grasshoppers, a wild man sticking her in a barrel and sending her down the rapids, thugs in her home, a remote, uncivilized land, no money, no family, no means of fleeing . . . She paused. No money. The vandals had taken all she had, but perhaps Rob had saved some. The idea took hold. Tomorrow, if the grasshoppers moved on, she would walk into Piedmont and talk to the banker.

Maybe — oh, please God — Rob had some savings that would come to her. Why hadn't she thought of the bank before? Her brother had been frugal and would surely have saved a handsome sum from his work at the flour mill. At sunup she would walk into town and claim her inheritance.

Stretching out on the floor, she wrapped her arms around her shoulders to ward off a sudden chill. Rob was sensible; he would have provided for her. Closing her eyes, Trinity dozed through the remainder of the night, listening to the sound of grasshoppers eating their way across the land.

THREE

Silence woke her. Utter stillness. Sitting up, Trinity cleared her head and looked down, taken aback when she saw a man asleep beside her. Springing to her feet, she clasped a hand to her heart . . . until her mind caught up and she remembered the grasshoppers.

She moved to the window, removed the blanket, and looked out. The creatures were gone . . . and so was every blade of grass, every leaf, every stalk of corn . . . even the hair off the man's mule.

A voice startled her. "Pitiful sight, ain't it?" Trinity turned as the stranger sat up, working a kink out of his left shoulder.

"Does this happen often?" Rob had never written a word about the insects. He'd spoken of a harsh land, but this was beyond severe. This was insane.

"Not often," the man said. "Had a big plague a few years back and there's talk the

26

critters are on the move again." He slowly struggled to his feet. "Last time they stayed a while. Ate everything within a hundred miles." He scratched his stomach. "Got any coffee?"

Trinity shook her head. "I was robbed," she said. "They took everything."

"I got some chicory in my saddlebag, unless the critters ate through the leather." His worn eyes roamed the broken furniture and strewn objects. "Mighty glad to hear you was robbed. I was startin' to question your housekeepin'."

She smiled weakly as he opened the door and walked outside. She needed to feed him, but what? The kitchen was empty. There might be a broken jar of peaches, but . . .

He returned with a bag of coffee, a slab of fatback, and four eggs. She nearly cried when she saw the bounty. "Where did you get those?"

"Had the coffee and fatback, and I've been known to help myself to a few fresh eggs when I happen across a farm." He tucked his head. "I ask the good Lord's forgiveness, but I figure if a hen lays one egg she can surely lay another."

Trinity took the items and hurried to the stove. Once the fire was going she set an iron skillet — only a little dented, thank goodness — on top and laid strips of fatback in the cold pan. The old man set to work making coffee. "What's a little thing like you doing out here in the wild?" he asked.

She explained about Rob, the thievery, and how she'd come from Sioux Falls to sell the property to the railroad. And the sooner the better. "I know it's been in the family for generations," she finished, "but I can't work it — don't want to work it — and with my brother passing, well . . ." She turned the slabs of sizzling meat in the skillet as the room filled with the delectable scent. "The railroad will pay a good price for the property."

"Yes, 'spect they will. They're buyin' up everythin' in sight. Hear they're gonna run the line clean past Dwadlo this time."

"This time?"

"The railroad line only ran to Dwadlo when they built it, but they had a couple of ugly incidents up there last winter. Hear tell they're gonna build it right this time."

"Is that so?" The man seemed excited about the prospect, so it must be a good thing. The news made her feel better. "Have you lived in these parts all your life?"

"Not yet — still got another mile or two

28

left in me — but I was born here, if that's what you're askin'. Born and raised a fer piece down the road." Smiling, she glanced his way. Old-timers had a quaint way of stating the obvious. The smell of coffee wafted through the air and seemed to make the surroundings less dismal. "Fact is, I used to come by this place every day or two just to look at your aunt."

Trinity turned, fork in hand. "Really?"

He nodded, his eyes mirroring memories. "She and her little sister was about the prettiest little fillies in the state, and that's a fact. I was moony-eyed in love with your aunt."

"Which one?"

"Why, the prettiest one."

Trinity wondered what it meant to be "moony-eyed" in love. She had yet to meet a man who made her heart skip. There had been lots of men who came through the café — tall, short, fat, thin — but none took her breath the way she'd heard other girls talk about. She'd been a bridesmaid twice, but never a bride. Not that she was in any hurry. She figured when the right one came along she'd notice, and so far she hadn't seen a one that caught her real interest.

"So you courted my aunt?"

"Courted her? No, ma'am, she wouldn't

hear of it — not that I didn't try. No, your aunt was older than me and she thought of me as a pesky kid. When I grew up, she was a woman, and she'd shush me off the porch and tell me to go away." He grinned. "I never did, but she didn't tire of running me off."

"So what happened?"

"Beats me. One day she up and followed her daddy off on some crazy ex-pe-di-tion. Never laid eyes on her again. I looked here and there, but wherever she went it was far away."

Lost love. Trinity sighed. She supposed it was better than never finding it. She dished up the meat on the lone unbroken platter and then broke the eggs into the hot grease.

Right now, love was the last thing on her mind.

It wasn't long after that the old man pushed back from the table and stretched. "I'll be getting out of your hair now, missy."

"I'm sorry to hear that. I've enjoyed your company," Trinity admitted.

Pausing, he fixed her with a stare. "You can't stay out here. What do you plan on doin'?"

"I'll walk to town today and speak to the banker, inquire if my brother left a bank account. Any amount would help."

He nodded. "Sounds reasonable. If you'd like, you can walk with me."

"I'd like that very much." She glanced down at her clothing. She was wearing Rob's pants and a shirt that was too big for her.

"You look fine," the old man grunted as if he'd noticed her concern. "You learn to make do with what you have."

That she knew all too well. "I'll run a brush through my hair and be right with you."

He went outside to wait, and as Trinity washed her face and tidied her hair with a broken comb she prayed that Rob had left a small sum. It didn't have to be much — just enough for a train ticket home.

Just get me back to Sioux Falls, Lord, and I'll never ask for another thing.

But she wondered if that was a promise she could keep. One did not make bargains with God. He knew her circumstances and the eventual outcome . . . but in the meantime, she didn't know where her next meal was coming from.

Trinity and her companion reached Piedmont within half an hour. The sun was beating down — no doubt the town was in for a scorcher. Four buildings, an alcove, and a saloon. Not much, but it would do. She located the small bank on the corner and smiled. Just enough. She read the signs as they walked by. General Store. Livery and Feed. Undertaker — with a small sign that read, "Knock loud for service." Saloon. Gert's Café. The smells coming from the last establishment were enough to tease Trinity's nose.

"If I had any money I'd buy you a hearty dinner," the prospector said. "I'm not panning much these days."

"Oh, the fatback and the eggs were plenty," she said, then glanced at him. "I'm sorry. I don't know your name."

He broke his stride and affected a regal bow. "Benjamin Henry Cooper, ma'am."

Curtsying low, she returned the friendly play. "Trinity Rose Franklin."

"Trinity — now that's a right purty name."

"Actually, it was supposed to be Teresa. The doctor was pretty hard of hearing, so he wrote *Trinity* and Ma didn't catch the mistake until he'd left. Once she'd thought about the name it seemed to fit."

"Well, it's a nice-sounding mistake to live with."

Benjamin stopped as they approached the bank. "I'm going to the stable to have the blacksmith take a look at my jenny's hoof. I think she needs a new shoe, and he might have some salve for her hide."

The little mule did look pitiful without a trace of fur. "Thank you so much for your help." She extended a hand and they shook. "It was a pleasure to make your acquaintance."

He tipped his battered hat. "The same, I'm sure." He reached for the mule's reins and started off toward the blacksmith.

Trinity stepped into the bank. A lone female clerk sat behind a wire cage, staring at her over her spectacles. "May . . . may I please see the president?" she asked, keenly aware of her mismatched, too-large clothing. The clerk nodded, and a moment later a young man with slicked-back hair rounded a desk and straightened his vest.

"How may I help you?" His eyes were skimming her brother's pants and shirt. Trinity's cheeks warmed.

"My name is Trinity Franklin. I'm Rob Franklin's sister."

The banker's eyes lit up. "Trinity! I've been expecting you, young lady!"

Trinity's heart soared. "You have? You knew my brother?"

"Knew him well. We played a friendly game of poker Saturday nights." He ducked his head. "Never bet money, mind you. Just matchsticks."

Smiling, Trinity extended her hand. "I'm here to inquire if Rob left an open account in his name."

The man's smile died, and he ushered her to his desk and a comfortable chair. When she was seated, he walked around the desk and sat down. "I wish I could say that Rob was frugal, but he wasn't. He spent more than he took in, but he does have a small balance in his account. It's not much, but what he had is yours." He glanced up and called to the clerk. "Will you get Rob Franklin's bank balance and close out the account?"

"Right away, Mr. Price." The clerk rose and went to consult a large book that sat on a ledge near the cage.

Rob had left her something. Trinity's heart pounded. *Please, let it be enough to get me home.*

"I've had a most frightful experience recently," she said. "Grasshoppers. They came in a swarm and ate everything."

"Yes," said the banker. "They're moving east. They've hit several areas but so far the town has escaped. Had quite a large infestation a few years back. We're praying we'll escape another plague."

34

The clerk returned and laid three bills and a small handful of coins on the banker's desk. Trinity stared.

"That's it?" she asked. "Twelve dollars and" — she reached out to sort through the coins — "sixty-two cents?"

The banker's face softened. "Considering that I knew and thought highly of your brother, I could make you a small loan . . ."

"No." She held up her palm. "I wouldn't be able to repay it for . . . for some time." By the time she got home she'd have less than nothing. It would take every cent she made at the café to keep a roof over her head.

Twelve dollars and sixty-two cents. She didn't have enough money to return to Sioux Falls. She might be stuck on this wasted, grasshopper-infested land for the rest of her life. She rose, pasting a smile on her face. "You have been most kind. Thank you."

"I wish I could help." He stood, extending an arm to escort her to the front door. "If you should need anything during your stay . . ."

"Thank you, but I won't be staying."

"Yes, uh . . . I heard about the raid. Most unfortunate. We've put up with these thugs and grasshoppers for a long time, and not a one of us knows what to do about either of them."

"I understand. Thank you." When the door closed behind her, Trinity drew a deep breath and bit her lower lip. Now what?

The blazing sun bore down, and Trinity realized she was parched. She crossed the street and went straight to the water barrel, cupping her hands and drinking deeply of the clear tepid water. Two older women passed, casting critical eyes over her apparel. Smiling, she nodded a greeting and then wiped her mouth on her sleeve. Men had the advantage over women. They could spit, scratch, and wipe their faces on their sleeves and never encounter so much as a raised eyebrow. Maybe the old prospector could offer a bit of advice for someone in her situation. Right now she needed all the wisdom she could get.

The livery. He'd said his mule needed a shoe and her hide needed salve. She looked up and down the street and found the livery not far away.

The owner was wearing a big apron over his clothing. A thick black beard hung nearly to the middle of his chest, and she noted specks of his breakfast still evident in it. His beefy arms worked two huge bellows to stoke the flames in a roaring pit. "Good

36

morning," she called.

He looked up, his eyes assessing her. "Mornin'."

"I was hoping Mr. Cooper was still around."

The man shook his head. "Had me check his mule for a broken shoe and treat her hide, but she was in fine shape. He went on a bit ago."

Tears formed in her eyes, emotion she'd managed to stave off until now. Never could she remember feeling so hopeless, so alone, so helpless. She didn't like the mood.

"Can I help?"

"No. Thank you. I thought . . . I just thought I'd walk with him a ways if he was still around."

Nodding, the man turned to stoke the blazing fire even hotter. She left the building and walked on. Where to now? Back to the house? She couldn't. There was nothing left there, not even a blade of grass. And there were thieves roaming around. Mother had taught her to pray when trouble arose and she had, day and night, but so far her misery had only increased.

She dropped down onto an empty bench in front of the general store. How could the heat still be rising? She picked up a paper fan to stir the air, studying the colorful advertisement on the back. It pictured a coffin laid out in style with the words "We make the final journey memorable" written in script beneath. The Undertaker. Knock loud.

As though the journey itself wouldn't be noteworthy.

She fanned the humid air, her gaze skimming the nearly empty street.

What about Dwadlo?

The thought came to her suddenly. Benjamin Cooper had said that her aunt had gone to Dwadlo . . . but she had surely passed by now. Trinity counted back and came up with a staggering number. Pauline Wilson would be ninety-four — much too old to still be living. But she could have left an inheritance. Unless Trinity was mistaken, she was the last of the Wilson kin. The thought stung. Her bloodline had run out. There was no family left.

People *did* live to be ninety-four, but not often. She had known a woman in Sioux Falls who claimed to be ninety-nine and she chopped her own wood, carried her own water, and plowed her cornfield every spring, so she guessed it was possible.

A couple passed and she glanced up. "Excuse me — can you tell me how far it is to Dwadlo?"

The gent paused. "Dwadlo . . . North Dakota?"

"Yes, sir." She hoped it was so far that she couldn't at least investigate the possibility that Aunt Pauline was there.

"About a hundred miles? I don't rightly know, but it's a fer piece."

Not that fer — far, she mentally corrected. Sioux Falls was a lot further, and she'd made that journey without incident. She glanced at the bills crumpled in her hand. Twelve dollars would surely be enough to purchase a train ticket to Dwadlo.

Trinity's eyes pivoted to the train track that ran behind the back of the undertaker's. Swiveling, she noted the sign tacked to the door of the general store: Train Tickets Inside. Slowly rising, she straightened her shirt and trousers and went inside to purchase a ticket to Dwadlo. There was no need to go home and pack. She had nothing but the clothes on her back. That, and hope. If by some miracle her aunt was still alive, she would surely know what to do.

And surely she would loan her the money to get home.

FOUR

Mae Curtis glanced up at the sound of the backfiring. The obnoxious noise shattered the summer morning stillness and the dogs went wild. Wiping her hands on a cloth, she stepped to the general store's front door and watched her best friend, Lil, climbing off the funny-looking contraption she'd been working on lately. "Lil!" Mae called. "You're stirring up the animals!"

Her friend climbed off the strange machine she had built, removed her grimy gloves with her teeth, and started up the steps, grinning all the while. Both cheeks and a strip of her forehead sported dark grease. "Boy, she's running like a top today!"

"Everyone in town is sick of that — what do you call it?"

"Motorcycle."

"Murdercycle's more like it. Either you're going to break your neck on that thing or someone is going to wring it. You rile up the old folks and the animals every time you ride that thing to town."

Lil shrugged, still grinning. "How long have we been friends?"

"Most all our lives."

"And didn't I clean up real nice and put a silly ribbon in my hair and wear a pair of them fancy boots for your weddin' three months ago?"

"You did. You looked beautiful."

"Then why does anything I do surprise you? You're just upset because you don't have the nerve to ride my machine." She flashed an ornery grin and reached into the barrel for a root beer. "When Cousin Bert shipped the material for me to build it I wasn't sure I'd be able to ride it, but she's a jewel."

"It's a loud, three-wheeled nuisance," Mae grumbled. "Fix that motor so it doesn't keep backfiring. Miss Prawley is going to drop dead of heart failure and you'll be the cause."

Mae's husband, Tom, had laughed when he'd seen her friend's newest gadget. Mae claimed her best friend had finally lost her mind, but Tom admired the three-wheeled, iron-banded contraption and its charcoal-fed two-cylinder engine. He said the whole

41

thing was a "bonecrusher" — and Mae didn't doubt it. But it was junk, noisy junk, and Lil was going to break her foolish neck.

"Well," said Lil, popping the lid off the bottle, "it ain't the newest motorcycle they got — they're building 'em better now — but Bert had the parts left over from a machine he built a couple years ago. He showed the machines at the circuses and thought I'd like 'em, and I do." She drank deeply from the bottle.

"For heaven's sake, Lil, you've turned into a hoodlum." It wasn't enough that she kept an elephant as a pet and took in every stray that Pauline missed. Now she had to build a motorcycle.

Lil eyed her friend. "Where's Tom this morning?"

"Where he always is lately — working with the crew building the new rest home."

"Rest," Lil chortled. "That's a good way of pulling the wool over a body's eyes. Rest. They'll be resting there all right." She took another swallow. "How many do you suppose will live there?"

"Hard to say, but right now there are four people on the waiting list. When word spreads there's a new facility to care for the aging, I imagine the list will grow."

"Fifteen rooms ain't all that much."

"It's a start." Mae stepped to the postal cage and sorted the day's mail. The trains were running again after two major derailments in the past months, and life in Dwadlo was slowly returning to normal. Well, nearly normal.

Lil's eye caught something out the front window. "Well, lookee there!"

Mae glanced up to see a horse and rider pass the mercantile. The stranger was trail-worn, but a coat of dust and grime couldn't disguise his uncommon good looks. "Looks like we have a visitor."

"Shore does." Lil wiped absently at the grease streaks on her face. "Could be he'll stop for a meal."

"Could be you'll have time to wash your face and comb your hair," Mae noted pleasantly. Lil was the salt of the earth, but Mae had long ago faced the fact that her friend was a tomboy to the bone. She had a heart as big as the Rockies, but when it came to matters of the heart she didn't appear interested — unless she was fussing with the blacksmith and livery owner, Fisk. Those two mixed like oil and water, and yet Mae had seen a spark of romantic interest lodged in both sets of dueling eyes. But Fisk had lost his wife the year before, and he didn't yet have eyes for anything but his work. Especially a red-headed pig-raising tomboy named Lil. She got under his skin like a deep splinter.

The outsider rode back into view and reined up in front of the store, then dismounted. Lil's eyes were fixed on him.

"Looks like he's coming inside," Mae noted. She handed Lil a cloth. "You have grease on both cheeks."

The front door opened and the man stepped inside. He removed his dusty hat, revealing a thatch of damp, curly black hair. "Afternoon, ladies."

"May I help you?" asked Mae, pausing in her mail sorting.

"I'm looking for Tom Curtis. Would you know where I could find him?" The man's gaze shot to Lil, who was frantically scrubbing both her cheeks.

"You're looking for my husband?" said Mae.

"You're Mrs. Curtis?"

Mae's smile broadened. "For three months now."

The man returned the smile, revealing a set of even white teeth. "Congratulations, ma'am. I'm proud to meet the woman who's able to corral Tom Curtis."

Mae leaned in close. "I'm right proud to be that woman," she said, then extended her hand to him. "You must be the friend Tom is expecting."

"Yes, ma'am. The name's Jones."

"Jones?"

"Just Jones." He flashed a boyish grin. None of the single women in Dwadlo were going to be safe around that grin.

"Tom's most likely working on the new rest home," said Mae. "Follow the street down the road a piece and you'll see the activity."

Dwadlo was small. Most of the homes and businesses were built of brand new lumber. At one time the town had been so cramped that if a body sneezed their next-door neighbor reached for a hanky, but when the train derailed last winter, taking out the whole town, they had been forced to rebuild. Now the businesses and residents had good-sized yards and picket fences, all thanks to the CN&W Railroad.

"Thank you." The stranger's glance slid back to Lil before he turned and started back out the door. "Morning, ma'am."

"Hey," Lil mumbled.

There was a low rumbling in the distance, and the whole building shook as the train pulled into town and released a noisy *whoosh!* of steam. One thing in Dwadlo remained the same: Every train arrival

45

jarred the teeth of anyone close by.

The stranger seemed not to notice the racket. "That's a strange contraption sitting outside the store. Is it yours?"

Lil's face turned four shades of crimson. "Yes sir. How did you know?"

He flashed that boyish grin again. "Just a hunch. It's a motorcycle, isn't it?"

"Shore is. Folks here usually call it a bonecrusher, but *motorcycle* is the proper name, and it's a right fine thing" — she slid an accusing eye toward Mae — "that some folk have the manners to call it by that name."

Jones nodded. "Didn't know you could buy one yet."

Lil stood up straighter and Mae cringed, noticing that Lil had only managed to smear the grease instead of removing it. "I didn't buy it. I built it."

Jones let out a slow, appreciative whistle. "Is that right. How many hours have you got in it?"

"Not exactly finished yet. I'm gonna switch out the charcoal-fired carburetor and put in one of those new spray ones."

He whistled again. "Hear they have a two-wheeler now that uses a five-cylinder engine built as the hub of its rear wheel."

Lil nodded, eyes aglow. "The Millet. The

46

cylinders rotate with the wheel, and the crankshaft starts the rear axle."

He replaced his hat and adjusted the brim. "Nice machine. Well . . . hope to see you around, ladies." He nodded a polite good-bye and turned to leave.

Mae stepped to the front window, watching as he paused to inspect the funny-looking contraption. A moment later he mounted his horse and rode off.

"Now there's a prime example of a very nice looking man," she said. "And he appears to share your . . . passion for progress."

"You're not supposed to be looking at men anymore."

"I'm not. I'm merely observing on your behalf."

"Well, I ain't blind." Lil set her empty root beer bottle on the counter and left the store, and it wasn't long later that Mae heard the familiar earsplitting backfire.

Honestly. There wasn't a ladylike bone in that woman.

The door had barely closed behind Lil when Mae looked up to see a customer trying to enter the store. Pauline Wilson's pack of dogs barked and leaped on the newcomer as she tried to squeeze through the narrow screen door. She was a pretty little thing — she had Lil's red hair and deep brown eyes — but she was dressed in a man's shirt and trousers. Mae hadn't seen her around before. She must be new to town. She didn't have any letter in hand, so this would likely be store business, not postal.

"May I help you?"

The young woman jumped as if she'd been shot when Lil roared past the store again, motorcycle backfiring as usual.

"I'm sorry." Mae flashed an apologetic smile. "The noise is on its way out of town."

The young woman crossed the room, seeming uncertain as the ruckus faded into the background with one final bomb blast. "I . . . I came in on the train and I wonder if you could point me to a boardinghouse."

Dropping her pen, Mae eased around the counter with an extended hand. "Of course. Welcome to Dwadlo."

The girl flashed a travel-worn smile. "Thank you." She removed a hanky and wiped her brow. "The town seems very . . . lively."

"Not on most days, just when Lil comes in from her pig farm. And those dogs are a nuisance, but they won't bite. Usually." Mae studied the girl's attire. "You're not from these parts." *Women around here wouldn't*

48

be caught dead in men's clothing, she thought privately.

"No. I'm from Sioux Falls, but I've been staying near Piedmont recently."

"So far away? You must be exhausted." Mae stepped to the barrel, took out a root beer, and removed the cap. "Please sit and have a cold drink."

The young woman accepted the hospitality and drank thirstily. Moments passed before she came up for breath. "This is most refreshing."

"Isn't it? We sell more root beer than flour during the summer. Well — what brings you all the way to Dwadlo?"

The young woman said it all in a single breath — something about thieves ransacking her home and grasshoppers and an old prospector and long-lost kin.

"I'm . . . I'm sorry for the trials you've undergone," said Mae when she seemed to be finished. Mae had experienced her fair share of problems in the past year. There had been the long, unsuccessful search for her elderly neighbor's family, two train wrecks, and more bad weather than a town should have to handle. But the trials had been tempered by blessings — so many she'd lost count. "The grasshoppers haven't

49

come this far yet, and we're praying they won't."

The young woman shuddered. "I've never seen the likes. They ate the fur clean off Benjamin's jenny."

Mae looked up, startled.

The woman nodded. "Literally."

"How . . . awful."

"It was, but at least the animal survived. She looks mighty strange, but the hair will grow back. Eventually." She finished her drink and set the empty bottle on the counter. "How much?"

"Oh," Mae dismissed the offer. "It's free on your first day in town." She noted the relief that crossed the young woman's features. Her eyes strayed to the scuffed bag, no larger than a hatbox. Odd that she would be traveling so light.

"Do you know a reasonably priced place to stay?" the young woman asked.

"How reasonable?"

"Very."

"Well . . . when they rebuilt the town the café added four rooms over their establishment. They rent for fifty cents a night, but that includes breakfast."

She could see the girl calculating in her head. She sighed. "I won't be able to stay long."

50

"I'd be happy to walk you across the street and introduce you to the café owner."

"I wouldn't want to be a bother. I can cross the street."

"All right, then. Be sure and remind Belle that Mae Curtis sent you."

"Mae Curtis. I'll do that. And I'm Trinity Franklin."

"Pleased to have you in town, Trinity."

Trinity reached for the scuffed bag and stood up. "Thank you again for the root beer. It was most refreshing."

Mae trailed the young lady to the door, pausing to adjust the slow-turning fan blades overhead. The slightest breeze caught the flats and stirred the dormant air. The newcomer's winsome expression tugged at her heartstrings. It didn't take much to see that she was alone. "Why don't you get settled in your room and then come back and have dinner with us tonight? Jeremy — that's my brother — he's fixing pork chops, and when he cooks he makes enough for an army."

"Oh." A blush crept up Trinity's neck. "I couldn't . . ."

"Of course you can." Mae draped an arm around the girl's thin waist. "You can eat and return to your room early." Leaning close, Mae whispered, "Besides, the food they serve in the café is a bit overpriced."

The subtle reminder hit home. The girl turned pensive, and then nodded. "Thank you. I'd be glad to join you."

"Good. Six o'clock?"

Trinity nodded.

"Six o'clock it is." Mae smiled. "I'll have Jeremy set an extra place, and we can all talk about helping you locate your kin. I've lived in these parts all my life, so I know just about everyone."

Relief flooded the girl's fine features. "That would be most helpful."

"See you at six."

"I'll be there."

FIVE

Tom Curtis hefted a two-by-four to a rafter and held it in place as the town blacksmith pounded in the nails. On sunny mornings like this, Fisk usually stood behind a forge, but not today. Today the crew was framing, and everyone that could lend a hand was here to help. Once the new rest home was built Dwadlo would be able to offer housing to the elderly, something the area sorely needed. Folks took care of their own, but those with no kin needed looking after. Thanks to the railroad, the new home had been completely funded.

Board securely in place, the two men stepped back to admire the work. Taking a hanky from his pocket, Fisk wiped the sweat off his brow. "She's comin' along real nice."

Tom's critical gaze ran the length of the building site. He had to agree. "That she is. Come fall, Pauline and the others should be able to move in."

Fisk grinned. "The old lady getting under your collar?"

"A little," Tom admitted, and then flashed another smile. "Pauline's a fine woman, but . . ."

"But newlyweds need their privacy."

"It's better now that Miz Farley took her in until Mae gets to feeling better. She's been a little under the weather lately and the two get to stepping on each other's toes." Uncorking a water jug, he poured a stream over his head, letting the coolness trickle down his collar. The last three months had been the best in his life. When he'd come to Dwadlo last winter he'd never imagined that instead of kin, he'd find the woman of his dreams.

Pauline Wilson had turned out not to be kin, but the point was moot. He was as fond of the ninety-four-year-old woman as any family member he'd ever known, and by fall she would be safely tucked away by the Missouri River in a brand new home for the aging.

Then it would only be Jeremy, Mae, and him.

The men turned as they heard a rider approaching. Tom lifted his hand against the sun's glare to see the new arrival. "Must be more help coming. We could use it this morning." Dropping his hammer, Tom stepped out to greet the rider, an even wider smile breaking across his tanned features when he recognized the man. "Jones?"

The visitor reined up and slid off his horse, and the two men pumped hands. "Jones, you old son-of-a-gun! It's good to see you!"

"I'd hoped to be here sooner, but a rainstorm delayed me a couple of days." The newcomer's eyes assessed his friend. "Marriage agrees with you."

"I highly recommend it." Turning, Tom introduced Fisk. "Fisk, meet one of my best friends and coworkers, Jones."

Jones stepped up and shook the man's hand. The blacksmith nodded a greeting, then returned to his work. Tom and Jones fell into step. "Work holding up in Chicago?" Tom asked.

"Have more than the line can handle. By the way, did I mention that I rented your old room when I heard you weren't coming back?"

"Lucky man. Bessie Helman sets a fine table. She still make those fat cinnamon rolls for breakfast?"

"Every Wednesday morning. You can set your watch by it. Six dollars a week and a man's got all he can eat and a clean bed to sleep in every night."

"Chicken and dumplings every Thursday night?"

"With hot rolls right out of the oven."

Tom shook his head. "She's one fine woman. Too bad she's in her sixties."

"When I'm slathering butter on those steaming rolls I'm tempted to overlook her age," Jones confessed with a chuckle. His gaze roamed the strip of land they were walking. "So this is the new project you gave up the single life and the big city for."

"The land didn't have anything to do with my decision. It was a feisty young postmistress with dark blonde hair and toffee-colored eyes," Tom admitted. "But by necessity, I have been rebuilding track in addition to the new town."

"I understand the hair and eyes thing, but something puzzles me."

Tom paused. "And what's that?"

"How did you manage to derail two locomotives in the span of a few weeks?"

"It wasn't easy."

The two men burst into laughter. The cost wasn't a laughing matter — the railroad had lost its shirt — but both were accidents, albeit mighty costly ones.

"Heard you never want to see a piece of herring again."

Tom's laughter faded and his stomach churned at the thought of all the herring that had been destined for Joann Small's wedding. The shipment had derailed, and Dwadlo had smelled like rotting fish for weeks. Joann's mother had had to serve beef at the wedding reception, and she was still harping about it.

The men matched long strides as they walked the banks of the river that ran along the back of the new rest home, catching up on recent developments with the railroad. "I was grateful for the advancement," Jones was saying, "but I've got to say I still have a lot of learning to do."

Tom reached over to slap him on the back. "I was glad to hear you'd replaced me. It's a well-deserved promotion." Jones had joined the railroad three years after Tom, and together they'd watched the business grow and prosper. "But what's this I hear about a piece of land you want to buy?"

Jones sobered. "The owner is wanting a fortune for the property. It's prime, Tom, and sitting exactly where we need to run the line."

"Then what's the problem?"

Jones shook his head. "Can't bring myself to spend the money when I know it's worth half the amount."

"Maybe in your eye, but you have to consider the railroad's need."

"I don't hold with highway robbery, and the price they're asking is pure thievery."

"You've bartered?"

"All that I'm going to, and the owner won't budge."

"Then pay the price."

"That's easy to say."

"Only because of where I'm standing today. I refused to pay the price for this particular piece of land. I walked away, the railroad built where I bought property instead, and the result was two lost engines, fourteen boxcars, six passenger cars, and the cost of rebuilding a town. Give them what they're asking."

By late afternoon, the men had covered the entire railroad property line. Jones admired the new rest home and even added a board or two, and the sun was starting to ease to the west. Tom picked up a few scattered tools. "I'd offer you a bed tonight, but our place is small. I can set you up at the café, though. They have four boarding rooms on the second floor now."

"Sounds good."

"And you're coming home to have supper with us, of course."

"Not until I have a hot bath and shave,"

said Jones.

"Fair enough. I'll take you by the café and you can rent your room, clean up, and come over around six. Our place is over there." He pointed to a white bungalow enclosed by a neat white picket fence. "Mae's little brother fries a mean pork chop."

Jones flashed a grin. "Does he make pie?"

"Pie, cake, anything you want. Mae's a fine cook herself, but Jeremy does most of the household chores. He's a little on the slow side — he had a birth injury, I think — but a finer kid you'll never meet."

"You're on." The men shook hands. "I'll be there at six."

Pausing before a glass storefront, Trinity checked her hair. According to the clock on the bank tower it was precisely two minutes until six o'clock. She wanted to be neither early nor late for her first Dwadlo dinner engagement. Mae Curtis seemed helpful and friendly, and she'd need both qualities tonight.

Her gaze roamed the Curtises' homey porch with its wide white railings. Three rocking chairs and a comfortable wicker chair sat empty. Six pots of geraniums lined the railings, lending bursts of color to the home. A buzz caught her attention and she spotted a hornet's nest tucked deep in the rafters. Stepping back, she squinted, leery of the insects darting in and out of a hidden nest. She swallowed back the urge to run. She'd been stung by the critters more often than she cared to remember, and afterwards her face would always swell like a dead pig in the hot sun. A hornet darted her way and she ducked and covered her head. The insect flew past in a whir.

Straightening, she readjusted her hair and was about to knock on the Curtises' front door when another hornet buzzed past. Then two.

Then a swarm.

She shrieked, furiously batting at the attackers. Hornets poured from the rafters, joining the assault. The ruckus attracted the dogs and they came running, howling all the way. They hit the porch and all bedlam broke out. Barks. Shouts.

Trinity's screams turned to screeches when a bucket of cold water hit her full in the face. The hornets thinned but quickly regrouped. Gasping, she pushed the wet hair back from her eyes before a second bucket of water knocked her to her knees.

This time she sat down.

The hornets retreated and a steel arm jerked her upward. Water blinded her and she staggered beside the assailant, allowing herself to be dragged through the front door like a sack of grain. The door slammed and a male voice rang out. "Tom!"

Pushing the soggy strands out of her eyes yet again, Trinity peered out from under her drenched hair, her jaw dropping. Him? Again? The same brute who had shoved her in the barrel and allowed her to go over the rapids?

This was not happening.

A tall form appeared in the kitchen doorway, a broad grin forming on the man's handsome features. "Jones! I didn't hear you knock." His eyes switched to Trinity.

"I didn't. Tom, you have hornets in the rafters."

"I know. I've been promising Mae to burn them out . . . ma'am? Can I get you a towel?"

"I don't want to be a bother," Trinity muttered, mortified. Water rolled off her chin. She plucked at her shirt, holding it out to let the water run off.

"It's no bother. I'll be right back. Jones, where are your manners? Show the lady into the parlor!"

Jones nodded, mumbling under his breath, "I don't know where his parlor is."

It was a moment before Mae returned

61

with Tom, chuckling over Trinity's appearance. "How dreadful! But I suppose a cool bath felt good on such a warm evening," she laughed.

"Ordinarily, yes, but . . ." Trinity reached for the towel and mopped her eyes. Loons. They were all loons.

"No harm done!" Tom slapped Jones on the back. "You look better." He bent and sniffed. "Smell better too."

"You need to do something about those hornets, Tom. They could kill a person."

"They're pesky critters. After supper you can help me burn the nest."

Mae put her arm around Trinity and walked her to a small room. They had indoor plumbing, something Trinity had heard about but never seen for herself. There was a stool, bathtub, and washstand. "Tom added them when he rebuilt the house," Mae explained. She stood back to focus on Trinity's sopping shirt and pants. "We look to be about the same size. I'll fetch you one of my dresses while your clothing dries." Stepping to the small closet, she thumbed through her clothing and took out a yellow-sprigged cotton. "This one should do nicely."

"Thank you. But you needn't go to so much trouble. My clothing will dry . . .

eventually."

"Nonsense." She flashed a smile. "It's no trouble at all. Oh — I smell the biscuits. You change, and there's a brush and comb in the top dresser drawer. I'll be dishing up the food."

The door closed and Trinity sank onto the funny-looking stool, her head swimming. This was undoubtedly the strangest town she'd ever experienced.

Six

The occupants were already seated by the time Trinity entered the kitchen. Mae sprang to her feet as she came in. "You look lovely!" she cried.

"Thank you." Smoothing her skirt folds, Trinity slipped into her chair. What an entrance she'd made, dressed in Rob's clothing. And the two hornet stings blazing on her forehead must be puffy red welts by now. Her eyes lifted and fixed on the source of her misery.

Jones.

The name stuck to the top of her mouth like peanut oil. What was he doing here?

"Trinity, this is my brother, Jeremy," said Mae, introducing the boy who looked to be somewhere in his early teens. He flashed a youthful grin in greeting, then returned to plating the pork chops he'd made. As soon as he'd finished, he excused himself and left the room. Tom frowned.

"Has he eaten already?"

"Yes. One of the dogs is ill, and he asked permission to stay with her until bedtime."

Tom accepted a bowl of potatoes. "Seriously ill?"

May shrugged. "We'll see."

After the prayer, Mae passed a basket of steaming biscuits around the table and Trinity tried to focus on the meal. The men appeared to have a great deal to discuss. Apparently Tom and Jones had once worked for the same railroad, which explained the presence of that ill-mannered beast. She gathered from snatches of conversation that Jones was in doubt about a plot of land he'd like to purchase.

Trinity broke into the conversation. "I have a piece of land you can buy that's well worth the price."

Jones glanced up. "Where?"

"Near Piedmont. Fine land, heavily timbered, sitting on a prime water source . . ." She paused, meeting his eyes. "But then you know about the water."

"No, I don't know much about Piedmont." He sliced into his pork chop. "How much?"

"How much is it worth?"

"Wouldn't know. I haven't seen it, and

anyway we're not looking for land in Piedmont."

Tom reached for an ear of corn. "Well, not yet," he said, "but the railroad is always looking for property. They're not in Piedmont yet, but they could be in five years."

Jones smiled and handed Trinity the salt dish. "Sorry."

"No need for sympathy." She sprinkled her potatoes lightly. He didn't recognize her. He didn't recognize her! Maybe the red welts on her face had thrown him. Or else he hadn't really looked at her that carefully when he'd shoved her in the barrel. "But I do have an interested party who's willing to put up a handsome price."

"Oh, really?"

"Yes. The Milwaukee Road. They should offer an attractive sum."

"Should?" Jones laid his fork aside. "They haven't yet?"

She shook her head. "But my brother assured me they would."

Tom chuckled. "Maybe you're being a bit hasty, Jones. If you don't buy the lady's land, someone else will."

"Buy land I haven't seen?"

"Speculation. It's part of your job."

Jones chewed for a moment as he considered. "What's your asking price?"

"I'll sell to the highest bidder."

He flashed that disarming smile. "And how do you know that's not me?"

"I don't. Mae, will you pass the cream, please?"

Mae reached for the white pitcher. "Trinity, tell us more about your life in Sioux Falls," she said, apparently eager to change the subject. But Jones wouldn't let it drop. He was baiting her and Trinity knew it.

"How much land are we talking about?"

"Two hundred thirty acres."

"Level ground, good water source?"

"Perfect land. Especially for railroads." She'd read enough to know that most railroads were buying any land they could get to establish future lines. So why was Mr. Fussy so reluctant to buy hers?

"What's your price?" he repeated.

"My brother said it would bring seventeen to twenty — at least."

"Thousand?"

She nodded, and he burst into laughter.

She turned a cool eye on him. "Is something amusing?"

"Your price."

Mae held up the bread basket. "More biscuits, anyone? Got plenty."

"What's wrong with my price?"

"You're too high."

Color crept up the back of her neck. The nerve of him — and in front of Mae and Tom. "Well, no matter. I wouldn't sell to you anyway." She was aware that she was being very ugly, but the man stirred her fighting spirit.

"I wouldn't buy." He looked at Tom. "Pass the sorghum, will you?"

Trinity, momentarily speechless, gathered her thoughts. Rob had always addressed people with the utmost civility, but she could stoop to this man's abrupt ways. She'd best him at his game, goad him into compromise, and then, at the last minute, refuse to sell and prove him the fool. She added a touch of cream to her coffee. "What would you pay?"

Jones dribbled sorghum on a biscuit. "Sight unseen? Five hundred. That's two dollars an acre and a fair price, ma'am."

Five hundred dollars. The staggering amount bounced around in her mind. It was a handsome offer to one whose total worth was less than four dollars. Although it wasn't nearly as high as Rob had predicted, it was more than she could dream of in her current situation.

"I presume you're making a joke?" she inquired lightly.

"No, ma'am." He brought the biscuit,

dripping with sorghum, up to his mouth. "I'd give you five hundred tonight."

She looked at Tom, and he shrugged. "It's a fine offer."

She dropped her gaze to her plate. "Maybe."

A dark brow lifted. "Maybe?"

"I'll think about it."

"I don't conduct business with maybes. Take it or leave it." He winked at Mae. "Mighty fine food. I can see why Tom fell so hard for you."

Mae blushed at the praise. "Jeremy's the cook. I just made the biscuits."

And with that, the subject of land purchase ceased. Mae chatted between bites, filling Trinity in on Dwadlo's recent history. "And that's why all of the homes and buildings are new," she finished.

"Yes, I noticed. Those train wrecks sound ghastly."

Once the men had polished off two thick slices of chocolate fudge cake, they pushed back from the table. Trinity finished her wedge and accepted a second cup of coffee.

"I should introduce you to Lil," Mae said. "You heard her fly past earlier today on her motorcycle."

Jones glanced up. "That friend of yours is quite a lady."

"Lady?" Mae snickered. "That's one word to describe her. She raises hogs, keeps stray cats and dogs — she's even acquired an elephant. Tom, you should take Jones to meet Esau. He came in real handy when we had to clear the train wreckage."

Jones frowned. "Your friend's got an elephant?"

Mae dabbed lightly at her mouth with a napkin. "Sounds like the woman for you."

He turned a sour eye on her. "What gave you the idea I'm looking?"

Mae grinned. "Lil's behavior can be a bit eccentric, but she's a perfectly wonderful woman and any man would be proud to claim her."

Tom sat back in his chair with a laugh. "Well, Trinity, tell us about this kin of yours. Mae says you're on the hunt for some long-lost relative."

"Yes, that's right. I've got a great-great aunt . . . well, at least I had one. I didn't even know where to look for her until a prospector who had known her happened by my place shortly after the raid."

"Raid?" Tom frowned.

Trinity glanced at Jones. Would the reference prompt his flagging memory? "My home was ransacked by a group of thugs. What they didn't tear up and destroy, they

70

tried to burn. Fortunately for me, the flames didn't catch and the house was saved."

Jones glanced up, focusing his gaze on her. She met his eyes. "Ring a bell?" she said drolly.

Recognition dawned. "That was you?"

"We do seem to meet in the oddest circumstances."

Mae looked back and forth between them. "The two of you have met previously?"

"Not really," Jones said.

"Only a brief encounter," Trinity assured them. There was no need to go into detail — and they would hardly believe the story if it were told. "There's nothing for me in Piedmont but the house. I plan to return to Sioux Falls as soon as I locate my kin. If she's alive, I'm hoping she'll have the deed to the land. And then I can sell" — she shot Jones a look — "to the other railroad."

"You're trying to sell the land without a deed?" He snickered.

Snickered!

"There *is* a deed — I just have to find it." She knew her reasoning had some holes in it, but how was she to know that Rob hadn't kept the document in his bank box? For all she knew it was somewhere in the house, shred into a thousand pieces along with everything else.

71

"I'm sure the other company will give you a fine price," said Tom. "Most lines are buying up everything they can get their hands on. But exactly who are you looking for here in Dwadlo?"

"My great-great aunt. Coming here is most likely a wild goose chase, but I took the chance. She would be very old now."

Tom shook his head. "You never know. I guess Mae mentioned that we're building a new facility to house the aged?"

"She did, and I see the work is well underway. It's going to be lovely, and what a pretty setting with the Missouri running right beside it."

"Exactly," said Mae. "Tom wants to put chairs along the waterfront so the residents can fish or enjoy the warm sun when weather permits."

Jones was still staring at Trinity. "That was you back there?" She gave a curt nod, and he sat back in his chair. "It's you. I can't believe it."

"What's the story here?" asked Tom. "When did you meet?"

"Tom," Mae cautioned, "perhaps they don't care to say when." She turned to Trinity. "I'm sorry. You were about to tell us who you're looking for."

"Pauline. Pauline Wilson."

72

A dead silence fell over the room.

"I beg your pardon?" said Mae.

"Pauline Wilson. Do you know her? Is she still alive?"

Mae's fork clattered to her plate. "Pauline is your aunt?"

"Yes. So you know her?"

Tom sprang up so quickly the dishes on the table rattled. "Know her! We've been looking everywhere for you!" Jones reached out to steady the gravy bowl.

Trinity lowered her cup to the saucer. "You've been looking for me?"

"Yes!" cried Mae. "We've searched high and low for Pauline's family!"

A tender shoot of hope sprouted in her heart. Pauline must have left an inheritance! She could go home, go back to her former life. "I would have written to inquire about her, but I regret to say I've lost all track of distant kin."

"No need to apologize," said Tom. "You're here now."

"How long ago did she pass away?" asked Trinity.

"Pauline isn't dead," said Mae. "She's still very much alive, and you will be a godsend to her."

Trinity's smile faded. "She's still living?"

"Alive and well — right here in Dwadlo."

73

"Really?"

"Really." Mae reached out to squeeze her hand. "The new nursing facility is being built in her honor."

Trinity's head was swimming. Jones nudged her water glass closer to her hand. "Better have a drink — oh. I forgot. You don't like water."

She shoved the glass back, sending him a steely glare. What was it with this man? She turned to face Tom. "Is Pauline . . . in good health?"

"For a woman her age, I'd say she's in excellent health. She has a few spells, but that's only natural, and her memory is going. She's ninety-four, you know."

Trinity nodded. "Who cares for her?" She saw a look pass between Mae and Tom.

"Actually . . ." Mae began, but then hurriedly picked up the cream pitcher and started it back around the table. The dish passed through three hands and landed back in Mae's.

Trinity peered at the woman curiously. "Who cares for my aunt?"

"I did for several years, but it grew increasingly hard to look after her when I had Jeremy and my work to think about. She's staying with Widow Farley right now, but the two of them . . . well, let's just say they look at things differently. Both like to have the final word, and it never matches. Pauline will move to the nursing home once it's up — we hope by late fall."

Trinity groped blindly for her glass. "That's . . . encouraging, but I'm not sure I'm in a position to care for her. I'm so sorry . . ." Nearly broke, and now a ninety-four-year-old aunt to care for?

Mae put her hand over hers. "We understand. You needn't apologize. Did you ever meet her?"

Trinity shook her head. "I think maybe when I was an infant. I've only heard stories — and there's a daguerreotype in the family album."

"Well, you'll love her. She's a splendid woman and" — she paused, glancing at her husband — "fairly easy to look after."

"She gets confused easily," Tom added.

Trinity took a deep breath. "Well, at least it's comforting to know that I do have living kin after all."

"Your parents are deceased?"

"Yes, and I lost my brother a few months back."

Mae sighed. "I'm so sorry."

"I was very small — I barely remember them, but I always knew Rob would be there if I needed him."

75

Mae patted Trinity's arm sympathetically. She knew what it was like to make do without parents.

Tom turned to Jones. "Where are you heading from here?"

"Back to Chicago. I'll send a wire in the morning to let them know I'm going to buy the land, high price and all — on your advice."

"Covering your bases, huh?" Tom stood and started to clear the table. "You're doing the smart thing."

Trinity wasn't sure what land they were speaking of, but she felt confident that Jones didn't intend to buy her property.

And she sure wasn't going to ask for clarity.

Mae poured hot water into the dish pan. "Trinity, come around midmorning and we'll visit Pauline together."

"That would be nice, Mae. Thank you again for supper." The meal had saved her twenty-five cents, and she could use the money. The food was quite good and the company, with one exception, was pleasant.

She eased past Jones and tried to beat him out the door. He would probably be all nicey nice and offer to walk her back to her room.

That was a definite no.

SEVEN

The bank tower clock struck eight as Trinity and Jones stepped out of the Curtis home. They descended the steps together and began to walk down the street, their steps perfectly in sync.

"You don't have to walk me across the street."

"I'm not. I'm going to my room."

Trinity glanced up. "You're staying at the café?"

"Tom said they were the only available rooms in town."

She couldn't argue, but she resented that he would be so close by. It felt too . . . personal.

Jones absently reached for the sack she was carrying. Before leaving, Mae had appeared with the bag, saying that it contained a few dresses and other personal items. Trinity could return them later. "I'll carry that for you," said Jones.

"It's light. There's no need." Their hands froze, locked in a duel to secure the bag.

"I'll carry it," he repeated.

"There's no reason. I'll carry it."

He tugged, and the sack spilled open, trailing personal garments all over the ground.

"You . . . !"

Trinity dropped to her knees and started stuffing frilly items in the bag. Jones calmly handed her a chemise and heat crawled up her face. When she stood up, he affected a mock bow and handed her the bag. "You carry it."

Straightening, she faced him. "You, sir, are a cad."

"And you, ma'am, have hornet stings on your face. Do you need salve?"

She arched her brow. "You are despicable."

"It appears we may have started off on the wrong foot."

"You nearly drowned me!"

"But I didn't. Here you stand, bright, cheerful, and in robust tongue. Now give it a rest. You did not drown."

Clutching the bag to her chest she stomped off toward the café, fairly bursting to inform him that he was ever so right. He had started off on the wrong foot and he was likely to remain there.

The strained walk took all of three minutes. When they got to the café, he tipped his hat and bid her goodnight. The fresh smell of soap and men's cologne mingled with the light scent of asters blooming nearby. Lifting her nose, Trinity turned to the right and went up the stairs that led to her room. An identical staircase led to two rooms on the left.

She could hear him snickering as she slipped the key into the lock.

Hopeless.

The insufferable beast was hopeless.

It was early the next morning, and already Lil's dirty boots were propped up on Mae's desk. "Did you tell the girl anything?" she asked.

"Tell her what?"

"About the dogs and cats, for example?"

"No. Why would I want to scare the living daylights out of her? She went a little pale last night when she realized she had an aging aunt who needed care," said Mae.

"Those dogs have torn up how many sofa cushions?"

"I have no intention of telling her anything. She'll see for herself." Mae closed the ledger and sighed. "I'm banking that she'll have the grit to handle Pauline's . . . eccentricity."

"You're playing with dynamite." Lil took a swig of coffee. "So you got to eat supper with Jones. How come you get first try at any good-looking bachelors who happen through Dwadlo?"

"I don't. I have my man. You are welcome to any and all who come through here."

"Mighty big of you."

The bell over the door rang and Mae looked over, brightening when she caught Trinity's eye. "Good morning, dear! Did you rest well?"

Well enough, Trinity supposed, knowing that the beast was sleeping nearby. "I did, thank you." She nodded a greeting to Lil.

Mae glanced at Lil. "You can handle the store?"

"I always do, don't I?"

"We won't be gone long." Mae smiled at Trinity. "Jeremy delivered a note to Mrs. Farley earlier informing her that we were coming to visit this morning."

Nodding, Trinity tried to calm her nerves. Meeting kin was a special event and she looked forward to the occasion. If only Pauline had some savings she might be willing to loan her enough to get home. Of course she'd pay every cent back.

The women left the store and stepped into

the street — nearly empty at this time of day. The fifteen-minute walk to Mrs. Farley's house provided plenty of time for conversation, as well as the chance to gather blackberries along the roadside.

"Tom loves blackberry cobbler," said Mae, straddling a thicket to access a particularly juicy patch.

Trinity waited near the road. Mae was so bright, her happiness bubbling over. "You sound like a happily married woman," she said.

"I never thought anyone could be so happy," admitted Mae. "What about you? Anyone special waiting back in Sioux Falls?"

Frank Logan came to mind. He was a young widower with two small children who ate most of their meals in the café. Their casual relationship was comfortable, but Frank was still grieving his wife and Trinity didn't feel all gushy and tingly around him. "No. No one special."

"You're still very young. There's plenty of time." Mae emerged from the thicket with a full basket of berries. The women fell into step and walked on.

"Lil seems rather . . . different," said Trinity slowly.

Smiling, Mae shook her head. "I love her like a sister, but she is, shall we say, unique.

She's brimming with life and can't get enough of it."

"That's not a bad attribute."

Mae paused to gather a handful of wildflowers. "Did you see her elephant behind the store yesterday?"

"How could I miss it?"

Laughter spilled out. "That's Esau. Perhaps you'll stay long enough to ride him."

Trinity grinned. "I seriously doubt that." She had done some silly things in her life, but riding an elephant would not be among them. "Where did she get an elephant?"

"Purchased him from the circus. They came through on the rail one day, and Esau was real sick. They were going to put him down, but Lil got to him first. She bought him and nursed him back to health — even built a nice heated shed next to her place to house him. He's the most pampered pet around. She dearly loves that animal." Mae fashioned the white prairie clover into a pretty bouquet and handed it to Trinity. "Pauline will enjoy these. She always kept fresh summer flowers on her kitchen table."

Their destination came into sight. A woman sat on the front porch, rocking. She didn't look up when Trinity and Mae approached.

"Morning, Pauline! We've brought you

some pretty flowers today!" called Mae.

The chair slowly creaked back and forth. Stepping onto the porch, Mae bent close to Pauline's ear. "Good *morning*!"

"I heard you."

"Then why didn't you answer?"

"You won't like what I have to say."

Turning to Trinity, Mae rolled her eyes. "I'm afraid she's in a mood today. She and Mrs. Farley have it out once in a while. Could be they're feuding this morning."

Nodding, Trinity knelt beside the rocker and placed the bouquet on the woman's lap. "Aunt Pauline, I'm Trinity. Trinity Franklin."

Pauline snubbed the gift and the greeting.

"Aren't you going to speak to me? I'm your kin, Trinity."

The old woman's voice turned sour and harsh. "That's what they all say. I got more kin than beggars have lice. You've come to haul me off somewhere. I don't want to go."

"No." Trinity's hand closed around her spindly arm. "I'm here to visit you. I won't take you away."

"Did you come on the train?"

"Yes."

"Ah *ha!*" She leveled a gnarled finger at Trinity. "The train done derailed!"

Mae intervened. "That was months ago,

honey. It's running now, and your niece is here to visit."

She sniffed, then turned her eyes on Trinity. "You're my kin," she said. It was a statement, not a question. Tolerant, but disbelieving.

"I am. I'm Francine's daughter."

"Francine who?"

"Francine — my mother — your . . ." Trinity mentally counted up the generations and came up blank when she reached the first *great.* "Francine's . . . daughter."

"Which would be," Mae helped, "Trinity's great-great . . ."

"Not great-great. Great, perhaps," Trinity offered, "but not great-great."

"No, it would be great-great . . . then maybe another great?"

Trinity shook her head. "I don't think the third *great* is correct. Wouldn't it be great-great . . ."

The old woman's eyes bounced back and forth between the women until she threw up her hands. "Stop!"

Mae patted her veined arm. "Now, now, it only seems proper we should have the generations accurate."

"I don't understand a word you're sayin' and it don't matter. I won't remember five minutes from now. So move on to something else."

Mae brightened. "Trinity is the kin we've been searching for, Pauline. Isn't it good that she's found you?"

"You're here to make me live in that nurse's home."

Shaking her head, Trinity smiled. "The nursing home isn't built yet, and I . . ."

Pauline shoved herself out of her chair and went inside. Trinity looked at Mae.

She shrugged. "This isn't one of her better days. We'll come back tomorrow."

Trailing Mae off the porch, Trinity had to wonder about her aunt's good days.

EIGHT

Jones dodged a buggy as he crossed Dwadlo's main street and proceeded to the general store. He noted the elephant tied to the hitching post and shook his head. Mae's strange friend was up and about early today. Entering the store, he spotted Lil behind the counter.

"Howdy!" she called.

"Morning." His gaze roamed around the room. "Mrs. Curtis around?"

"Nah. She took that Trinity woman to meet Pauline. Dale — he owns the store — he's off visitin' family in Texas so I'm watchin' the store." She came around the counter, all grins. "What can I do for you?"

He removed his hat. "I need to send a wire."

Lil nodded. "Mae'll be back shortly."

Delay. Now it would be hot as blue blazes before he could get on the trail. He absentmindedly wiped the sweat from his brow.

"I'll wait at the café."

Lil nodded. "You want a sody or root beer? I wouldn't complain none if you wanted to keep me company."

The woman definitely had the hunting gleam in her eye. She was pretty, if you favored your women boyish and a bit scuffed up and, unless he missed his guess, feisty. The screen door opened and the town blacksmith stepped inside. Lil's smile faded. "What do you want, Fisk?"

The man ignored the less-than-hospitable greeting and marched to the back of the store. He returned moments later, a swath of white cloth bundled around his bulging jaw and tied in a knot at the top of his head. Until now, he hadn't said a word.

Lil eyed the bandage. "That tooth botherin' you again?"

He grunted.

"You in pain?"

Shifting, he glared at her.

"Yaw. I can see you are. You better let me pull that tooth."

His eyes widened and he took a step back.

"Don't go gettin' all squirrely on me. I ain't gonna pull the durn thing until you let me." She marched around the counter and located a small vial under the shelf. "You're going through this stuff like water. Dale says

87

he don't have another shipment due in 'til next month. That'll be five cents."

Nodding, he fished around in his pocket, a stony glare fixed on her.

"Fork it over."

Five coins landed on the counter.

"I said fork it over, not throw it over."

Fisk picked up the vial, meeting her glower before he gave Jones a silent greeting, turned on his heel, and left.

Scowling at his back, Lil scooped up the coppers and dropped them in a box. She turned a hopeful smile on Jones. "Well, want that sody?"

Jones watched the blacksmith exit. She'd been a mite hard on a man in obvious pain.

"Thanks, but I'll wait at the café." He turned to leave when he caught sight of the elephant again. It was tied in front of the window. "You didn't ride your motorcycle this morning?"

"Nah, she's cuttin' out on me. I think my carburetor's gone crazy." She stepped around the counter and trailed him to the door. "Sure you don't want that sody or root beer?"

"No, thanks."

"You can ride my cycle if'n you want."

"No, but I appreciate the offer."

"Esau? You want to ride him?"

88

"No."

"Say, do you know anything about carbu-retors?" She peered up at him. Her hair looked like she'd thrown it up in the air and jumped under it.

"No, ma'am. Fact is, your motorcycle's the first one I've ever seen. Heard about them, but never seen one."

"That's too bad. I was hopin' you might be able to give me some advice."

"Sorry." He opened the door and Esau trumpeted, shattering the morning serenity. Jones mentally shook the oddity aside. For the life of him, he couldn't see why Tom had decided to leave Chicago and stay here.

As he passed the alleyway a shadow ducked behind a row of barrels. Intrigued, he turned and followed the silhouette. He went up to the barrels and jiggled them. The wooden containers tipped but fell back into place.

You're seeing things, Jones.

He turned and had started back up the alley when he saw a flash of material behind one of the front barrels. The culprit was a mole — a sneaky mole. Pausing before the suspicious container, he nudged it with his boot. Then nudged harder. Kneeling, he pushed it aside and came face-to-face with an old man. The guilty party lowered a half-

89

eaten pancake, forcing a remorseful smile.

Jones eyed the pile of trash lying beside him and realized he was eating the café's garbage. Shoving the barrel clear, he sat down with his back against the café's outer wall. "Is this where you eat?"

"First time I ever et here, but it's fine fixin's." He extended a pancake. "Want one?"

Jones shook his head but couldn't shake the memories the sight evoked. He'd lived on the streets as a young man, and had eaten many a meal from the same source. "Thanks, but I had my breakfast earlier."

They sat in silence. "Name's Benjamin," the man said finally. "Benjamin Henry Cooper."

Jones took the grimy hand. "Jones."

"Mighty glad to meet you, Jones."

"You lived in these parts long?"

"No, just got here." He rummaged in the trash for a moment. "You live here?"

"Just passing through. I work for the railroad."

"That a fact? You like what you do?"

"It's a living." Jones eyed the soggy pancake. "Why don't you put that away and come inside the café? I'll buy you breakfast, and you can keep me company while I have a cup of coffee."

The old gent glanced up, pancake halfway

90

to his mouth. "Why would you waste the money?"

"Let's just say I don't like to see folks eat garbage." He'd left home when he was fifteen — though by that time it had ceased to be home. When his father married a woman who didn't take to children other than her own he'd become an outsider, a nuisance. Something to be ignored.

"Perfectly good eats," the old fellow argued. "Folks nowadays are wasteful. Now, this here pancake's still got a little warmth in it." He studied it. "Right amount of butter, good and soggy with plenty of maple syrup."

"Indulge me. Let's go inside and get you some hot food."

He shook his head. "Can't." He glanced out at the street. "She might see me."

"Who might see you?"

"Her." He pointed. "That purty little lady lookin' for her Aunt Pauline."

Jones glanced toward the alleyway entrance. "Do you know her?"

"A bit."

The old-timer wasn't making a lick of sense. Why would he follow a stubborn, impractical young woman like Trinity to Dwadlo? He shifted. "What do you want with her?"

Benjamin licked butter off his fingers. "Used to have feelin's for her aunt. Real powerful ones. Made my heart all ajigger. I figgered she was dead by now, but I got wind that she was still alive and living here in Dwadlo."

Settling back, Jones sorted the information. "You used to be sweet on Trinity's aunt?"

"Yep, that little lady's her great grand-niece . . . or somethin' like that. There could be another *great* in there. I wasn't listenin' overly close."

Jones lifted his hat and wiped his brow. Dwadlo just got stranger.

"You ever been in love, son?"

"No, sir. Not the marrying kind of love." The last thing he needed was a woman ordering him around like his stepmother.

"Seems odd for a feller your age. Most men are lookin' if they're not already taken."

"No time, sir. No time. I'm headed out to purchase a piece of land and then I'll be riding back to Chicago."

"Eager to get there, huh?"

He flashed a quick grin. "Mrs. Curtis should be back by now. Once I send a wire, I'm heading out."

"Miss Mae took Trinity out to visit Pauline this morning."

Jones shook his head. "You've been spying on her?"

Behind him there was a sharp intake of breath, followed by an angry female voice. "You've been following me?"

Both men started. The two women had approached without making a sound.

The old-timer scrambled to his feet, dropping a third pancake. Jones slowly rose to meet Trinity's flashing eyes. Mae Curtis stood beside her, cheeks flushed. "Don't sneak up on a man like that!" Jones snapped.

"You should talk," Trinity noted.

She could not get that barrel incident out of her craw. He met her stare. "You could get hurt."

Her chin lifted. "Are you threatening me?"

"Take it any way you want, lady."

"Jones. Trinity. Let's retain a smidgen of good manners," Mae cautioned.

Trinity focused on the prospector. "And what are you doing here, Benjamin?"

He held up his hands. "Now, before you bust a gusset, let me explain."

"You followed me."

Benjamin nodded. "I did. Guilty as accused."

Trinity turned to Mae. "He had feelings for Pauline years ago. Decades ago. Seems he never got over it."

Benjamin shook his head. "Never." He pointed at his chest. "Still pains me right here, real hurtful, like a bullet shot clean through the heart."

Jones spotted a grin starting at the corner of Mae's mouth, but she caught it before it broke out. She nodded, her face perfectly straight. "Don't you know, sir, that a gentleman should not follow a woman?"

He bristled. "I ain't followin' Pauline. I've left her alone for forty-five years."

"Look." Jones held up a hand, hoping to put an end to the conversation. "The fellow is about to move on."

"I ain't either. I've come to see my woman." His whiskered chin quivered with determination.

"She isn't your woman," Trinity said, and then her tone softened. "I'm afraid she wouldn't remember you."

He looked at her sideways. "Is she actin' nuttier than a squirrel in the fall, and don't know if up is down or front is sideways?"

Trinity glanced at Mae. "Well . . . yes."

He shook his head. "That's just Pauline. She was always nuttier than a pecan pie, but purty. Real purty." He clasped his hands to his heart. "Her smile could melt the coldest snow in winter."

Jones shook his head. "I need to send a wire, and then you can ride out with me."

Half an hour later, the wire had been sent and Jones was saddling up. The prospector brought his jenny to the rail and prepared to leave. Jones glanced at the old man and almost felt sorry for him. He had to be up there in years. He'd carried a torch a long time for a woman nobody would claim. "You're welcome to ride with me until Fargo. That's where I'll veer off and head for Chicago."

The man shook his head and went about tightening the straps in silence. He was put out, but Jones wasn't his nanny. He shouldn't be hanging around bothering the womenfolk.

Jones mounted up. Trinity stood on the front porch of the store, watching him. For a moment he felt sorry for her — and then he remembered their squabble last night and his sympathy died. She was a hard-headed one. He tipped his hat politely. "Goodbye, Miss Franklin."

Her gaze locked with his. "Goodbye, Mr. Jones."

"Stop by anytime you're out this way!" Mae called. "We loved having you!"

"Yes, ma'am. Tell Tom to behave himself."

95

With a final glance at Trinity, he made a clucking noise and was on his way.

The rattle of pots and pans accompanied the two men out of town.

Trinity watched his back as he left. A niggle of doubt remained. She'd love nothing more than to see Jones ride off and bring their bizarre relationship to a close. But what if he was her last chance at selling her land? The Milwaukee Railroad wasn't going to offer the sum Robert had suggested . . . but Jones got under her skin. She'd sooner eat a skunk than sell him her land.

Mae's voice broke into her troubled thoughts. "Mercy, it's hot. Shall we go inside and have something cool to drink?"

"Thank you, but I think I'll go back to my room and rest." It was sweltering, and she had some thinking to do. Some serious thinking. Was she actually going to let Jones ride away? She could easily catch up with him and accept his offer, though it would pain her . . . but better misery than poverty.

At least one of them was being very foolish. Quite stupid, actually.

"Mae . . ."

She turned in the doorway. "Yes?"

"Am I being illogical?" Trinity hardly knew this woman, but instinct told her she could trust her. "Should I have sold the land to Jones?"

Frowning, Mae removed her hat, fanning her face. "Perhaps you were being a mite hasty last night."

"Yes, I fear that I was. Hasty is the word. Do you think I should go after him and accept his offer?"

"That's a question only you can answer."

"The man annoys me. Greatly."

Sighing, Mae smiled. "It doesn't take much to see that, but all men have a way of getting under a woman's skin. My Tom and I had quite a merry chase during our courting period, but perhaps a body ought not to cut off his nose to spite his face."

"Courting! I wouldn't see the man socially if he were the last one on earth." She fumed, but had to acknowledge the wisdom of what Mae said. "But . . . thank you. Thank you for your honesty." She started off the porch.

"Supper tonight?" asked Mae.

"I'll let you know. I may decide to take a ride in a bit."

NINE

Spotting a pond, Jones reined up a few miles out of town. His horse was already breathing hard and this might be the last water for a while.

Since they passed a pumpkin patch the old-timer had been steadily dropping behind until he was a good distance away. The heat must be getting to him: in the past half hour his form had slumped down, draped on the animal's neck. The jenny's hooves plodded along, pots and pans rattling.

Jones removed his hat and wiped away the sweat. Why had he invited him to ride along? They still had a fair ways to go before they separated, and the old man couldn't or wouldn't keep up. But then, he didn't appear to be the sort who got in a hurry.

What to do? He didn't want the man dying on him, but neither could he afford a long delay. As the jenny drew closer, he squinted. Then he muttered under his breath and slapped a hand against his thigh. The old coot had pulled a fast one. What he had assumed was the old prospector barely hanging on was a couple of rolled-up blankets and a pumpkin with the old man's hat on it. Jones took a closer look. The man had cut a hole in the bottom of the pumpkin and impaled it on the saddle horn.

He looked up, his gaze focusing on an approaching traveler. Benjamin? Had he changed his mind and decided to come back?

Trinity removed her hat and dabbed the moisture off her forehead as she approached Jones, leading her rented horse. She'd vacated the saddle some time earlier. The animal had a terrible gait and she'd prefer blisters on her feet to sores on her backside. "Is it always this hot?" she complained.

"I wouldn't know, ma'am. Just passing through." He peered around her. The old prospector was nowhere in sight.

Trinity tucked her hanky into her waistband. "You must be wondering what I'm doing here," she said.

"The thought did cross my mind." He looked at her, realizing in spite of himself that she was pretty — big brown eyes and strawberry red hair. Freckles, but skin so clear a baby would envy her. The tiny brown fleck near her mouth intrigued him. Made a man tempted to explore it . . .

Her gaze swept the area, landing on the pumpkin. "Where's Benjamin?"

"That's what I was wondering. He was behind me half an hour ago but must have pulled a fast one."

She turned questioning eyes on him.

"The old fellow rigged up his mule to look like he was still on it. I don't know where he went, and I'm in no mood to go searching." His gaze scanned the area, then turned back to here. "Why are you here?"

She drew a breath and straightened her shoulders. "I've reconsidered your land offer, and I accept if you add another fifty dollars."

"Fifty dollars."

"Yes, and I would like the money wired to Sioux Falls. I'd not want to carry such a large amount on my way back."

"I reckon you wouldn't."

"And I want to complete the transaction as soon as possible. I'm anxious to go home."

Grabbing the jenny's bridle, Jones mounted his horse. She'd come all this way to demand money? Well, she'd had her offer. Chances were he'd bid too much for a piece of land she didn't have a clear deed to anyway. She'd refused his proposition, and he was free to rescind the offer. Her loss. Brown eyes and red hair didn't sway him. Or that cute mole at the corner of her mouth. "Sorry, ma'am, but the offer's off the table. I've been doing some thinking, and I've decided that I'd have to see the property before I purchase it."

She sucked in her breath audibly. "You would go back on your word?"

"No, ma'am. I'd have stood straight by my word last night." He flashed a grin. "But that was yesterday. It's morning now — late morning — and I'm having second thoughts." He nudged his horse's flank and started to ride off at a trot. Running after, she dogged his heels.

"That's *completely* unfair!"

"No, it would be unfair of you to take advantage of me," he pointed out. "I haven't seen the land — don't even know for certain it exists."

"You were there!"

"Near there — and I wasn't concentrating on the land. And you need a deed to sell. That's just plain fact. I'd have to take your word that you own the property outright, and I don't know you."

"You know Tom, and he said it was a good buy!"

"Could be, but Tom isn't purchasing anymore. I am, and I'm responsible for my own actions." He clucked, picking up the horse's pace.

"Wait!" She slowed, winded now. Kicking himself, he reined in the horse and rode back. He stared down at her.

"What?"

"I'll take twenty dollars less."

He whistled appreciatively. "Twenty dollars less. For prime land?"

Nodding, she tucked stray wisps of hair under her straw hat. "Twenty-five . . . and not a penny less."

He sat, considering, and then shook his head. "That makes me suspicious. Why would you take less for a prime piece of property?" By the set of her jaw, he knew that if she were prone to violence he would be felled like an oak. She pressed her lips together and swatted at a gnat. He sat atop the horse, grinning.

She finally answered through clenched teeth. "Thirty dollars, and there isn't a thing wrong with my property. It's the best land around, but I want to go home, Mr. Jones . . ." She paused. "What's your name?"

"Jones."

She met his laughing eyes. "Jones. Your name is Jones Jones?"

"No. Jones. Period."

"Your parents didn't give you a first name?"

"They didn't figure I'd need one." His grin widened. "Anyone ever tell you that you can't hide your feelings? I think your hair gets redder when I get your goat."

She jerked herself up straight. "Then tell me, Jones, what am I thinking?"

"That you'd like to knock my head off."

"Close," she admitted. "But back to business. Thirty-one dollars less — but you close the deal right now."

"Right here in the middle of the road? With no deed?"

"Right here." Sweat was rolling down her temples now. "The deed has to be somewhere. I'll find it."

"Thirty-one dollars less." He looked up at the cloud, studying the offer. "You have any livestock you want to throw . . ."

"Thirty-one! Don't try to back out!"

"Now there you go, talking like we have an agreement."

She clamped her lips shut. She knew that he had her. She could stay around until the cows came home and *hope* to get back to

Sioux Falls, or she could loosen up and admit she was stuck. He'd probably give her the money to get home if she'd be a tad more agreeable. Her hair was curling in the humidity. She must look a mess, but she refused to be beholden to him.

Jones dismounted, keeping the reins tight in one hand. Approaching her, his smile faded. "Let's sit a spell. The heat's fearsome."

She trailed him to the roadside and they sat down beneath a tall maple. Shade mercifully canopied their heads. Uncapping a canteen, he offered her a drink of water. She carefully wiped the rim, aware of the devilment in his eyes. "I'm desperate," she said. Relief filled her eyes as the admission tumbled out. She needed an ally.

"What makes you so desperate? Your land will sell even if I don't buy it."

She briefly explained what had happened after he'd ridden off on the first day they met. "I had gone down to the water to do the wash when the ruckus started. I wasn't really aware there was a problem until you shoved me in the barrel, though."

"About that," he interrupted. "I didn't mean to startle you, but when I saw what the men were up to and then spotted you at the water's edge, I figured I didn't have time to explain my actions."

"Apology accepted."

"I'm not apologizing. I'm explaining."

She fixed him with a schoolteacher stare.

He took another swig of water. "Go on."

"Anyway, the men ransacked the house and left me nothing. And then the grasshoppers came." His frown told her she didn't have to elaborate.

"The house is the only thing left standing?"

"The house . . . and not much in it. I didn't know what to do until Benjamin happened along and told me I might have an aunt in Dwadlo. I used the last of the money for a train ticket and came here to find Pauline, hoping she could give me the money to get back home to Sioux Falls."

"How old is she?"

"Ninety-four."

He whistled.

"I know, ancient — but she looks to be faring well for one her age."

"How did your visit go with her today?"

"Not well. She didn't know me, of course — but that's no great surprise, since I was very young when she last saw me."

Leaning back, Jones took another long swallow of water. He lowered the tin and frowned. "Maybe your aunt will eventually recognize you — you or your name."

"I doubt it. Like Benjamin said, she doesn't appear to know front from sideways. It's highly unlikely that she would share any of her meager savings with a great grand-niece she doesn't recognize."

Jones replaced the cap on the canteen, tapping it tightly into place. "So that's how Benjamin fits into the picture. I wondered."

"It was pure providence that he came by just as the grasshoppers swarmed in."

Chuckling, he studied the ground. "Sounds like he had quite a hankering for your aunt."

"Still does, if he followed me here."

Jones paused to study her. Her cheeks reddened even more under his slow perusal. "I'll have to have a clear deed to your land."

Her heart sank. She had only Rob's word that the land belonged to the family, and Pauline wouldn't even speak to her.

He seemed able to read her thoughts. "Your aunt could have one tucked away somewhere," he said gently.

"Maybe . . . but her memory's so bad."

He stood, mounted his horse, and turned back toward town. He looked down at her. "You bring me that deed, and we have a deal."

"I thought you were leaving."

"Changed my mind. I'll stick around another day or two — give you time to get your business in order. No point missing out on a prime piece of land."

What were the odds that a ninety-four-year-old woman would remember where she kept the deed to land that had been in the family since she was a girl?

"How long do I have?"

"Two days."

She nodded. "I'll go to Pauline's right now."

"Good." He stopped just before pressing his heels into the horse's flanks. Trinity followed his gaze as he eyed Benjamin's jenny, its hair still stripped clean. "How did that happen, by the way?"

"Grasshoppers. They ate her fur."

He grinned. "Well, let's hope those hoppers don't have a craving for property deeds." He kicked the horse and trotted off, leading the jenny behind him. Trinity set off behind him. She'd be fine. He'd buy her land and she could return to her life in Sioux Falls. All she had to do was locate the deed.

Like that would be a stroll in the park.

Ten

Early the following morning Trinity sliced white bread and then spread a thin coat of butter on the four crusty pieces. Mae stood at the counter rolling out a crust for her fresh peach pie. Trinity gritted her teeth as she worked. She was not a quitter.

"I can't get her to acknowledge me, but I have to try something. I thought a picnic would allow us time to become acquainted." Beyond the question of the land and the deed, Trinity had so many questions to ask Pauline. What had her mother been like? Her father? Had they been giddy in love that morning when they'd struck out for town and supplies? Her life before she was orphaned was a blank slate, and her aunt might possibly be able to fill in the blanks. Family ties were distant, but surely Pauline knew part of the family history. Surely the stories hadn't been lost completely.

"Well, she never particularly favored

picnics, but I suppose it wouldn't hurt to try." Mae slid the peach pie in the oven and then closed the door. She fanned away the heat from her rosy features. "She wasn't receptive to you yesterday. What makes you think she would accompany you on a picnic today?"

"I have no reason to believe that she will." Trinity layered thick slices of ham on one of the buttered pieces of bread. "But I'm not going to give up until she agrees to spend time with me. There are so many things I'd like to know about the family if she can remember them — or perhaps she's recorded names in journals. It would be nice to know who I am and where I come from. I can't remember much from before my parents died."

Mae paused beside the work table and eyed her work. "Put a little sugar on Pauline's bread and butter. She has a dreadful sweet tooth."

Trinity reached for the sugar bowl and pinched a few grains. "Won't you come with us?"

"Not today. The mail is always heavy at the end of the month and I want to catch a nap this afternoon once I finish sorting it. The hot weather is dragging me down."

Trinity wouldn't have pegged Mae for a

woman who napped. She was constantly on the run, working at the store or doing an errand or making supper for an ailing neighbor. She was a marvel.

Trinity wrapped the sandwiches in white cloth and slid them into a wicker basket.

"There are plenty of peaches," Mae reminded her. "No use letting them go to waste." She swatted a gnat away from a piece of overripe fruit.

"Thank you." Trinity added a few of the plump fruits and two cloth napkins before she closed the lid. "Well, wish me luck."

"Luck?" Mae turned from the sink and grinned. "I'll be praying for an act of God."

The sun was reaching its highest point in the sky when Trinity neared the Farley place. Nothing seemed to be stirring. The front porch rocker sat empty and when she hesitantly paused and listened she couldn't hear a sound coming from inside the cottage. Most likely Pauline and Miz Farley were chatting away, working on hand stitching or piecing a quilt. Miz Farley had been so good to welcome Pauline into her home. The women must spend long hours enjoying each other's company.

Meadowlarks chirped and flittered overhead.

Approaching the porch, Trinity gripped the wicker basket and mentally rehearsed her invitation. "Good morning, Aunt Pauline!" she would say. "It's such a beautiful day that I thought a picnic was in order. I brought ham sandwiches and peaches!" She prayed her aunt wouldn't recall her earlier visit and might even welcome the company. Folks had warned her that one never knew where Pauline's mind was from day to day.

She lifted her hand and started to knock when the door flew open and she gasped as a pan of dishwater hit her full in the face. Staggering backwards, she dropped the wicker basket, wicked words forming in her mind. When she cleared her eyes, she saw Pauline staring at her. "Great balls of fire! Are you back?"

Trinity fisted water from her eyes. "I . . . yes . . . Why did you . . . I mean . . . Do you have a cloth?"

"Yeh . . . Hold on a minute." The door shut and Trinity sank to the porch, still half blind and her eyes stinging. Pauline returned shortly carrying a damp dishcloth. "How was I to know that you were standing in the way of me dumping the dishwater?"

No apology. No polite "I'm sorry!" Aunt Pauline made it sound like it was Trinity's fault that she'd thrown slimy dishwater in her niece's face.

Trinity took the damp cloth gingerly and mopped at her eyes, cheeks, and hair. "Do you not have a back door?"

"I ain't got *no* door, missy. None I can call my own." The old woman lifted her by the arm and hefted her to her feet. "You're startin' to be a pest, do you know that?"

Wringing out the cloth, Trinity was tempted to sass but then thought better of it. "I hope you haven't eaten dinner."

"Dinner? I just finished the breakfast dishes." She turned and shaded her eyes to stare at the sun. "It's another hour or two afore dinner."

Trinity returned the cloth, and then hefted up the wicker basket to show her. "I brought a picnic lunch. I thought perhaps you would enjoy an outing. It would give us a chance to visit and get to know each other."

"I don't like picnics."

"But you like bread and butter sandwiches sprinkled with sugar, don't you? And Mae sent along fresh peaches!"

Pauline appeared to consider the offer, and then tossed it aside. "I'm not hungry."

"But you will be in a couple of hours." Determined, Trinity lowered the basket. "Let's walk a ways. It's a pretty morning and I noticed the wildflowers are particularly lovely today. Do you need to tell Miz Farley that you're leaving?"

"I'm leaving?"

"You're going on a picnic."

"I don't like picnics."

"Miz Farley?" Trinity called through the open door. It wasn't long before a stout white-headed woman appeared in the doorway, wiping her hands on a stained apron.

"I'm taking Pauline on a picnic." Guilt rushed through her when she remembered her manners. She really should invite the woman to come along, but this picnic involved personal business, so she couldn't. "We'll be gone for a while."

"Hallelujah and thank the good Lord."

Trinity wasn't sure how to take the comment. "We won't be gone long."

"The longer the better." She slammed the door.

Pauline tired easily. They hadn't walked far at all when she suddenly gave out and sat down under a tree. Trinity followed, carrying the wicker basket. The spot was as pretty as any along the roadside and the sun was starting to bake the earth.

"Did you bring anything to drink?" Pauline asked.

"Mae handed me a jar of fresh lemonade

just as I was walking out the door. She's always so thoughtful."

"Mae's a good girl. Always thought if I had a daughter, I'd want her to be like Mae."

She'd just opened the door to one of the subjects uppermost in Trinity's mind. "If it isn't too personal a question, why didn't you ever marry?" If what Benjamin said was true, Pauline had been pretty enough in her younger years to have her choice of available men.

"I came close a couple of times but always backed out." Pauline settled on the grass, perspiration gathering on her upper lip. "Decided I didn't need a man."

"Have you ever regretted your choice? I only ask because often I think the same thing."

Pauline's eyes grew distant. "There was one — once. A long time ago. Probably should have paid more attention to him, but that's water over the dam. Can I have a glass of that lemonade?"

"Of course." Trinity opened the basket, uncapped the jar, poured the contents into a glass, and handed it to her. Pauline drank thirstily.

"I suppose you and Miz Farley are having a grand time together, sewing and visiting

114

and cooking?"

"That old heifer? She's a wart on my soul. I wish a hole in the ground would open and swallow her up."

Taken aback, Trinity cleared her throat. "If you don't care for Miz Farley, why are you living with her?"

Pauline turned dour eyes on her. "Do I have a choice?"

Trinity hadn't thought about the arrangement. Obviously Miz Farley wasn't a bucket of sunshine, but the nursing home wouldn't be ready until fall. She changed the subject. "How often did you manage to see my parents when they were alive?" she asked.

Lowering the glass of lemonade, Pauline studied on the question. "Don't rightly recall. Who'd you say your folks were?"

"John and Francine Franklin."

"Oh, I remember them. No, didn't see them much. Once every few years, maybe, if they happened to come through Dwadlo, which they didn't — that I recall. So I guess I didn't see them often."

"Oh. Then you didn't know much about my mother?"

"She was a real nice woman. I recall she always had a good word to say about everyone."

"And my father?"

"That louse?" She took another swig of lemonade from the glass. "He was polite enough, but had a cowardly streak a mile wide if you were to ask me."

"Cowardly?" Trinity frowned. Rob mentioned that their father had a temper, but she'd never heard him called cowardly.

"I thought so — coupled with a mean streak. Your mother never took any guff off him, but I've heard family members say they didn't know why she put up with a man like that."

Cowardly and mean. Which of those traits had she inherited? Trinity tried to absorb the information. Somehow she'd expected glowing recollections of the man who'd fathered her. Rob's nature had always been pleasant and patient.

"Do you recall me and Rob when we were young?"

"Don't recall you now, young'un. I just tolerate you because you won't go away."

"Aunt Pauline," Trinity chastised, "you need to learn manners. It isn't nice to be so blunt with your words. You hurt people's feelings."

"You asked me, didn't you? If you don't want to know the truth then don't ask."

Trinity slowly unwrapped one of the sandwiches and handed it to her aunt. Pauline stared at the offering. "Not really hungry."

"I sprinkled sugar on it."

"Sugar?" She glanced up. "How'd you know I like sugar on my sandwiches?"

"Mae told me."

Her aunt eyed the sandwich Trinity was now unwrapping. "I shore do favor ham."

Trinity extended the sandwich to her. "You're welcome to this, but . . . you don't have teeth." Heat crept up her neck at the blatant observation, but the words slipped out without proper thought.

"Since when have missing teeth stopped me from eating ham?"

"I just thought . . . I'm sorry. I'll eat the bread and butter."

"Nope. Wouldn't be polite to eat your ham. I'll have the bread and butter." She settled back and bit into the fare, gumming the bread. "Then if you haven't finished your sandwich I might have a bite of ham."

Trinity made a mental note to save at least half of it.

They ate in companionable silence, watching an occasional wagon pass. The occupants waved and called a friendly hello. The people of Dwadlo were a friendly lot. Folks always seemed to have a smile and kind word for a stranger. Mae said they'd all pitched in and helped bring the town back to normal after the train derailments.

Time passed and Trinity knew she should question Pauline about the deed, but she was afraid to ruin the moment. They had formed a quiet truce and now that the ice between them was broken, there would be plenty of opportunities to convince Pauline that she needed help with her personal business and Trinity was there to serve her.

Around one o'clock, Trinity gathered the remains of lunch and packed everything into the basket. Pauline was tiring visibly, and the picnic had been most pleasant. They had chatted about ordinary things — Dwadlo and Pauline's intermittent recollections of years past. Trinity recognized that back in her day, Aunt Pauline would have been fascinating company. She was knowledgeable about a good deal of subjects even with her faulty memory.

By the time they'd returned to Miz Farley's and said goodbye, Trinity was convinced that she and Pauline were going to become good friends — and, with a little help from the Lord, close family.

Eleven

The smell of supper lingered in the air as Pauline pushed open the screen door and settled in the porch rocker. Trinity, still a ways down the road, could just make out her slight figure. She knew she was pushing her luck with two visits in one day, but the picnic had been so productive that she wanted more.

The evening heat was letting up for the day and the sun was sinking lower in the sky. When she was a child this had been her favorite hour of the day — still was, only she hadn't stopped much these days to enjoy the peaceful feeling. Good health wasn't anything she thought about either — one surely didn't at her age — but she paused as she watched Pauline struggle to lower herself into the rocker. One day, if the good Lord allowed it, she'd be like Pauline. Her footsteps would be slower, more uncertain. Her eyesight would be poor, and her

119

hearing would fade. Her patience might be fleeting.

Granted, her aunt had lived much longer than the allotted three score and ten years. Maybe God had forgotten Pauline, but Trinity didn't see how. She was a Wilson, and she made herself heard loud and clear.

The good Lord couldn't miss Pauline.

Approaching the house, Trinity touched a self-conscious hand to her hair. She should have dressed more properly. A hat would be in order. Mae had offered one but Trinity had refused. It was too hot to be proper. Right now she had to concentrate on her mission, and she didn't need anything distracting her.

Pauline nodded off as Trinity climbed the two steps leading up to the porch. A rose vine wound its way up the white column and around the handrail. The summer night caught the sweet scent and carried it on a soft breeze.

"Aunt Pauline?"

The old woman's head bobbed, her chin dropping lower to her chest.

Easing closer, Trinity approached the rocker. She didn't want to startle the poor thing awake. "Pauline?"

"I heard you the first time."

Trinity jerked back, startled. Her aunt

120

didn't have the most pleasant personality. She knew that old age often made a person persnickety, but this woman was downright ill-mannered. She cleared her throat. "I enjoyed our visit so much this afternoon that I thought I'd set a spell with you this evening."

Pauline opened one watery eye and peered at the setting sun. "Again? It's my bedtime."

Encouraged by the more hospitable tone, Trinity took the chair opposite her aunt.

Pauline's eyes were wide open now. They scanned Trinity's length, head to toe. "Ain't you the one that was here last month?"

"This morning," Trinity corrected. "We had a picnic together. A very enjoyable one. With bread and butter sandwiches and peaches."

"Don't recall."

"I promise I won't take much of your time." She scooted the chair closer. "I've come to ask a favor."

Pauline's eyes narrowed. "Mooching? You here to mooch off your kin?"

Mooching wasn't what she had in mind. Trinity briefly explained her plight. When she mentioned Wilson's Falls Pauline appeared to stir, but then sat back and listened. Trinity couldn't tell if anything she was saying made sense to the woman, but she plowed on. "My brother, Rob, was the last of our kin. Wilson's Falls must be sold. The proceeds will be yours, but we must have a clear deed to the land in order to sell."

"Clear deed," Pauline repeated.

"Yes." Trinity sat up straighter, confident she had her aunt's undivided attention. "Do you have one?"

"One what?"

"The deed to Wilson's Falls."

"Why would I have a deed to some falls?"

"Because you and your sister, Priss . . ."

"Priss?" She shook her head. "She passed a long time ago. Good woman. I miss her."

"My condolences." Trinity squeezed the old woman's hand. "But since no one is left to work the land, and the railroads are buying track sites, you need to dispose of the property."

"That right?" Pauline sat back, setting her rocker in motion. "Why?"

"Because I live in Sioux Falls and I want to go home."

"Sioux Falls is your home?"

"Yes."

"Had a friend there once. I think. Daisy. Darnell. No — Dixie. Not sure on that. What are you doing in Dwadlo?"

"I came here to find you so I can help you

sell the land. Once that's done, I can go home. As soon as possible." She didn't mention that she was counting on the money from the sale to cover her train fare. That would be an overload of information.

"Where's that?"

"Sioux Falls . . ." Oh dear. She was fading. "Wilson's Falls is the piece of land we're discussing." She was only confusing her more.

"We're in Wilson's Falls?" Pauling glanced up at the sun sliding down beyond the horizon. "Why, that can't be right. It's my bedtime."

Scooting closer, Trinity found her words rushing out. "Please, Aunt Pauline, stay with me. Do you have a deed to Wilson's Falls?"

"What's a deed?"

"It's a . . ." Sitting back, Trinity closed her eyes. *Grant me patience, Lord. She's old and I know she gets tired easily.*

Shoving herself out of the chair, Pauline shuffled to the screen door. "We're talkin' in circles. You need to go home and if you come visitin' again, don't wait till so late." She sniffed. "A body can't get a lick of rest around here."

A woman's voice came from inside the house. "Are you talking to yourself again, Pauline?"

123

"Ah, dry up," Pauline muttered. "Talk about not gettin' any peace. It's a madhouse 'round here." She opened the door and stepped inside.

Night birds called. Twilight had started to soften the heat. The setting was peaceful . . . peaceful as a tomb. Sighing, Trinity watched the screen door bang closed. A second later a woman with a mop of white hair appeared. She was round and jolly, but her tone was none too cheerful. "What do you want?"

"I'm here to visit my aunt."

"Pauline's your aunt?"

"Yes, ma'am."

"You're real kin?"

"Yes, ma'am."

"You wouldn't pull my leg, now, would you?"

"No, ma'am. Pauline's my great-great aunt."

"Ain't nothin' great about that woman. Hold on a minute." She disappeared into the house and Trinity listened to the rise and fall of muted female voices. From the sound of it, a heated dispute was in progress. She heard what sounded like a dish hitting the wall. Then shouts. Livid accusations.

Trinity began to sweat in spite of the cool evening breeze. Were the women fighting?

Was she supposed to go inside to defend her aunt? Perplexed, she stood and shifted on her feet. How she longed to see friendly faces and serve up a plate of fried catfish and cornbread to normal folk back in Sioux Falls.

A full five minutes passed before the white-haired woman returned with Pauline in tow. Opening the screen, she nudged the elderly woman out and stuck a sack in her hand. "Now get on out, and don't come back here no more."

"I'll come if I want . . ."

The screen door slammed and Trinity's jaw dropped as the woman flipped a hook over a nail. The defiant act struck her. Pauline had just been handed off. To her. To a long-lost niece who didn't have the slightest idea of what she would do with a ninety-four-year-old relative she hadn't known existed until a few days ago.

Pauline was muttering. "Let's go. That woman's not playing with a full deck."

Still reeling, Trinity sputtered. "Go where?" Her room over the café had one small cot and a dresser.

"How should I know? 'Pears you're my keeper. You figure it out."

Her keeper! The words ricocheted through Trinity's brain. The entire situation was getting out of hand. She'd come for a deed and gained an old woman. Her gaze fell on the small bag in Pauline's hand. Could it contain the deed?

It couldn't be that simple.

"May I see your bag?"

Pauline drew the sack closer to her breast. "No. It's mine."

"I know it's yours. I just want to make sure you have everything."

"It's all here."

"How do you know?" She'd packed in such haste. Something like a deed could have easily been overlooked.

"I just know. It's personal and you're not looking."

Obviously the matter would have to be dealt with later. For now, Trinity would have to find a place for her.

Find a place for Pauline. This was insane.

Jones leaned back, cold drink in hand, and let the warm breeze ruffle his hair. The store was closed to business, but a few late shoppers trickled by and ventured a knock. Mae would good-naturedly let the person in for a tin of powder or sack of sugar. The elephant and a couple of saddled horses stood hitched at the railing. Benjamin's hairless jenny grazed beside the building.

His gaze traveled over the near-empty street. Nice town, Dwadlo. Small, but friendly. Had a few weird characters, but he supposed all towns had their share. By now he'd have been nearer Chicago, but a few days' delay wasn't going to make or break him. Except in Violet's case. The banker's daughter had played coy long enough and had finally consented to have supper with him when he got back. Hopefully the delay wouldn't cost him his social life.

Sliding lower in his chair, he closed his eyes and pictured the dark-haired, blue-eyed beauty. She was quite a prize. Pretty, sensitive, and knew how to laugh. A smile twisted the corners of his mouth. Maybe it was getting to be time to settle down, have a few children. Stay put for more than a week at a time. But he'd never leave the railroad like Tom. He needed the open space. When the time came he'd put in for a desk job. Push a pencil instead of scouting remote territories for land to buy up.

The screen opened and Tom stepped out of the store. Taking in a deep breath, he patted his stomach and sucked in the night air.

Jones motioned to the opposite chair. "Looks like Mae's feeding you well."

Grinning, Tom dropped into the chair and propped his feet up on the railing. "I have to say I like married life real well."

"That a fact?"

"That's a fact. You should try it."

Chuckling, Jones focused on the quiet street. "I might consider it. In time."

Tom closed his eyes and rested his head on the back of the chair. "Where is everyone?"

"Can't say. The streets seem empty for so early."

"Everyone must be out looking for the old prospector," Tom guessed.

"Might be. The old coot got away faster than a greased hog."

"Mmm."

"Lil still in there with Fisk?" asked Jones.

"Yep. She's still trying to fix that toothache. He was in pain when he got here and the two of them have been squabbling for the past half hour. One of these days one of them is going to tear the other's head off."

Jones chuckled. "This could be the day."

"They've always fought, Mae says. They can't get along, but if either of them are in trouble they run to each other first."

"Fisk isn't married?"

"He was," said Tom. "Lost his wife about a year and a half ago. Nice guy. Quiet — if Lil isn't around. Unassuming. Nothing like Lil."

128

Shouts came from the back of the mercantile. Fisk's raised voice tangled with Lil's bossy jeers.

Jones dozed, only half-listening to the ruckus. Settling down with someone like Mae would be nice, but what if he got a hooligan like Lil? Violet, now, was as meek as a kitten. But what if she turned out to be like his stepmother?

The screen door flew open and Fisk stalked outside, holding his swollen jaw. Jones watched as he marched off the porch and walked up to the jenny grazing at the side of the building. He sat up straighter when the blacksmith bent and kissed the donkey. Smack on the lips.

Bolting upright, Jones watched as he did it again. "Hey!"

Tom's eyes flew open. "What's wrong?"

"Fisk just kissed that donkey."

"Kissed the donkey?" Tom turned to look, then broke into a grin. "Old folk tale. Kissing a donkey is supposed to relieve toothache."

"You aren't serious."

"I sure am. Ask Lil — she knows all about those old remedies. I guess Fisk is willing to try anything at this point."

The man in question straightened, spit a couple of times, and then wiped his mouth

129

on his sleeve, wincing. He turned and stalked back into the store without looking at either man.

Jones sat back in his chair. "There isn't a woman alive who could convince me to kiss a donkey."

"Speaking of women," said Tom, "here comes a mite pretty little thing."

Jones turned to see Trinity and someone walking beside her. It wasn't the old prospector. It was a woman, moving slowly and laboriously.

"Good grief." Tom got to his feet. "She's got Pauline with her."

"Her aunt?"

Tom stepped off the porch and went to meet the two women, offering a supportive arm to the elderly lady.

Another shout erupted from the back of the store and Jones winced. If Lil couldn't fix that tooth he needed to see the doc and have it yanked out of there.

Trinity approached, her cheeks flushed from the walk. Jones stood up to greet her. "Evening, Miss Franklin."

Trinity nodded to him and sat down on the porch steps. Tom helped Pauline into a chair. "Now, what are the two of you doing out this late?"

"Mrs. Farley just threw Pauline out of her house."

"Threw her?"

"She packed her things in that little sack and ordered her to leave. With me." She lifted her eyes, and Jones could see that she was close to tears. "Where will I put her?"

"Mae! We need you out here!" shouted Tom.

The screen door of the store opened and Mae poked her head out. "Pauline?" She let the door swing closed. "What are you doing here at this hour?"

"I'm homeless. Again."

"Oh, dear." Mae glanced at Trinity.

"I went for another visit this evening," said Trinity, "and Mrs. Farley and Pauline had some sort of . . . dispute." Her words trailed off as shouts came from the rear of the store.

Mae shook her head. "Just ignore that ruckus. Lil is trying to help Fisk with his toothache."

Another yell. Jones shuddered. "Can't they do that somewhere else?"

"No. Lil has a dental chair set up — or something that acts as a dental chair. Just ignore it."

Yelps filled the summer air.

"I'm plumb tuckered out. Where's my bed?" asked Pauline.

131

Mae looked at Trinity and sighed. "I'll make up a pallet for you. Tomorrow we'll find a more permanent place." Her eyes drifted to her husband. "How much longer before the rest home is complete?"

"A few months yet, honey." His eyes reflected his apology.

Shaking her head, Mae took Pauline's arm. "Come on, sweetie. We'll give you a nice sponge bath and put you to bed."

Trinity stood to follow, but Jones reached out and took her arm. "Come on. I'll get you a cold lemonade."

Her eyes brimmed with gratitude. "Thank you. I'd be ever so grateful."

The shrieks from the back of the store heightened and Lil's voice rose. "I'm pulling that tooth! Now you get a firm grip on the chair. That sucker's coming out!"

"No, it ain't!"

"Yes, it *is*!"

"Good Lord, help me!"

"The good Lord's sent me, so hush up!"

Listening to this was excruciating. Frozen into place, the expressions of those on the porch changed from agony to revulsion to panic as the noise swelled. From the sounds, there was an all-out war going on in the back — one that none of them were inclined to join.

The sound suddenly ceased. A blanket of silence dropped over the group.

Jones felt sick to his stomach. Trinity's eyes were larger than they'd been the day he stuffed her in that barrel.

Mae and Tom stood, speechless.

"Well? Is anyone going to put me to bed?" Pauline demanded. "I can't stay here all night."

The front door flew open and Fisk stalked past, his jaw wrapped in a large white cloth and tied in a knot at the top of his head. He nodded a silent hello as he passed, then stepped off the porch and strode toward the livery.

Jones just watched, shaking his head. Just suppose he did decide to settle down. What if he got a girl like Lil? Then what?

Trinity set the sponge aside with a sigh. Pauline had been bathed and dressed in one of Mae's soft cotton nightgowns. Jeremy came into the house and paused in the open bedroom doorway. "Mae, Pauline can't sleep on the floor. She can have my bed."

"Thank you, sweetie. That's kind of you, and I'm sure Pauline will appreciate a good night's rest. How's the sick dog?"

"Twelve's better today."

"That's good." Mae looked at Trinity. "He

133

gives each of Pauline's strays a number. It's easier to keep up with."

The boy turned to leave, then came back. "Mae, can I walk out to Lil's place? She told me I could help wash Esau if I got there in time. He hasn't had a bath in weeks."

Mae glanced out the window. "It's getting late. The sun will be down before you get back. Be sure to take a lantern."

"I will. Thanks!"

"He's a delightful young man," Trinity said when she heard the front door bang shut.

"Was that a gunshot?" Pauline asked. She sat up straighter. "Is someone robbing the bank?"

"No, that was just the door slamming shut." Mae led her to the bed in Jeremy's room. "Here we go. Nice fresh sheets."

Pauline slid onto the mattress, pulling the sheet up to her neck and grinning tooth-lessly. "Ah. Now this is better."

"Is your bank robbed often?" Trinity asked. It was such a strange town, filled with such eccentric people. Backfiring two-wheeled machines. Elephants. Excessive crime, apparently. And according to last night's dinner conversation two trains had derailed there within the past year. Why, a body wouldn't be safe here.

"No, but Pauline worries about things." Mae flashed a smile. "Everything, actually."

"Shall I put her sack in the closet?" asked Trinity. Truth be known, she was dying to see what the bag contained — but she could hardly rummage through someone's personal effects without good reason. If the deed was in there it would be a miracle. She was quickly learning that nothing in Dwadlo was ordinary.

"No, it'll be fine here until tomorrow." Mae paused, her pretty features pinched. "We're often forced to find Pauline a new home on short notice. I'll be so thankful when the rest home is ready. All this moving around has to tire a body out."

Trinity patted the edge of Pauline's pillow. "Goodnight, dear. Sleep well."

She trailed Mae out of the room and softly closed the door, already hearing soft snores. Jones and Tom sat on the porch, boots propped up on the railing. Fireflies danced about in the waning light.

A twinge of envy crept over her. Home. What a wonderful place to be. Her room in Sioux Falls wasn't a house, but a comfortable bed, chair, and washstand made it hers. She'd potted green plants and set them on the windowsill to catch the early morning sunlight. Until now she had been completely content, but seeing Mae and Tom together made her realize how much she still wanted. They had each other and Jeremy and a home where love spilled from every corner.

Shaking the melancholy thought aside, she trailed Mae to the kitchen and found a large glass of lemonade awaiting her. Jones. He'd poured the drink while she was bathing Pauline. Tears sprang to her eyes. She wasn't sentimental, but the small act touched her. She had been on her own for so long, so accustomed to taking care of her own needs, that she'd forgotten — or perhaps never known — how small acts of kindness made life easier. If she wanted a drink, she poured it. If she was hungry, she cooked. If she was sick, she made chicken soup. If she was having a bad day, she poured her heart out to Willis, Mrs. Oates's cat. But there was more to life than that. Her gaze roamed around her comfortable surroundings. Mae had found more to life than working at the post office. She'd found Tom. She'd found love.

"Looks like the men poured our lemonade." Mae picked up her glass and drank deeply. Trinity sipped the sweet liquid. "Delicious, isn't it? Jeremy uses way too much sugar, but . . ." Mae took another long drink.

Too much sugar wasn't necessarily a bad

thing, Trinity reasoned. Especially for someone who rarely experienced this kind of attention.

TWELVE

Nodding goodnight to the men, Trinity stepped off the porch steps and started to her room above the café. Twilight turned to dark. Lantern light spilled from the café. The night was so lovely she found herself meandering past her room and further down the road, following the trailing scent of blooming honeysuckle. In the distance she spotted Jeremy running toward town, his legs pumping hard as his long strides ate up the ground. He came to a halt, breathless, as he reached her. "Miss Lil needs help. She's got problems with the elephant."

Trinity started, then stopped dead in her tracks. "We'll need the men."

"No, she said just get you or Mae. She said not to bring any men."

Trinity started off again, running now. Why no men? Did Lil think she had the strength to move an elephant? She clearly didn't know her limitations. There was a

stitch in Trinity's left side now, but she ran
harder. How did one control an elephant?

Jones. They needed Jones, not her.

They reached Lil's home and Trinity
paused to take in her surroundings. Lil lived
in an old shack with a tarpaper roof, and
every imaginable object littered the yard.
Pigs snorted and scattered. Dogs barked.
Cats lined the rough timber railing. She'd
never seen such disarray.

A large shed sat a hundred yards from the
house. Lantern light spilled out the open
doorway and silhouetted Lil, who was waving to catch their attention.

"Hurry up!"

Trinity raced toward the light, Jeremy
leading the way. When she entered the
primitive building she stepped back. Esau's
massive rump was in her way.

"I need help," said Lil, pushing past the
mound of gray flesh. "Move it, Esau!"

The animal didn't budge. Trinity's heart
raced. She'd never faced anything so massive. The animal's sheer height snatched her
breath away. The elephant was fixed in
place, not moving a muscle.

"What's wrong?"

"See for yourself! Git on over, Esau." She
whacked the animal's rear, but he didn't
budge.

139

Peering around the elephant, Trinity spotted a cowering figure, his arms thrown over his head to shield it. A man . . .

Her eyes narrowed. "Benjamin! We've been looking everywhere for you. What are you doing?"

"Afearin' for my life!"

She glanced at Lil. "Will Esau hurt him?"

"Naw, but he ain't above scarin' him to death."

Stepping cautiously around Esau, Trinity crept closer, reaching out her hand to Benjamin. The elephant had him trapped.

"Oh, help me, Miss Franklin! I'm in a fine mess!"

"I should say you are. How did you get back there?"

Lil shouted from the other side of the animal. "I told him he could stay with Esau but I warned him not to crowd him. He don't like to be cramped." Bending, she peered through the elephant's fleshy hind legs and called out. "Did you crowd him? I told you not to crowd him."

"I didn't crowd him! He jest takes more than his share of space!"

Jeremy's summons now made sense. Had he brought Tom or Jones they would have had a field day with Lil. It seemed the people of Dwadlo weren't overly fond of

140

having an elephant parade through their streets. She met Lil's troubled eyes. "What do you want me to do?"

"I'm gonna give him a good whack and see if he'll move back."

"Benjamin?"

"Esau!"

The elephant shifted and swished its tail. Trinity jumped back.

"Are you ready?" Lil called.

She was as ready to have an elephant trample her as she was ever going to get. "I don't think this is smart. Perhaps the men . . ."

"No one's going to say a word to the menfolk about this. Now when I whack him, you grab his tail."

Trinity's mouth gaped open. Grab his tail? "Then what?"

"Then let's hope Esau gets the message and takes a step back — just far enough to get you outta there, old feller."

"Jest hurry up!" cried Benjamin. "If that thing takes a notion to charge, I'm a goner!"

"Esau ain't gonna charge anything but his supper. Hold on. You ready, Trinity?"

"Jeremy, step outside the shed," Trinity ordered.

"But Miss Franklin . . ."

"Outside," she repeated. She might be

risking her life for a strange redheaded ruffian she didn't know a thing about, but she wasn't risking his.

Jeremy turned and left the shed, but stayed close enough to keep an eye on the action.

"I'm ready!" Trinity called. Maybe she wouldn't need a train ticket back to Sioux Falls after all. This could be the end.

"Okay! I'm gonna whack him! Benjamin? You ready?"

"Jest whack the beast and git it over with!"

Smack!

Esau surged backward, pinning Trinity to the doorframe.

"That did it! I'm free!" Benjamin hollered.

Trinity turned horrified eyes on Jeremy, who was waiting patiently outside. "I'm trapped."

"Want me to go get Tom?"

"No!" If he brought Tom then Jones would come as well, and wouldn't she look the fool, pinned behind an elephant? As if she hadn't already made a complete imbecile of herself in front of him.

Whack!

The animal lunged and Trinity jumped free, collapsing to the ground in front of Jeremy. Pain seared her right shoulder. Sucking in her breath she struggled to get to her feet with one hand, the throb almost unbearable. The boy gently helped her upright and dusted off her dress. "Are you hurt, Miss Franklin?"

"No, I . . . I'm not sure." Clamping her eyes shut she fought the white-hot pain radiating through her limb. She'd fallen hard.

"You sure? Oughta let the doc take a look at you."

Lil stepped out of the doorway, followed by Benjamin. The old-timer took one look at her and frowned. "You need a doc, young lady."

Cradling the arm, Trinity allowed herself to be led to a nearby stump. After shooing half a dozen pigs away, Lil made her sit down. She examined the arm with a furrowed brow. "I'll git my doctorin' kit," she said finally.

Stark terror flooded through Trinity. She'd witnessed the tooth pulling ordeal earlier, and she wasn't about to let this woman touch her. "No. I'll go to the doctor."

"Why? I'll set it for nuthin'. Doc'll charge you as much as two chickens and a dozen ears of corn."

Trinity had neither chickens nor corn, but neither did she have a death wish. She held firm. "I prefer to let the doctor look at it."

If this woman's doctoring skills matched her dental proficiency, she wouldn't survive the ordeal.

The next morning Dwadlo was buzzing with the news of the incident at Lil's the night before. The doctor had been woken from a deep sleep to set Trinity's shoulder, and had been none too happy about the interruption.

Jones brushed his mare, Sue, with a heavy stroke, a grin forming at the corners of his mouth as he thought about the elephant. But the flash of humor quickly faded. Trinity could have been seriously injured, and the old-timer had been lucky to get away with his life. Fact was, Esau was still a wild animal and he needed to be handled with caution.

He spotted Trinity coming out of the café carrying a wicker basket in her left hand. Her right arm had been lightly wrapped in white gauze. The bandage would come off soon. Guilt plagued him. He'd been a mite hard on her. And the chance of her coming up with a deed to Wilson's Falls was next to nothing if it involved Pauline. Jones didn't know why he was still hanging around. He wasn't using common sense.

Trinity crossed the street and walked his

way. A grin forced its way out and he ducked behind Sue, pretending to focus on the mare's hindquarters. She paused beside the horse and stood there while he worked. Finally she spoke. "I see you smiling, Jones."

Straightening, he forced a stern expression. "What smile?"

Shaking her head, she rounded the mare to face him. "I wasn't hurt. The arm is only sprained."

"You could have been killed. What were you doing there at that hour? Last I saw you were heading for your room."

"The night was so lovely I thought I'd enjoy a short walk. Jeremy came after me and . . . well, you know the rest of the story. Apparently everyone in Dwadlo does."

Chuckling, Jones bent to examine Sue's left ankle. "So you found Benjamin."

"Lil said he could sleep in Esau's shed, but he's looking for other quarters today."

"Did you mention that I wasn't any too happy about the fast one he played on me?"

"No, that's between the two of you. I have my own problems, thank you."

Jones straightened, grinning.

"Stop that insipid smiling."

"Fine, but I'd think you would be happy. Now that you've found Benjamin, maybe he can help."

145

"How could he help? He hasn't seen Pauline in years."

"Could be he could get her to remember where she put the deed — if one exists."

"From what he tells me she wouldn't give him the time of day forty-five years ago. I hardly think she would share personal information with him — even if she does remember him."

Jones ran the brush over Sue's glistening hide. "You never know about women."

"And you do?"

"Just enough to say they're unpredictable. One minute they're hot to tell you everything they know and the next they clam up and you can't get the time of day out of them."

"You sound as if you've dealt with a few."

"My fair share." He glanced up and smiled. "In my business I have to deal with women sometimes."

She dropped to a hay bale and set her basket aside. "And otherwise?"

He frowned.

"Otherwise — is there someone special waiting for you in Chicago?"

His hand paused and the grin widened.

"I merely ask to be civil," said Trinity. "I'm afraid we began our acquaintance under a strain and it appears to be continuing."

"I'm not mad at you."

"Nor I with you." She adjusted her skirts and kept her eyes on the ground.

She needed something. Jones felt it in his bones. A woman like her didn't sashay into the livery and make small talk with a man who got under her skin.

"Really? I think you could have skinned me alive that first day. I didn't intend for you to go over those rapids. You must know that."

"I'm afraid of water. And I don't like dark, cramped spaces."

"Granted, but what about dinner at the Curtises' the other night? You didn't much care for my company. It was all you could do to be polite."

She lifted her chin and met his gaze. "I don't believe I said anything rude."

"Oh, honey, your eyes said it. Loud and clear."

She bristled. "My name is not *Honey.* It's Trinity."

"I know your name." He moved to the horse's mane. "So what's on your mind this morning?"

"I'm not going to find the deed within our agreed-upon time."

A fact he had already anticipated. "I'm sorry to hear it."

147

"Could you possibly delay . . ."

"No, ma'am. The railroad pays me a salary and I'm not earning it hanging around here. Fact is, I'm not supposed to be in Dwadlo at all, but considering I needed Tom's advice I decided to detour." The brush paused in its strokes, and Jones rested his hand on the mare's back. "Tom Curtis knows more about a land's worth than any man around."

"I'm sure he does — but would a delay of another day or two really hurt?"

He pulled the brush through the mare's coat absently. "You still have tomorrow."

Her thin shoulders slumped with silent defeat. He could have given her more time, but he seriously doubted the deed would be located — if it even existed. Accurate records hadn't been kept that many years ago, and there were a thousand places to lose those that had been documented.

"What am I going to do? I think I'm in trouble." Her wistful inquiry touched a heartstring. What *was* she going to do? She had no family other than a senile aunt who had outlived everyone's expectations. She was in a pitiful state, and she had every right to wonder.

"Look." He set the brush aside and came around to drop down on the hay bale beside her. She smelled pretty — like the purple hyacinths that bloomed in the spring. "I'll loan you enough to get back to Sioux Falls. You can pay me back whenever you save up enough that the ticket won't run you short."

"Thank you, but I can't accept it. Mae and Tom have offered to help as well, but the train ticket isn't my biggest problem. I can't walk away and abandon Wilson's Falls. My ancestors worked too long and hard for me to just give away their sweat and toil. Pauline and I both deserve the funds from the sale."

"And if the search proves worthless? How long are you prepared to look?"

"I couldn't say." She lifted troubled eyes to meet his. "I haven't thought about it."

She had spunk. Most females would have hightailed it out of here once they'd been saddled with a senile great-aunt. Jones reached out and tweaked her nose, and then tucked a stray lock of hair into place. "I once had a friend who gave me some sound advice."

"And it was?"

"Take heart — things could always get worse." He winked. "About that question you asked earlier . . ."

She looked up to meet his gaze.

"The one about whether I have a woman."

149

She blushed and ducked her head.

"Were you just being sociable when you asked that?"

"It's none of my business," said Trinity.

"I don't have a woman," said Jones, "but I intend to get one soon."

She nodded, her head low. "That's nice."

"Very nice. I've worked hard to get her attention." He sat back, smiling. "It's going to be a pleasure to win her love."

"You're very smug about it."

"No." He stopped, seeming to think about it. "She's been giving me the runaround for a year now, but she's interested. And you? Anyone in your life?"

She shook her head. "I see a widower who comes into the café every day, but it's nothing serious."

"Does he know that?"

"We haven't spoken about our feelings."

She stood, carefully gathering her basket. She winced as her arms shifted position.

Jones focused on the bandaged arm, frowning. "Is the arm giving you much pain?"

"Some, but it will heal soon. I have to go now." The conversation had become too personal for her taste. "I'm on my way to find Benjamin and see if he'll accompany me to Pauline's."

Jones stood and straightened his hat. "Won't this come as quite a shock to Miss Wilson? She hasn't seen the man in half a century."

"I'm sure his appearance will be like a bolt from the blue — if she remembers him at all." Trinity met his eyes. "I have one more day, correct?"

"One more day. And good luck." He sobered when he thought about the task that lay ahead of her. Not an enviable one for anyone involved. "You're going to need it."

"You're such an encouragement." She flashed a smile and he knew that she was warming up to him. For some reason he liked the thought. He picked up the brush and returned to the horse.

"Hey — Miss Franklin?"

She turned. "Yes?"

"Remember to take heart."

Nodding, she walked on. He watched her go, hand on Sue's back, wondering who the lucky man would be who won her heart.

"Then you'll come with me?" Trinity had spent an hour searching for Benjamin, looking in alleyways and on the outskirts of town. She'd finally located him half a mile outside of Dwadlo, near the river. He'd been none too happy to have his camp discovered, but Trinity was none too happy that he'd followed her to Dwadlo. As far as she was concerned, she'd evened the score.

Benjamin scratched his bearded face. "You want me to go with you to see Pauline?" His bushy brows drew into a tight knot. "I don't know, ma'am. I don't want to make her heart give out. It's been a mighty long spell since we've laid eyes on each other."

Trinity doubted either one would recognize the other, but if anyone could prompt her aunt's memory it would be him. "Seeing her is the reason you followed me all the way here, isn't it? Why have doubts now?"

"Yes, ma'am — that's purely the reason, but I sorta thought I'd take my own time showin' my face. She probably ain't gonna be too happy to see me. Kind of like your worst nightmare come a-knockin' on your back door."

"You never know. The years have a way of changing folks and softening hearts, but since you've come all this way you can't not see her."

"Well, I reckon I can do what I want, but" — his gaze shifted to the road — "maybe I'll just go on back to Piedmont. Ain't no harm done. She'll never know I've been here."

"No." Trinity snagged his arm and gently urged him ahead of her. "You must help me, Benjamin. She might respond to you." Goodness knew Pauline didn't recognize a great-grandniece she'd only seen as a baby.

"I cain't leave my camp and my jenny!"

"Your personal belongings won't be noticed, and we'll only be gone a short while." No one but a desperate soul would tramp through the heavy thicket and poison ivy to get to him.

"I don't like this, missy. Not one bit."

"Nor do I, Benjamin, but I don't have a choice." Without that deed and the money it would mean, she'd have no alternative but to stay put here in Dwadlo.

And there was no way she was that desperate.

Pauline was entertaining herself in the small yard, catching fireflies. Her stained pink housecoat looked out of place in the setting, but Mae said the gift had come from Tom and the old woman rarely gave it over for the wash. Her ruddy face was wrinkled like an old apple, but her eyes shown with childlike delight as she clutched a fruit jar to her chest. She stood perfectly still and let the insects fly to her, and then, once they were close, she snaked out a hand, captured them, and stored them in the jar. Trinity motioned for Benjamin to stay back. Best that she clear the way before she sprung the old fellow on her.

Pauline focused on her prey, hand poised in midair.

"Pauline?"

"What?"

"Remember me? Trinity? I visited you earlier."

"Yeh, yeh." Her hand snatched a bug. "You don't give up, do you, young'un?"

If Trinity were thin-skinned she'd be strongly inclined to take issue with her aunt's exasperated tone, but she wasn't — and locating the deed was far more important than her etiquette.

Pauline seized a bug.

"I've brought someone to see you."

"Don't want to see anyone. I'm bug-catchin' and after that I'm goin' to bed."

"I think you'll want to see this particular person." She motioned for Benjamin to come closer. He took a hesitant step forward, twisting his battered hat in his hands. Trinity frowned. She should have taken more time to spruce him up a bit. His dirty shirt, strong odor, and unkempt beard would hardly endear him to Pauline. But the way his eyes softened as he focused on the woman catching fireflies in the gathering dusk was that of a young man smitten with his first love. Moisture gathered in his eyes as he stepped closer.

"Miss Pauline?"

She stopped mid-snatch. A twinkling light fluttered by, ignored. Trinity stood still as a winter's night. "Pauline?" she said softly. "Look who I brought."

She sensed the hesitancy — the woman's almost visible uncertainty, as though she questioned her hearing.

"Aren't you going to look at me?" Benjamin's voice filled the silence.

"Don't need to."

"Do you know who I am?"

"Benjamin Henry Cooper, I told you to stay away. Why have you come?"

"Can't stay away. I told you I loved you years ago, and nothin's changed."

She turned, her eyes squinting to adjust to the fading light. In the softest tone Trinity had ever heard her use, she said, "I don't want you to see me like this."

"Like what?" His dull gaze ran her length, love lighting his features. "You haven't changed a bit."

"You always were a smooth talker."

155

"Never smooth enough to convince you that we were born to be together."

Pauline turned her eyes to Trinity. "See what I have to put up with? The man won't leave me alone."

"I would take that as a compliment, Aunt Pauline." If a man — any man — looked at her the way Benjamin drank in the sight of Pauline, she would feel blessed indeed.

Pauline snatched a firefly out of the air.

Time was brief. Her aunt's lucidity would fade quickly. Trinity edged closer. "We've come to ask you about the deed to Wilson's Falls."

"What about it?"

Trinity glanced at Benjamin, encouraged. "Do you know where it is?"

"Of course I know."

"You do!"

Pauline snared another one. "I said I did."

"Where do you keep it?"

She held up the jar, her gaze focused on the twinkling lights captive there. "It's a secret."

"I know what I'm asking is delicate, but I'm here to help with your personal business. You'll have to cooperate . . ."

"Don't need any help."

"Yes, you do." Benjamin reached to help her tighten the lid of the jar. "We're not

156

young'uns anymore, Pauline. Our memories aren't so good as they used to be. Tell your niece where you keep your papers, and she can sort things out."

"Why should I tell anyone my personal business? That's what *personal* means. That you don't tell anyone."

He took the jar from her. "The day's coming — and it's right around the corner — when you're not going to be able to handle your business anymore. Now this little gal is trustworthy, and you can tell her anything she needs to know. I'll personally testify to her integrity."

Benjamin spoke with dignity. His English was perfectly proper.

"There you go, using all those fancy words." Pauline met his gaze. "You still doctorin'?"

"Naw, gave that up years ago. Tried to take a bullet outta a man's stomach and couldn't see. My eyesight wasn't good enough. I walked away and never practiced again. I jest got old. We all do."

"Not me. I'm fit as a fiddle."

His smile broadened. "I can see that. Now tell your niece where you keep the deed."

"In a lockbox."

Trinity's jaw dropped. The old-timer was a doctor? Pauline remembered where she'd stored the deed? Would wonders never cease? *Thank You, God!*

And it seemed to Trinity that she heard a voice in her head that replied, *You see? My ways are not your ways.*

Benjamin was nodding. "In a lockbox where?"

"In Piedmont. Priss and I put it there a long time ago so we wouldn't lose it."

Trinity edged closer. "Piedmont!" For goodness' sake! She'd just come from there. What sort of crazy circus was this?

Nodding, Benjamin turned to Trinity. "Looks like you got your answer."

"You've been an immense help. I couldn't have done this without you."

A blush spread up the old-timer's neck, and he extended his arm. "Miss Pauline, would you sit on the porch with me for a spell?"

"I can't. It's my bedtime."

Benjamin winked at Trinity. "I think I can get permission to delay your routine for this one fine evening."

"Don't know as I can stay awake." Pauline looked up at the slit of a moon, and then took his arm. "But I'll give it a try. Bring my bugs. I poked holes in the lid so's they can breathe."

"Doesn't matter how long you can stay

awake. If you'll just sit with me that will be enough."

Pauline sighed. "You always could charm the birds right outta their trees."

Trinity watched the old folks slowly making their way around Tom and Mae's front yard, arm in arm, each leaning on the other. Deep inside, a romantic sigh surfaced. It seemed that love could be grand no matter one's age, though she'd hate to think she'd have to wait for her nineties to discover her soul mate. A face popped into her mind — Jones, looking down at her from under his hat — but she shook the mental image aside. She couldn't be thinking about Jones in a starry-eyed way — that was insane. He had big plans to court the woman in Chicago. Envy swelled through her. A man like him would have a woman waiting in every town, eager to provide for his comforts.

Jones was certainly not her focus. Her life was back in Sioux Falls with a man she had yet to meet. She had to concentrate on selling Pauline's land, though even her most merciless inner critic had to admit that Jones did have the most captivating, heart-shattering grin.

He'd have no trouble snaring a wife. None in the least.

THIRTEEN

Sunlight streaked the rosy dawn as Jones walked into the livery. Fisk was there already, his grin as wide as Texas this morning. The usual white cloth that cushioned his bad tooth was gone. "You look a mite happier," said Jones as he reached for his saddle on the stanchion.

"Feel like a new man!" The blacksmith motioned to the coffee. "Want a cup of java?"

"Already had more than my share." He hefted the saddle onto Sue's back and reached beneath for the wide belly strap.

"Shore hate to see you go," Fisk said. "Been a lot of comin's and goin's around here the past few months. I'm 'bout ready for things to settle down a mite."

"You ever think about getting married?"

The blacksmith shook his head. "Been married once, don't plan to do it again."

"You and the wife didn't get along?"

160

"Oh, I loved the missus. Loved her more than life itself, but she took sick and it weren't long afore the good Lord took her home."

"Sorry to hear that."

"Hardest thing I ever faced, losin' her. Won't nobody ever replace my little Petunia."

A shadow appeared in the doorway and Jones looked up to see Trinity, breathless and holding a small sack. "Oh, thank heaven," she said. "I overslept and thought I might have missed you."

He lifted his brow. "Miss me?"

"I thought you'd leave before I could catch you. Pauline knows where the deed is."

A snort escaped Fisk. "She don't know her right foot from her left most days. How's she supposed to remember where she keeps a deed?"

"She says it's in a lockbox in Piedmont."

Jones shook his head skeptically. "Can you trust her memory? She doesn't appear to be . . . in control of her faculties."

"That's a nice way of saying she's nuts, and she is, but I think the information's correct. I took Benjamin to see her last night and he made all the difference. She remembered him and she remembered the deed."

161

Jones slipped the bit into Sue's mouth. "Then I suppose you'll be taking the train back to Piedmont?"

"That's what I wanted to speak to you about." She eased into the livery, her eyes searching the stalls. "You're riding in that direction, aren't you?"

"Could be. Why?"

"The train isn't due here until Sunday. I can't wait that long." She glanced at Fisk. "Can I rent a horse?"

"Yeah, I got a couple of small mares. I won't rent you one, but I'll sure enough loan you one."

"Thanks." She flashed him a grin before addressing Jones. "You don't mind if I keep you company?"

"Let's say I don't. How do you plan to get back?"

"If the deed's there, we'll make the transaction and be done with our business. Fisk? You're not overly attached to the mare you're loaning me?"

"No, ma'am. Some feller came through a while back and wanted me to reshoe the animal. He never came back for her. I'm out the price of shoes and feed."

"Good. Once I get the money from the land I'll sell the horse, wire you the money, wire Pauline *her* money, and take the train to Sioux Falls."

Jones wasn't sold on the plan. She'd slow him down. "Piedmont is a good two-day ride."

"That will still put me there sooner than if I wait and take the Sunday train," she said, turning needy eyes on him. "We have a deal?"

"I wasn't aware I was given a choice. Aren't you concerned for your reputation? A single man and a pretty woman traveling alone together?"

She shook her head. "Not in the least."

Fisk laughed. "Don't say much for yer appeal, does it, Jones?"

Smiling, Jones swung himself into the saddle. "Mine or hers?" He focused on Trinity. "You can ride along. I intend to get a good look at Wilson's Falls before I hand you a wad of money. How soon can you be ready to ride out, Miss Franklin?"

She lifted the sack. "I'm packed and eager to go."

Jones studied the girl. Now he had her on his back for another couple of days. "What are you planning on eating during the trip?"

"Mae and Jeremy are packing my supplies as we speak."

"Pretty sure of yourself, aren't you?"

She nodded. "Since I'll be paying for your

services, I can assume that you will see me safely to Piedmont."

He lifted a dark brow. "Now I'm a hired escort?"

Her chin raised a notch. "I thought it was a natural assumption. Of course, I won't be able to pay until you give me the money for the land."

Fisk chuckled and Jones groaned inwardly. Having her along for the ride wasn't all that unpleasant a thought, but Jones resented the way she took his services for granted. He was not a paid man, not in any woman's eyes. And babysitting her would slow him down when he was overdue as it was.

"Well?" She faced him, waiting.

"I'm thinking about it."

"If you're worried about propriety, I'll ask Benjamin to ride along, or Lil . . ."

"Not Lil. And certainly not the old-timer." A two-day ride would take six if Benjamin was along.

"Well, then?"

He adjusted the brim of his hat. "I'll ride slowly. You get your grub and catch up."

"Deal." She turned and half ran, half skipped to the store.

Jones met Fisk's dancing eyes. "Don't say a word."

He saddled up and rode out, hearing that

164

wicked chuckle behind him. Jones could tell what Fisk was thinking — that he was going to fall for Trinity.

That would not happen. Paid man — hogwash! She'd regret the day she hired him.

FOURTEEN

"You're not much of a talker, are you?"

The monotonous trail stretched ahead, hour after hour. Trinity hadn't spoken a word since leaving Dwadlo. She didn't appear to be the chatty sort, endlessly going on about insignificant matters. He wasn't accustomed to riding with women, but she focused on the trail and he had to admit they were making good time. At this rate they'd be in Piedmont by early tomorrow afternoon, weather cooperating. It had been hot and dry, but the dark bank of clouds building in the north promised rain.

The animals smelled water. Jones gave Sue her head and she galloped toward the river.

Trinity reined up short fifty yards from the placid stream. He turned in his saddle, recalling her abnormal fear of water. "Want me to take you across?"

It didn't take much to see that she was scared. "Throw me your reins and I'll lead you safely across."

She flushed. "I can make it!"

Shrugging, he kneed Sue and walked her into the water. Rain had been scarce and the river was low — not more than waist-deep in the middle. He kept an eye on Trinity as her mare approached the water. Reining in, she seemed to be gathering her courage before she gently nudged the horse forward. Something in that little gal's life had spooked her around water.

A crack of thunder split the air. Sue jolted beneath him, and Jones turned in the saddle to watch Trinity struggle to restrain her animal.

Lightning streaked across the sky and another clap of thunder came — louder this time. Both horses started. Jones turned and took the mare's reins from Trinity. "Hold on! We'll be out of this in just a minute."

Her knuckles turned white but she gripped the saddle horn and held tight. The first drops of rain pelted the riders as they rode clear of the river.

Jones tossed the reins back to her as they clambered onto the far bank. "That wasn't so bad."

Offering a hint of a smile, she nodded. "Not bad at all."

She was at least a discriminate deceiver.

The shower turned out to be brief. The sky cleared and the sun popped out. At noon Jones pulled up under a spreading tree and dismounted. A fresh spring gurgled in the distance. "Thought we'd eat dinner and rest the horses a spell."

Trinity obediently climbed down and went to the creek to wash her hands. Jones joined her to clean up, studying her out of the corner of his eye. They'd ridden half a day and she hadn't said a word but the few she'd offered while crossing the river. She hadn't seemed lost for words before.

"What makes you tick, Miss Franklin?"

She looked up, curiosity shining in her eyes. "I'm not sure what you mean."

He pulled a piece of soap from his pocket and lathered up. "Well, what's up with you and water, for example?"

"I can't . . ."

"Other than you can't swim and you don't like tight places," he put in. "Seems like you'd learn — there's a lot of water and root cellars around."

Her eyes focused on his hands. He passed her the bar of soap and continued. "I was swimming before I cut most of my teeth." He remembered the warm summer days when his pa had taken him to the river and they'd played on a rope swing overhanging the water. Some of the best memories he had.

She worked up a lather, focusing on her task. "Sounds like you had a nice childhood."

"You didn't?"

"My ma and pa set off for town one day and never came back. Rob was fourteen that year and I was five. They were gone for days. Rob said something must have delayed them and I shouldn't worry. We didn't have much in the way of supplies — that's why Ma and Pa went to town. After a few weeks a passerby told Rob that a woman's body had washed up downstream. No man, no buggy, no horse — just a woman about Ma's age. Rob said the rains had been heavy that year." Shrugging, she rinsed her hands. "We never knew for certain what happened."

"Your brother raised you?"

"We lived on a small piece of land — not too close to any settlement. Rob figured we were making it well enough on our own. By the time I was eight I could cook as well as he did. We planted a garden every year, and I canned our food for the winter. Rob hunted and trapped and sometimes he sold the pelts to traveling peddlers."

Jones listened with growing admiration.

The woman wasn't all fluff. "No family member came to check on you?"

"There were only the two aunts, Pauline and Priss. But we didn't know how to reach them. Rob couldn't figure out where to send a letter, and I couldn't either. But what about you?"

"Me?" He shook his head. "My ma died shortly after I was born. Pa remarried later, and his new wife didn't take to a stepson. It wasn't long before I decided I could make it on my own. I left the cabin when I was fourteen and lived with a bunch of drifters for a while. I was sixteen when I hired on with the railroad."

"Then you worked with Tom?"

"Yes. He was hired a few years before me." He handed her a cloth to dry her hands. "So you never knew what happened to your parents?"

"No. After a while we just stopped looking out the window. They weren't coming back." Her eyes darkened. "Rob said it didn't matter. Pa had a temper, and Rob said he wasn't afraid to use the whip on either one of us. I was too young to remember, but I can recall him locking me in the cellar when I misbehaved. It was dark and cold — and there were spiders." She shuddered. "I could hear the water dripping and

Pa said that if I wasn't good the cellar would fill up with water and . . ." She stopped.

"That explains your fear of water and tight places."

"For a while Rob wouldn't allow me in the cellar, but then we had to store canned goods. He'd fetch anything I needed, but there were times he wasn't around and I had to go down there alone." She shook the thought away.

"Well, don't feel bad. We all have our dislikes and peculiarities. I don't like the sight of blood."

She caught back a snicker.

"I know — it's not a manly trait, but I get all lightheaded when I see it. I try to avoid the sight as much as possible."

She smiled. "Did you mention dinner?"

"I've got cold biscuits and ham waiting for me."

She stood. "I'll get the canteens and get some fresh water."

His gaze followed the petite form. She was quite a woman. Her story explained a lot — her fear of water, her fear of dark places. He made a mental note to steer her clear of the things she dreaded.

Trinity returned from the spring and they opened their sacks. She glanced up when she discovered the contents of the brown paper-wrapped bundle. "Cold biscuits and ham."

They looked at each other and burst into laughter.

"It appears we have the same cook," said Jones.

A twinge of dread filled his empty stomach. That wasn't all they had in common. *Jones, don't go falling for a woman with brown eyes and a tragic past. You've steered clear this long. Don't let your guard down now.*

The last thing he wanted to do was hook up with a woman; she might turn out like his stepmother.

The mares' hooves ate up the miles that afternoon. Clouds overhead at least made the building heat bearable. The cold biscuits and ham sat hard in his stomach. Jones's thoughts were on supper, and his plans to roast a fresh rabbit over a spit. No sooner had he thought of it than the unthinkable occurred. Looking back when he heard a scream, he saw Trinity's mare plunging headlong to the ground, pitching her rider into the air. Trinity slammed down onto the path.

Jones swung Sue around and galloped back, springing from the saddle before the animal had stopped.

Trinity's hand was gripping her side.

172

Gently rolling her to her back, he searched for broken bones. "It looks like you've hurt the same arm." When he was certain she had no major injury he gently sat her up.

The mare's sides were heaving from the pain, and her whinnies shot straight to his heart. He'd always had a soft spot when it came to animals.

"Is my arm broken now?"

He tested it, frowning. "I don't think so. You've aggravated it more, but I'll rewrap it for you once I put the mare out of her pain."

Her eyes brightened with unshed tears. "Is that necessary?"

"Believe me when I say I would avoid it if I could." He braced himself, then rose and moved to squat beside the animal. One eye gazed up at him, glazed with agony. He stroked her head, speaking softly. "It's okay, girl."

She snorted, her eyes wild with pain.

Trinity stood and approached, her gaze fixed on the scene. "Must you put her down? She doesn't belong to me, and maybe we can find someone to help her when we reach Piedmont."

"She belongs to the good Lord now." Jones gently touched the damaged fetlock. Trinity could see the exposed bone. She turned away.

Taking her by the arm, Jones led her to the side of the road and sat her down before he examined her injury more closely. "It's starting to swell. You may have a break after all. Does it hurt?"

"It's throbbing like the dickens."

"I have bandages in my saddlebag." His gaze met hers. They could both hear the panicked whinnies filling the air. "Will you be all right here for a few minutes?"

Anxiety filled her flushed features. "I don't want to see this."

"Then you won't." Scooping her into his arms, he carried her up an overgrown trail, deep into the woods. She'd hear the shot — there'd be no escaping that — but the timber would mute the sound. Lord knew he didn't relish what he was about to do.

"I'm sorry, Jones." Her words spoke more than empathy. She felt his reluctance.

He straightened and removed his hat, running a sleeve over his forehead. "No matter how many times I'm forced to do it, it never gets easier."

"Rob had to put our old plow horse down. Ed — he was like family. I'll help . . . if you need me."

"You don't want to see this."

"Neither do you." She met his eyes.

"I'll handle it. Now stay here." He turned

174

on his heel and walked off, the tight knot in his throat threatening to do him in.

The sun was dipping low in the west as Jones changed Trinity's arm bandage. A sizzling rabbit slowly turned a golden brown over the open fire. Getting the mare's carcass off the road hadn't proved easy, but Sue had managed the load. Trinity had appeared minutes after the shot.

"Go back. You can't do anything."

"I can keep you company." She hadn't shirked the unpleasantness, and she worked beside him to clear the road just like a man.

Losing an animal meant they were now down to one horse. Jones had helped her into his saddle, thrown the dead mare's saddle over his shoulder, and walked. His gaze swept the ugly site they had just left. Blood. Carcass.

"I'd just as soon camp elsewhere tonight," he said.

She hadn't given him any trouble on that suggestion.

Wrapping the arm snugly, he sat back on his heels. "I don't have anything for pain, unless you want a shot of gin. I carry a bottle for incidents like this."

"That isn't necessary." Her eyes roamed the camp. "I would love a bath."

"There's a river nearby. Want me to walk you there?"

"I can manage." She struggled to her feet as his hand supported her. "May I use the soap?"

He walked to his mare and dug around in the saddlebag. "What about clean clothing? You have blood on your shirt and trousers." So did he — a reminder he'd wash off as soon as she returned.

"I'll wash off in the river." She offered a grateful smile as he handed her the bar of soap. "I'll be back shortly."

Crossing his arms, he grinned. "You don't need my help? Where's your fear of water?"

"In the proper place, where yours obviously isn't." A grin escaped her. "I have no fear of a good scrubbing."

"I'm happy to help."

She offered him a look he couldn't decipher — and didn't care to at the moment.

The water was shallow and Trinity waded in up to her waist, then stripped down and scrubbed her clothing, hair, and body. The stench of death gradually washed away, and when she returned to camp she smelled pretty again.

The spit was empty, her portion of the rabbit lying on a tin plate. Her gaze swept the small camp and she smiled when she spotted Jones. He had spread his bedroll in the nearby pasture. Stars twinkled overhead, a few bright ones seeming to outshine the rest.

Carrying her plate to the pasture, she went to sit beside him. He had proven himself to be a good man. A decent, compassionate person. He had handled the mare with calm and care. Easing down beside him she picked at the meat, savoring the light breeze that lifted and dried her hair. The slight wind felt good on her sunburned skin. She ate quietly, gazing out at the night's splendor.

"Ever seen anything prettier than a summer sky?" Jones asked in his soft baritone.

"I haven't," she admitted. The heavens outdid themselves tonight. She thought that if she could reach high enough she could pluck out one of the twinkling lights and put it in her pocket. "In the beginning God created the heavens and the earth. Then God said, 'Let there be light'; and there was light," she murmured. On the long winter evenings Rob had always read to her from the family Bible, and she loved recalling his voice reading those passages.

Jones rolled to sit up, his gaze focused on her now. "The night is almost as pretty as you, Miss Franklin."

Heat crept up her neck. "I prefer fall, when the leaves turn golden and the air is crisp and the moon is round as a dinner plate — but I admit it would be difficult to create a night more spectacular than this."

"Our Creator has quite the touch." His gaze swept the twinkling brilliance.

"It's nice to hear you believe in God."

"Yes, ma'am. Have for a long time." He was silent for a moment, watching the sky. "Name me one other Being that could do this."

The sky stretched limitlessly across the horizon, more lovely than a rare jewel.

Trinity sighed. "Penny for your thoughts."

He chuckled. "I thought you'd be too tuckered out for conversation."

"I am, but this — how often does one get to observe such beauty?"

"Not often." His eyes trailed over her, and the intensity in his gaze made her blush. She was glad it was too dark for him to see. She hoped he didn't think she had invited a personal — almost intimate — observation. She'd only meant . . .

He put his hands back behind his head and sang softly.

Lift up your head, find a smile, and search for the rainbows.

"That was very nice," she said. "You have a lovely voice."

She drew her knees to her chest and rested her chin, her eyes shifting to the mare pastured nearby. The grass was dry but plentiful. "And you have a lovely animal."

"Sue?" Leaning back on his elbows, his eyes followed her focus. "She's my lady."

"Had her long?"

"Since she was a yearling." Lying back on his pallet, he smiled. "Bought her with my first paycheck and we haven't spent a day apart since."

"I wondered why you spent so much time in the saddle. You could ride the train anywhere you like."

"I could, but I love the outdoors, and I don't work by a train's schedule. So I ride. She's good company."

"She sounds like she's found a very loyal owner."

"She'll be with me as long as the good Lord keeps her here on earth." He ran a hand through a mass of dark hair. "Strange how you can get so attached to an animal."

"Sue sounds more like family than an animal."

"She is."

"And your real family — are they still living?"

179

"I couldn't say."

Trinity straightened. His tone had turned cold. She had struck a nerve. She nibbled on the rabbit.

"What about you?"

She started, surprised that he wanted to continue the conversation. "I have no family — none but my aunt."

"I'm sorry."

"No need. The Franklins were never close." She sighed. "You know how you meet people who have brothers and sisters and cousins and they're all close? Lovingly joined at the hip? My family was never like that. It was just me and Rob, fighting to survive." She turned to look at him. "But we don't have to talk about our pasts."

Yet after a moment he did, his throat tight with emotion — perhaps resentment. "The Good Book says to honor your mother and your father, but sometimes it's mighty hard."

"That's true. There are . . . varying circumstances in every family."

The silence stretched. She ate her meal, sensing that if he needed to say more he would. She needed to hear more.

The thought took her by surprise. They'd had their differences, but the man appeared goodhearted and solid — the sort of man a hovering mama would be delighted to welcome into the family. She studied him out of the corner of her eye. How had he escaped matrimony all these years?

"I had another horse I cared about. Jeannie."

"You appear to favor mares."

"I didn't name her. Pa gave her to me when he found her alongside the road, limping. He wrapped the ankle and when she healed he said she was mine. Her name was Jeannie. She was ornery and had a will of her own, but she was mine and I loved her."

She set her plate aside. Something in his tone suggested he would continue, given sufficient time to swallow the knot crowding his throat.

"My stepmother resented that horse about as much as she resented me." His chuckle was as mirthless as the bombshell that followed. "She gave her away to a stranger while I was putting up hay in the field. Swore she was eating us out of house and home."

Trinity reached over and took his hand. His grip tightened in hers.

There was a light bouncing across the prairie, coming straight at them. Trinity lifted her head and peered closer. "What is it?"

There was an earsplitting recoil followed by a shower of light. Jones jumped to his feet, scrambling for his holster.

"Marauders?" Trinity sprang up, cowering against his tall frame.

"It sounds like" — Jones grunted — "It's Lil. On that blasted machine."

"Lil?" Trinity stepped around him to peer more closely at the approaching light. Another backfire convinced her. "What's she doing here?"

Lil skidded to a stop and killed the engine, her smile radiant even in the dim light. "Good! I was hoping it would be you two!"

"What in the world are you doing here this time of night?" Trinity planted her hands firmly on her hips as she spoke. Jones didn't look all that pleased to see her either.

"Sorry to interrupt your trip, but you gotta come back, Trinity."

"Go back?" Visions of the long day on the trail washed across her mind. "Why must I go back?"

"It's Pauline. She collapsed in the post office late this morning. They can't get her to wake up."

Bile rose to Trinity's throat. "Is she . . ."

"Not yet — at least, she weren't when I left — but the doc thinks it could be close. He sent me to get you. Benjamin's with her,

182

and he says you'd better hurry."

Trinity felt the touch of Jones's hand on her elbow. "I'll saddle the horse," he said.

"Yes. Thank you." Stunned, she was turning to follow him when Lil's voice broke her concentration.

"You won't make it back in time if you ride that horse — especially double. Climb aboard. I'll have you there in a few hours."

Trinity stared at the noisy contraption Lil was straddling. Her pulse thudded in her chest. She could be killed on that thing — and not be there when Pauline drew her last breath.

"I'll get you there." Lil's upturned lip suggested she resented Trinity's obvious reluctance.

"I . . ."

"She's right," said Jones. "You ride with Lil and I'll follow after."

Lil gave the throttle a couple of hefty twists and the monster roared to life.

Numb, Trinity allowed Jones to lead her to certain doom. "What if I don't get there in time?" she asked. Not only would she lose a lovely old aunt she had just found, but Pauline would take the deed's location to the grave.

"Worry about one thing at a time." Jones helped her onto the machine and she

183

wrapped her arms around Lil's waist. "Hold on tight. Lil, drive safe," Jones warned. "I want her there in one piece."

Lil arched an eyebrow. "She'll get there. You questionin' my ridin' abilities?"

"Right now I'm questioning my sanity. You get her there safe, understood?"

"I ain't deaf!" She popped the clutch and the machine shot forward.

. . . to certain, agonizing death, Trinity was absolutely convinced.

FIFTEEN

"Lil, slow this thing down! You're going to kill us!"

Trinity clung to Lil, burying her face in the woman's shoulder as the motorcycle bumped and lurched over the rough road. The lantern tied to the front bars barely provided enough light to travel the jagged terrain. Fence posts and fields flew past in a blur. The machine hit a bump, and Trinity gritted her teeth and prayed. *Please, please let this be over soon!* She didn't know how far they'd traveled today. There'd been the dead mare, and they'd eaten a leisurely lunch. How far back to Dwadlo? The moon rose higher, and the occasional loud belch spewing from the back of the machine distracted her thoughts. Pauline was dying. She'd just found her family and now their time together was fleeting.

The machine hit a bump in the rutted road, and Trinity groaned. She should have stayed with Jones. Sue was fast, but this fire-breathing fiend was steadily eating up the miles.

"That thar's a mighty fine-lookin' feller you've snagged."

The women had ridden for over an hour when Trinity pleaded for respite. Grabbing Lil's shirt collar, she'd begged. "Stop this thing or I'm going to slap you silly!" She'd never struck anyone, but Lil was tempting her. Every bone in her body rattled.

Lil had slowed to a stop and finally cut the engine. Trinity rolled to her side and slowly lifted her leg over the machine and touched ground. Firm, solid ground. She closed her eyes in silent gratitude. If she lived to be a hundred she would never forget this ride.

Lil was sliding off the machine and stretching. Trinity tested her legs, and when it appeared they would hold her she hobbled around in a circle trying to bring life back to her limbs, aware that Lil was watching from the corners of her eyes. She must look rather silly, but at the moment vanity was the farthest thing from her mind.

She recalled Lil's earlier statement. "If you're referring to Jones, I barely know the man."

"That a fact? He ain't yorne?"

"He ain't." She mentally cringed at the use of improper language. Rob had always been adamant that she speak proper English.

"Well now, that's a real shame. Mighty fine-lookin' male."

"Looks aren't everything." She worked a kink out of her shoulder. Jones was a looker, but then she'd seen good-looking men before. She valued a man's personality and his moral traits more highly than his appearance. Looks faded but the core remained until death. She had witnessed many an unhappy marriage by women who had married for financial gain or the way a man wore his clothing.

"No, but they shore help if a man's got 'em." Fully stretching, Lil grinned. "Especially around these parts. Ain't many that would clean up real nice except Tom — and maybe the Estes boy but he's only sixteen. A bit young for my taste."

At least she knew her limits. Trinity guessed that Lil would have to be close to Mae's age and that would be looking at the later twenties — real later. Trinity couldn't imagine how Lil's taste in men ran. Surely not suave and sleek — not when she always looked like an unmade bed. Rough and

187

rowdy — that was more likely her type. But he'd have to be extremely rough and tremendously rowdy to best her, and she was surely a woman who'd need besting occasionally.

She bit back a grin when she imagined Lil pairing with Jones. The match would serve him right. He was so smug and sure about everything it would do him good for a woman like Lil to tear into him. Of course he'd tear right back.

"What about the blacksmith? I heard you two might be sweet on each other."

"Fisk? Me and Fisk?" Lil turned her face up and hooted. "He'd be the last man on earth I'd marry."

"Why? He seems pleasant enough."

"That ole coot? I'd sooner eat a bowl of spiders than marry him."

Trinity shrugged. "Just repeating what I've heard."

"Who'd you hear that garbage from? Mae?" She snorted. "Mae thinks she knows everything."

"She appears to know a lot about the town."

"Well, she should. She's lived here all of her life."

"What about you?"

"What about me?'

"Have you lived here always?"

"Came here when I was an infant. My ma married my pa when my real father took sick and passed shortly after I was born. Ma was one of them mail-order brides. Ever hear of 'em?"

"Yes." Trinity had certainly read about women who accepted proposals by mail or magazine advertisements. The practice seemed a bit extreme, but it appeared to serve a purpose. Widows and single women seeking matrimony found the homes and security they sought, and men gained female companionship and mothers for their children.

"You wouldn't catch me marrying a man I hadn't met," Lil said. "Fact is, I don't think I'll be marryin' at all."

"Nor I," Trinity mused. She had yet to meet the man she could imagine herself spending a lifetime with — or even a few months. She'd met nice men but there had never been that excited buzz others talked about. Not even a faint stir, unless she counted the occasional maddening awareness she felt when Jones was around. But that was usually annoyance. She was doing fine on her own and a man would only complicate things.

She glanced at the moon. "I guess we can

189

move on now."

"Yore bottom is in better shape?"

"The feeling's come back." She winced, dreading the long hours to come.

"Well, saddle up — or climb aboard I'd guess you'd say. We got a ways left to go." Lil slid onto the machine and stomped hard a couple of times before the engine roared to life. Serenity shattered.

Heaving a mental sigh, Trinity climbed aboard. Before they took off, she prayed out loud. "Dear God, please let Pauline hold on a little longer. And while you're at it, Lord, it wouldn't hurt to throw in a little strength for me."

She'd lost track of time when Lil wheeled into Dwadlo, heading straight for the post office.

She killed the machine. "Here you go. Safe and sound, and it only took a couple of hours."

Light spilled from the Curtises' home as bright as day. Trinity spat. Her mouth was full of dirt, and even without a mirror she knew her eyes were ringed like an opossum. She removed a handkerchief from her pocket and handed it to Lil. "Clean up a bit. We both look a fright." Lil's red-orange hair stood on end after the harried ride, and grime from the road covered her face. Trinity was certain they both looked like escapees from the insane asylum.

Lil scrubbed her face and absently tossed the hanky back to Trinity. The front door opened and Mae appeared as the women started up the steps.

"Thank goodness you found her." She wrapped Trinity in a grateful hug.

Trinity returned the embrace, her gaze straying to the post office. "Is she . . ."

"She's holding her own. Doc says she's had a light stroke, but we won't know how light for a bit yet. Come with me. She's awakened twice and asked for you."

Trinity tiptoed through the open doorway. A lantern burned low beside the bed. Benjamin sat up straighter when she entered. "My prayers have been answered. I feared you wouldn't make it in time."

She reached over and gave the older man a hug, noting that his dialect was missing tonight. Had he been putting on an act all these years? Acting like a lone prospector with little education in order to disguise his past as a doctor — a doctor who'd ceased his practice because of one mistake?

"Mae said she asked for me earlier."

"She's fretting about something. She's called for you several times."

191

Trinity stepped closer to the bed. The log cabin quilt had been drawn back to the foot of the bed and a light throw covered Pauline's fragile body. Bending close, Trinity whispered, "Pauline?"

When there was no response she spoke louder. "Aunt Pauline?"

Her eyes fluttered open, pale and unseeing. "Is that you, Trinity?"

"It's me." She grasped her hand. "What's this I hear about you taking ill when I'm barely out of town?"

"I'm not ill."

Benjamin quietly shook his head.

"No, but if you were you'd be better in no time."

"I had a little weak spell. Happens all the time." Her eyes opened more fully, focusing on Trinity. "Glad to see you're back. I've been worried about you."

Smiling, Trinity stroked the arthritic fingers. "I only left a few hours ago."

"I know. I fear I might have sent you on a wild goose chase."

"What do you mean?"

"The deed." Her eyes turned lively — the old Pauline. "Did I say that deed was in Piedmont?"

Trinity felt her smile freeze in place. The long saddle rides, shooting the horse, the harrowing ride back . . . Pauline couldn't be about to tell her it was all in vain. "Yes."

"That's what I feared." Pauline shook her head, then looked at Benjamin. "What are you doing here?"

"I've been sitting with you all morning."

"You got nothing better to do with your time than sit with me?"

"No, actually. I haven't."

Her strained features softened. "Well now, that's right nice of you. But there's no need." She pushed herself up on her elbows and then wilted back to the pillow. "Guess I need a bite to eat. I'm a mite weak this morning."

"Good. Doc wants you to eat and then rest for the next few days."

"Pshaw. What does this doc know?" She turned hopeful eyes on the old-timer. "What matters is what you think. Is it my time, Ben?"

"Only God can answer that question, but the doc's right about you needing rest, darling."

Something akin to fear formed in Pauline's eyes and then passed. She sighed. "Well, don't be buildin' my pine box jest yet."

Benjamin patted her hand lightly. "There'll be no talk about pine boxes."

"Oak then, if that suits you."

His eyes softened like a smitten youth's. "It would please me if you did what you were told and got better."

Pauline looked back to Trinity as if she'd suddenly remembered her presence. "The deed ain't in Piedmont."

Trinity groaned inwardly. She had spent this whole horrific day in vain?

"Then where is it?"

"Here, in the Dwadlo bank."

A startled hiss escaped Mae. Trinity turned to face her, and she returned a wry smile. "The bank — or what's left of it — is a pile of rubble just outside of town. The last train wreck destroyed the building."

Benjamin frowned. "All of it?"

"Every brick," said Mae. "If the deed was kept there, it's gone."

Trinity bent closer to Pauline. "Are you sure? Could it possibly be anywhere else?"

"I'm certain as I can be." She flashed an apologetic smile. "I'm not known for my accuracy, but I'm fifty percent certain the deed was in Dwadlo's bank. Seems like me and Priss put it there for safekeepin'. We put *something* there." She glanced at Benjamin. "Does that sound right?"

"Sounds right," he said.

"What about the land office?" asked

Trinity. "Was that destroyed as well?"

Mae nodded. "All the businesses in town were leveled."

Benjamin pulled up a chair and Trinity sank down on it. Gone. The land would fall to ruin and waste without proof of ownership. "Can I apply for a new deed?"

"Pauline can apply," Benjamin said, "but she'll have to get better first."

"I can apply right now." Pauline tried to sit up again and failed. She slowly sank back. "Fetch a lawyer over here. I'll sign the necessary papers."

"It's four o'clock in the morning, Pauline. No lawyer is going to conduct business at this hour." Benjamin gently stroked her hand.

"All right, then. I'll hold on until one can get here." She winced. "You'd best get him here early."

Benjamin glanced at Trinity. "I'll do what I can."

Nodding, Pauline closed her eyes. "Trinity, you can trust Ben to get the job done. Now, if you don't mind, I think I'll rest my eyes a bit."

Trinity tucked the light blanket closer around her and whispered, "I'll keep Ben company while you sleep." Exhaustion threatened to overtake her, but she wanted to be present when her kin passed over. Pauline would be the last one — the final person with the same blood running through her veins. The indelible bond overcame fatigue and gave her strength.

"That'd be right kind of you." Her voice grew faint. "Family's mighty good to have around at a time like this."

Family's good to have around no matter what, thought Trinity.

Dawn was streaking the sky when Jones arrived, riding Sue. Mae handed him a steaming cup of coffee when he came in. "Any change?"

"She wakes up briefly but drops back to sleep. Doc says she's awfully weak." She motioned toward a back bedroom. "We've moved her back there."

"Trinity?"

"Well, she survived the wild ride, but it's taken three cups of tea to settle her nerves. She's with Pauline and Benjamin."

Sunshine poured through the half-open bedroom door. Jones pushed it open and stole a look inside. Trinity sat beside her aunt while Benjamin dozed in a nearby chair. A smile lit the young woman's face when she recognized him.

"You're back," she whispered.

Entering the room, he kept his voice low. "Are you all right?"

"I'm alive — which I seriously doubted would be the case a few hours ago. That machine . . ." She shivered, and then her eyes met and held his. "I'm glad you're back."

"I pushed Sue hard." He reached for her hand and moved to Pauline's bedside. "How's she doing?"

"Weak. And Jones — she didn't mean to, but she misled us about the deed."

"I thought it was too good to be true. There isn't one, right?"

"There was one. Right here in Dwadlo's bank."

"Then what's the problem?"

"The bank was destroyed when the second train derailed."

A voice spoke softly from the corner. Benjamin. "Could we search through the rubble? It's piled in a heap nearby."

"It would be like looking for a hair in a vat of molasses." Jones shifted. "We'd never find a deed in that mess — much less a legible one." He'd seen the refuse. Even the town's scavengers avoided the dumpsite.

He looked at the sleeping form on the narrow bed. "We could get a lawyer, but will she rouse enough to sign the documents?"

Trinity's hand tightened on his arm. "We thought of that, and we've been praying. She's full of grit — and she wants to help."

"When the lawyer gets here we'll wake her just long enough to sign the papers." Benjamin stood up and approached the bed, his eyes lovingly resting on the patient. "She's strong. She'll sign those documents."

"Oh, Benjamin." Trinity stepped closer and grasped his hand. "This is so hard for you. To love someone so deeply . . ."

"We have time." He patted the young woman's arm. "Trust me. The Lord's assured me we'll have our time. Not as much as I'd like, but enough."

A soft tap at the door caught Jones's attention, and he turned to see a somber man with a hooked nose enter the room. He carried a small black satchel. The attorney had arrived. His ferret-like eyes skimmed the sleeping form. "I was told she was alert enough to conduct business."

Trinity took a protective step forward. "She can be awakened when it's time."

"Then wake her." He set the satchel on the bedside table and extracted a quill pen and bottle of ink.

"Aunt Pauline?" Trinity spoke softly.

No response.

Jones eased closer. "Pauline? Can you

open your eyes for us, honey?"

She didn't stir. Only the slight rise and fall of her chest told them she was still breathing. Trinity bent closer to feel for a pulse.

"Pauline?" said Benjamin. "Open your eyes, darling."

The waiflike figure lay still as death.

The attorney reached for a glass of water that sat beside the bed and dashed it all over the sleeping woman's face. Her eyes flew open.

Trinity gasped, and Ben took a threatening step forward. "She's awake," the attorney noted. He turned to rummage in his satchel and extracted a piece of paper. He spoke loud enough to rouse the dead. "Miss Wilson? Can you write your name on this paper for me?"

Pauline blinked, water still streaming from her hair down over the pillow. "Why should I?"

"You're applying for a new land deed!" He was shouting now.

"She isn't deaf," Trinity told him.

Pauline blinked. "I'm signing something?"

"Yes, ma'am. That's my understanding. You'll have to wake up enough to sign this paper."

"Huh." Clearly baffled, she wiped at the

water dribbling off her chin. "Oh, mercy me. I'm drooling."

Trinity bend to sop up the water. Jones shot the lawyer a dirty look. "Was that really necessary?"

"She must be awake to conduct business."

Jones hoped he never had occasion to deal with the man again. He would shoot the weasel.

Easing the older lady to a sitting position, Trinity held her firmly in place as Jones placed the pen and paper on a book and sat it in front of her. "Do you understand what you're doing, Auntie?" asked Trinity.

"I'm drooling."

"No, we lost the title deed to Wilson's Falls and we must apply for a new one."

"Lost it?" She peered at Trinity. "Why, I had it in a box at the bank. How could I have lost it?"

"Just sign the paper, ma'am. My breakfast's getting cold." The lawyer must have had frost running through his veins.

Trinity wedged the pen into her fingers. Pauline bent, drawing the paper close to her nose. "What is this?"

"An application for a new deed. You need to sign or make an X at the bottom of the paper." The lawyer shifted on his feet, waiting.

Pauline shoved the paper aside. "I don't sign anything without readin' it first."

"Good Lord, woman! That would take all day!"

"Sir," Benjamin interrupted sharply, "the lady needs a few moments."

Trinity reached for the document and skimmed it. The wording was simple and stated its true intent. "I've read it, Aunt Pauline. You can sign it."

Jones moved the paper closer and Pauline bent, but then shook her head. "No. I ain't signin' anythin'." She lay back down and closed her eyes. Trinity groaned, and the lawyer snatched back the application and stuffed it in his satchel.

"Call me when she's willing to cooperate," he said, and with a flurry he was out the room.

The search for the missing deed was on again.

It was late in the morning as Trinity stood at the mercantile window and watched Lil load sacks of feed across the street. The woman's powerful arms could squeeze a man senseless. She was fit and trim and had the strength of two strapping males. Shaking her head, she murmured, "Wonder what she'd look like in a dress?"

Mae glanced up. "Who?"

"Lil. I was wondering what she'd look like in a dress and bonnet."

"Not bad." Mae closed a ledger and rounded the mail cage to come and stand beside her. The women fixed on their subject.

"She doesn't look bad. She wore a lovely dress to my wedding. Her hair was clean and brushed — she even wore a bright ribbon. It was so unlike her."

"She needs a man."

Mae smiled, returning to her work. "Lil doesn't *need* anything. But a nice, even-tempered and extra-patient male would give her company, though she vows she doesn't need or desire male companionship."

"She mentioned that she has no intention of marrying, but actually I think she would make some man a fine wife. Why, she's as strong as two men and can outwork three."

"And when she isn't riled, she can be right good company." Mae leaned closer to the window pane. "What's she doing?"

"She's shoveling manure now. Mr. Grate has been down in his back and she must have offered to take over for him." Trinity shook her head. "You said she cleans up fairly well?"

"Well, I wouldn't say she has a womanly

side . . . at least none that I've noticed. She isn't one to fuss, but some men find more value in a woman's nature and Lil conforms to any situation."

"Yet she says she doesn't want to marry."

"Doesn't every woman contend the same when she's still single at her age?"

"She isn't ancient."

"No, but the bloom is certainly off the rose." Mae sighed. "I'm just lucky Tom favors perennials."

Trinity grinned. "Don't be silly. You're as lovely as any woman around."

Lil might not be a looker, but the pig farmer certainly had charm. Uncut and unpolished, but charm nonetheless. It was a shame for someone with Lil's gregarious and giving nature to be alone. She'd make a fine mama and a devoted wife.

"Mae? Ever thought about helping her a bit with her appearance?"

Mae laughed. "I've offered a thousand times. If lassoing a man means taking a weekly bath, combing her hair every day, and wearing a dress, she isn't interested. She prefers her pigs' company."

"It's such a shame." Trinity moved away from the window. "I would think you'd be curious to see exactly how you could transform her — you know, turn an ugly duckling into a beautiful swan."

Mae shook her head. "I love her exactly as she is. If I were to try and change her she wouldn't be Lil anymore. Can you hand me that stack of egg cartons?" She flashed a smile. "And help me put them out on the counter?"

A breathless Mae stopped Trinity when she emerged from the hotel later that day. "Trinity! I have news!"

"News? What is it?"

"You remember what we were talking about earlier today? Our chance has come — quicker than I thought and maybe not at the most opportune time, but we need to act if we're going to."

"Going to what?" Trinity reached up to tie her bonnet strings. She had sat with Pauline most of the afternoon and she needed a brisk walk to get her blood circulating.

"I'd forgotten about it with all the excitement, but Mary Grace and Luther Willis's children are having a get-together tomorrow night for their parents' fiftieth anniversary. I realize it isn't the most ideal time with Pauline so ill, and of course should the Lord call her home we wouldn't think of going, but Tom said we should think of dropping in. Mary Grace and Pauline used to sew together in the Women's Quilt Society."

Tying a snug knot under her chin, Trinity smiled. "I wouldn't think it improper at all. I'll sit with Pauline and you and Tom can take Benjamin to the celebration. The outing would do him good and he needs a distraction."

"Thanks — but Lil's known Mary Grace and Luther forever. She took food to Luther for weeks when Mary Grace had her appendix out last fall."

"Then she should go too." A grin formed when Trinity caught the implication. "You know, it would be a perfect time for her to wear a dress."

Mae winked. "I was thinking the same thing. And you know, there will be fiddle playing and dancing."

"Sounds like a good deal of fun." Trinity started off. "You convince Lil to go, and I'll be over early tomorrow evening to help."

"Wait!" Mae caught up with her. "Lil won't want to go because that would require bathing."

"Well, I must say she could use a good scrubbing." Trinity didn't particularly enjoy visits with the girl when she'd been mucking around in pig wallow all day.

"She won't take a bath unless it's for an

extra-special occasion."

"Isn't a party a special occasion?"

"Not for Lil — unless someone was to escort her. A good-looking man, for instance."

Trinity paused, her gaze going to Mae. "A date?"

"Yes. If a man were to ask her to go to the party with him she'd go."

"She doesn't like men."

"She *says* she doesn't like men. I don't believe her. I see the way she looks at Jones."

Irritation swept Trinity. "Jones? I've never noticed the slightest indication that he returns her — interest." And she would have taken note. The very idea of Lil and Jones together was laughable. Jones was suave — experienced. Lil . . . wasn't.

"No, he doesn't appear to have an interest — but if he were to ask her to the gathering she'd be pleased as punch."

Somehow the thought didn't sit well with Trinity. Jones wasn't interested in Lil — or in women in general. But then she wasn't his keeper. "He'll never do it."

"No, not if he knew he was taking her. But Tom could get him to come along and I could ask Lil to go . . ."

"*Trick* him? He'd never speak to you again, and besides you said she wouldn't go if she had to clean up."

"I could make her *think* she had an escort."

Stopping short, Trinity caught her breath. "Jones would skin you alive!"

"Not if he wasn't aware of what was happening. We can clean up Lil — make her look real pretty and smell like a spring flower and when we go to the party Jones is certainly gentleman enough to ask for a dance. One dance and Lil will think he brought her."

"You must think the man's addled in his head."

"Of course he isn't. He's very nice and most likely if I asked he'd grant me the favor, but I'd really rather not be so obvious." Mae's front teeth worried her lower lip. "And Tom wouldn't be real happy if he knew what I was doing, but I can pull this off." She reached for Trinity's arm. "You'll help, won't you?"

Trinity pulled back. "I don't want to lie to Jones."

"You don't have to lie. Nothing untoward will take place. I'll tell Lil that we're going to the anniversary party and Tom and Jones will take us. She'll just assume Jones will be her escort." She flashed a smile. "Simple."

"Maybe you shouldn't be dancing —

you've been awfully tired lately."

"Nonsense. It's the heat. We'll have a couple of dances, eat cake and drink punch and then come home. Neither Lil nor Jones will ever be the wiser. Now, are you going to help me make a woman out of Lil?"

Shaking her head, Trinity considered the notion. It wasn't actually a deception. Lil would get to enjoy the fun and not feel like a wallflower and Jones would never be the wiser. The idea seemed innocent enough — so why did she resent the notion that Jones would be with Lil? "What do I have to do?"

"I'll have Lil come early tomorrow evening. We'll give her a good scrubbing and then have her put on one of my dresses. You can fix her hair and we'll add a touch of color to her cheeks. I have extra slippers with the daintiest little heels. We'll transform her into a lovely woman."

"Lil? Lovely?"

Taking her arm, Mae picked up the pace. "Don't worry. Everything will be just fine. Be over no later than five tomorrow night."

"Won't Tom notice all the fuss?"

"Tom never notices what Lil looks like." She flashed a grin. "Or smells like."

As hard as that was to conceive, Trinity shrugged. She could do a good deed as well as the next person. "I'll be there, but you're accepting the blame if this backfires on you."

Sixteen

"A bath!"

Lil stood in the doorway, jaw agape. "What fer? I took one last month."

"A lady should always be fresh and clean for a party," Mae argued. Trinity stood in the kitchen in front of the filled wash tub, a towel draped over her right arm. A large bar of soap was waiting in her hand.

"I ain't takin' no bath." Lil whirled and started out the back door, but Mae blocked her exit.

"Don't make me hurt you, Lil. I want to go to the party and have a good time. Bathing never hurt anyone — and while we're at it we're going to give your hair a good scrubbing."

"Over my dead body!"

"If that's what it takes."

Squeals erupted from Lil's mouth. It wasn't an easy bath and it took the better part of fifteen minutes, but finally she was scrubbed and rinsed and dried.

Planting Lil in the dentist chair, Trinity grabbed a comb and began to work through the matted red rat's nest. Lil was still sputtering. "This here is an ambush, Mae. Jest you wait, you got one a-comin'."

"Hush." Mae touched her finger to her tongue and then tested the hot iron. "Once I press this dress I'll work on your face."

"My face! What's wrong with my face?"

Mae picked up the iron from the stove and ran it lightly over the lavender-sprigged cotton. "Nothing's *wrong* with your face. I'm just going to add a little color."

"Ouch!" Lil jerked away and reached for the comb, but Trinity held it out of her grasp.

"Sit *still.* I'm going to put a few curls in here and there and if you keep wiggling you'll get burned."

"There ain't a man alive worth all this trouble," Lil groaned. "Jones better look real good himself tonight."

Jones always looked real good, tonight and any other night. Trinity picked up the curling iron and tightly wrapped a hunk of hair around it. "Where did you get this thing, Mae?"

"The curling iron? It's a Marcel. Ordered it from a catalog a few months back. Isn't it marvelous?"

Trinity released the clip and a lovely curl fell into place. By simply laying the iron on a stove the rod turned hot and made beautiful curls almost instantly. "Fabulous. It must have cost a fortune."

"Tom bought it for our three-month anniversary."

Lil was muttering to herself. "Curly hair — shoot! Ain't never had curly hair and don't want it now."

"You're going to be the belle of the ball."

"What ball? I thought we was gonna eat cake and drink punch at Mary Grace and Luther's place."

"And dance," Mae added, shaking out the folds of the finished dress.

"Jones asked me to a dance? He did not."

Mae met Trinity's eyes. "Did I mention there would be dancing?"

"Jones did *not* ask me to the party — why, that's a boldface lie if I ever heard one, Mae Curtis. You should be ashamed of yoreself. There ain't a man in this town — *especially* Jones — that would invite me to that party."

Mae seemed to be grasping for words, then gave up and shrugged. "Well, you never know. Miracles happen."

"Jones takin' a shine to me would be like Eve mistakin' an apple for an orange."

"Lil, you're too hard on yourself."

"And I ain't never danced in public — I ain't that good."

"Just do the simple box step." Trinity wrapped another curl around the rod. "Let the gentleman take the lead."

"And don't fuss at him — whomever you're dancing with. Be polite," Mae warned.

"Then what do I yak about?"

"Talk about the weather. How lovely the summer has been. Does he enjoy the holidays?"

"The holidays are months off."

"Still, he will know if he enjoys them or not." Trinity released the last curl and stood back to study her work. "Oh my, Lil. You really do have beautiful hair."

Lil hesitantly touched her hand to her head.

"Careful," Trinity warned. "You don't want to muss the curls." The girl did have exceptionally workable hair. Clean, shiny, and curled. The wide arc of freckles dotting her complexion only added to her sudden allure.

Mae eased her out of the chair and slipped the freshly ironed dress carefully over Lil's head and then stood back to survey their work. Her hand came up to cover her

213

mouth. "Oh, Lil. You are exquisite."

Color crept up the young woman's neck. "Can I take a look-see in yore peerin' glass?"

"Of course." Mae reached for a hand mirror and gave it to her. Lil lifted the object and stared. And stared.

"Well? What do you think?" Mae prompted.

"Huh. I ain't looked at myself since I was a kid. Twelve, maybe?"

Trinity and Mae spoke in stunned unison. "You haven't looked in a mirror since you were twelve?"

Lil shrugged. "Didn't much care for what I saw then so I didn't look again." She turned to the right, and then the left. "Like what I see a lot better now."

Easing in, Mae touched a bit of rouge to Lil's cheekbones and then drew a thin line of kohl along her eyelids. Lil simply sparkled.

A hot knife of envy sliced through Trinity. Lil, while not exactly exquisite, was certainly eye-catching. And it would be Jones's eye that she caught tonight.

"Well?" Mae glanced at Trinity. "I have thirty minutes to make myself presentable. Want to help?"

"Of course," Trinity murmured, suddenly wishing that she hadn't been so accommodating. Jones wasn't likely to fall head over heels in love with Lil, but no one could help but notice that the woman did have a more presentable side. And he was fascinated by Lil's interests. He never failed to inspect the motorcycle when she roared into town, and Trinity had noticed the way he would sit on the mercantile porch and wait until she and Esau had ridden out of town before he got up. Their fascination for the unusual was identical.

She bit her trembling lower lip. In the future, the pig farmer could clean *herself* up.

Jones jerked the black string tie into a knot and frowned at his image. He should have his head examined for agreeing to this nonsense. He didn't know Mary Grace and Luther — never laid eyes on either one of them — and now he'd agreed to go to their anniversary party.

A knock on the door took his mind off his misery. He stepped to unlatch the lock and let the heavy door swing open. Tom appeared, grinning like a donkey eating green grass. "Ready?"

"Will be in a couple of seconds." He picked up a bottle of Bay Rum and splashed a little on his cleanly shaven jaw. A bath and a shave cost seventy-five cents in this town. Highway robbery, pure and simple.

Tom sidled into the room, his gaze roaming the furnishings. "Nice place. I haven't seen the rooms since the café finished them."

"It's not bad." Jones picked up the comb and ran it through his hair. "Remind me again why I agreed to go to this shindig?"

"Because Mae's been real close to these folks and she didn't want to go unless she took a friend. Said she'd feel real bad about leaving her behind — and she really appreciates you pitching in to help."

"But why do I have to go? I don't know the Willises."

"Mae thought it would be nice to have her friend escorted. For appearance's sake, you understand."

Leaning closer to the mirror, Jones scoffed. "Escorted? I'm supposed to escort this woman? Can't she get her own dates? Who is she, anyway?"

Tom pulled a watch out of his pocket. "Will you look at the time? We'd better get going. Don't want to be late, now."

Giving a final glance in the mirror, Jones decided he looked as good as he was going to get. He was clean, shaved, smelling good, and about to escort a woman he didn't know to a party. Never mind that he'd rather turn in early. He reached for his hat. "Is Trinity going to be there?"

"No, she's sitting with Pauline. Mae thought it would do Benjamin good to step away for a few minutes."

"He doesn't know the Willises either, does he?"

"I'm sure he doesn't."

Jones locked the door of the rented room and turned to take the long row of stairs leading to the first floor. Already the sound of guitars and fiddles filled the warm, humid air. The two men crossed the street to the Curtises' home. They climbed up to the porch, taking the steps two at a time. Mae appeared in the doorway to greet them.

Tom paused, a grin splitting his face. "Just look at her, Jones. Look at her and eat your heart out."

Jones had to admit that Mae was glowing tonight. She was prettier than a black cloud during drought. Pink was her color, and the love evident in her eyes for her husband only made her more comely.

His smile died when a second figure appeared in the doorway, looking every bit as pretty but apparently forgoing tonight's festivities. "Evening, Miss Trinity," he said.

She acknowledged the greeting with a

nod. She appeared unusually sober tonight. "Jones."

"Everyone ready to have a good time?" Tom asked.

Mae touched her hair and glanced toward Trinity. "I'll get Lil."

Still grinning, the name took a moment to register. When it did, Jones turned to note the motorcycle sitting at the hitching rail. "Lil's going to the party?"

"Yes, she is . . . Lil? Lil! We're leaving now!"

Another figure appeared in the doorway and Jones focused on her, trying to remember if he'd seen her around Dwadlo before. She was striking in a practical way. Her red hair shone in the fading sunlight and the freshly ironed calico dress hugged nubile curves. He didn't recall meeting her in town. Only when she stepped onto the porch and turned to face him was he able to make the connection. "Lil?"

Tom echoed the surprise in Jones's voice. "Lil Jenkins? That isn't you, is it?"

"Close your mouths, fellers. It's me." She spun on her toe and whirled, the hem of her skirts swirling around those satin slippers. "Don't this just beat all you've ever seen?"

Jones had to admit that he was floored by

the stunning transformation. Lil looked downright decent, all clean and perfumed to high heaven. He glanced at Tom, whose eyes were fixed on the woman. "Lil?"

"Aw, come on, Tom, you know it's me. Quit yore gawkin'. Now are we going to a party or not?" She stepped up and slipped her arm through Jones's. "Right nice of you to offer me an invite."

An invite? Jones glared at Tom, and he shrugged. Why, that lowdown, dirty rascal . . . He'd tricked him into taking Lil to the party!

"Let's go, gents, and walk slow now. Without my boots I feel like I'm gonna stub my big toe in these flimsy things Mae calls slippers."

"Stop fussing. You look lovely." Mae reached over to give Trinity a hug. "I wish you could come. We'll miss you."

Trinity nodded. "I wish I could too, but I'll be fine. I'll get Benjamin. He was still dressing a moment ago."

"Poor dear. He really doesn't want to leave Pauline, but we'll only be a few doors away."

"He needs the distraction, and I wouldn't be surprised if Pauline was asleep for the night. The doctor promised to check on her before he stops in to offer Mary Grace and

Luther his congratulations." She met Jones's eyes and smiled. "Everyone have a lovely time, now — and bring me back a cup of punch."

For the briefest of moments Jones allowed his gaze to focus on her. Though she wasn't dressed for a party, the heat had tinted her cheeks a rosy pink. A single light tendril fell across her forehead. Apparently transforming Lil had not been the easiest goal to obtain. He offered her a smile, which she returned.

Taking her to a dance tonight would have been much more pleasant . . . but he shook the unwarranted thought aside.

He wasn't taking anybody but himself.

The Virginia Reel had already begun when the small party reached the Willis place. Jones had reconsidered, deciding that he wasn't going to embarrass Lil in front of everyone. It wasn't her fault, after all. She didn't appear to be aware of the ruse, but Tom owed him one. Maybe two. He didn't have anything against Lil but he liked his women a little more — soft. Soft and pretty and smelling like Trinity. Or whatever it was that she bathed in.

The small house was overheated. Furniture had been pushed against the wall to form a small dance floor. Women from the church auxiliary were cutting various flavored cakes and pouring red punch. Fisk stood at the front of the room and called the dance, accompanied by a group of men playing fiddles and guitars. By eight o'clock, the roof of the Willis cottage threatened to lift.

Lil proved to be a seasoned dancer. Jones teased her when he whirled her through a second set of four corners. "Where did you learn to dance like this?"

"Shoot, I dance with myself!" she shouted above the din. "Me and the hogs and dogs and cats — we have us a big party every so often. Esau would join in if he could." She proved to be so adept on the dance floor that Jones didn't have to worry about entertaining her. The younger men kept tapping his shoulder, wanting to take their turn spinning Lil around on the dance floor.

He wandered to the punch bowl and accepted a cool cup of the refreshing drink, his eyes on the belle of the ball. He glanced up when Tom joined him.

Tom grinned. "Isn't that something? Who'd have thought Lil would clean up so nice?"

"Curtis" — Jones lifted his cup and took a drink — "you're a dead man."

Tom chuckled. "Blame Mae. This was her idea."

"She's trying to match me and Lil?"

"No, but she loves Lil and she worries that she needs a man. Mae's hoping a few of the local yahoos will open their eyes and see Lil for the fine woman she is." His gaze focused on the dance floor. "Seems to be working out real well."

"Fisk doesn't appear to be noticing."

Tom shook his head. "Fisk isn't and won't ever be romantically inclined toward Lil. The two like to annoy each other, but neither one of them is likely to make it permanent. They're too much alike. Hard-headed as they get."

Jones focused on a flushed Lil, who was in the middle of a mighty fine two-step with a man who looked to be about her age. "Well now, it looks like she's opening a few eyes this evening."

"Yeah." Tom grinned. "Appears so." A second man stepped to the couple and tapped the shoulder of Lil's partner.

"The way I have Lil figured, she doesn't need a man to make her happy." Jones took a sip of punch. "She's content with what God has given her. A man would get in her hair. Hold her down. If I was a betting person I'd say Lil won't ever marry — not for lack of asking but by personal choice."

"That a fact? And what about Trinity?" Tom's tone held a playful edge.

"Haven't paused to study her." He turned and smiled at the chubby woman pouring punch. "Hit me again, Miss Lucy. It's mighty warm in here tonight." His gaze traveled to Benjamin, who sat on the sidelines with the wallflowers. He was the only man who wasn't dancing. "Make that two cups," he told the woman. The poor man had suffered enough.

Briefly he stood in front of Benjamin. "Ready to get out of here?"

The old doc's eyes brightened and he sat up straighter. "Been ready since we got here."

Jones lifted the extra cup. "I promised to bring Trinity some punch. I say we leave now before the drink gets warm."

The gratitude he witnessed in Benjamin's eyes made the night complete. A good dance, a little punch, and chocolate cake did a man's soul good.

Lil lifted a friendly hand when Jones motioned that he was cutting out. She flashed a smile and swung into a do-si-do. No expectations. That's what he liked about that woman.

That and her motorcycle.

Seventeen

"Did you enjoy the dance last night?"

"It wasn't bad. The cake was good."

Crossing his arms, Jones stared at the rubbish pile. The size was staggering. The railroad's two derailments last winter had left an untidy heap. The first one had been sheer bad luck, while the other was caused by a runaway engine. The evidence lay before him, piled high as the newly constructed post office. Flies swarmed around the burdensome sight.

Tom shook his head. "Give it up. Searching for a single piece of paper in there would be insane."

Fisk nodded his agreement. "I ain't siftin' through that mess." A heavy stench still curtained the area.

The blacksmith was right, but the stubborn side of Jones wouldn't let up. "I thought a bank box might be easier to spot."

"That's crazy talk." Fisk pulled his kerchief over his mouth and tied a knot behind his head.

"Jones, you don't need to worry about this," said Tom. "Mae and I can handle anything necessary on this end. There's nothing holding you back from leaving today."

Jones could think of a reason. A toffee-eyed woman who, with a lift of her long lashes, could coil him around her little finger. He couldn't ride off and leave until he was confident that Wilson's Falls was hers and that she was financially secure — which she would be unless she married some jackal who took her for every cent she owned. He shook the thought away. She was a burr in his saddle. A responsibility he didn't need. The deed was her problem. He could leave those trusting eyes behind.

"What time do you plan to ride out?"

The harmless question struck a raw nerve. What was the big hurry to get out of town? His task was to complete his work, and he needed a few more days.

"I've changed my mind," he said. "I'll hang around until Pauline passes." Trinity would have Benjamin for comfort, but the old feller was going to take Pauline's death hard. He'd need a man's presence to assure him that life would go on — and Jones had

225

taken a liking to him. He couldn't ride away and leave the old man hurting. Not for another day or two. "The railroad understands my situation. And Doc says Pauline probably won't make it through the day."

Tom shook his head. "Strange to think of. Mae's going to need some time to get over the loss. Pauline's been like family to her."

Something deep inside Jones hoped the doctor was mistaken about the end. Pauline was weak, but she could have a few days left — days she and Benjamin could spend getting reacquainted. He chuckled at the thought of the untimely love match. There wouldn't be much time for old-fashioned courting.

Jones chuckled.

Tom glanced over. "What's so funny?"

"Benjamin and Pauline. I guess it's true what folks say: It's never too late for love." He glanced at Fisk. "Did you notice anything different about Lil last night?"

Fisk turned sullen. "Noticed she was makin' a blame fool of herself dancing with every man in the place."

"Didn't see you taking a whirl on the floor," Tom goaded.

"I was busy callin' the dances."

"Yeah?" Jones grinned, grateful for the lighter subject. "Well, by the looks of it, she

226

won't be in your hair as often. The men around her appeared to like the new Lil."

"New my foot," Fisk scoffed. "She'd be a burr in any man's saddle." He twisted his wedding ring absently. In a brusque tone he admitted, "I shore do miss my departed."

"Fisk, Tom tells me your missus has been gone a while and Lil would marry you at the drop of a hat."

"I ain't marryin' that bossy redhead!" Color suffused the blacksmith's neck. "Rather be tied to a polecat."

"That can be arranged too." Tom winked at Jones.

Jones noticed the whole town took delight in teasing Fisk about Lil. He enjoyed it too. The warring couple was a sight to behold. The two fought like dogs and cats and disagreed on everything — from the right way to churn butter to the way Lil dressed like a man. Pig farmer by trade and hoyden by heart — that was Lil. The woman was a might unconventional for most men, but whoever married Lil Jenkins wouldn't suffer from a single day of boredom. And yet he didn't see a love match in the making. If the couple fought now, marriage wasn't going to change the discord. Both Lil and Fisk were smart enough to recognize the fact.

He glanced up as cloud cover drifted

overhead. "Fisk, will you take a look at Sue sometime this afternoon? I think she's feeling poorly today."

The men turned from the rubble and walked to the mercantile. Mae was standing in the doorway, fanning herself.

"Tom?" Dark circles were sketched around her beautiful eyes, and Jones noted that she looked paler than usual.

"Yes, sweetie?" Tom's features sobered. "What's wrong? Is it Pauline?"

Opening the screen door, Mae waved his assumption aside. "She's sleeping. It's me. I don't feel so . . ."

She wilted like a flower closing for the night and landed on the porch, unconscious.

Chaos broke out when Mae hit the ground. Tom sprang to life and lifted his bride into his arms, carrying her inside. Trinity, who had left Pauline's bedside for a brief visit with Mae, gaped at the sight of her lifeless form.

"What is it? What's happened?"

"She fainted," Tom grunted. He laid his wife down and bent over her, murmuring her name.

A doctor. They needed a doctor. Before she knew it Trinity was running back to the Curtises' house. Benjamin would know what to do.

■ ■ ■ ■

The old gent bent over Mae's immobile form. Trinity stood close by, wiping the patient's face with a cool cloth.

"Could be too much excitement." His age-spotted hands made a slow but efficient examination of Mae's wilted body. Trinity realized how small and helpless her new friend looked in repose. When Benjamin looked up, he shook his head. "It's been so many years since I've practiced."

"Can you determine anything? Is it her heart? She's much too young for heart problems."

"A body's never too young or too old to give out." He frowned. "She appears to be fine. No breaks or open wounds. Her breathing is normal. Pulse is fine. I think she just fainted — probably overheated — but when the doc gets here we'll know for certain."

"I told her we should just have fruit and not light the cook stove this morning." Trinity released a short breath. "It's stifling in here. Let's get her to a chair and under the fan." The blades turned slowly in the thick air and provided a small measure of relief.

Tom stooped and carefully placed his hands under Mae's arms. Trinity took her feet and together they eased her to a chair in front of the window. She murmured, starting to come around.

"I'll get some water." Trinity straightened as Mae opened her eyes.

"I'm fine," she said.

Benjamin knelt beside her chair. "The doc's just outside of town making a house call. He's due back any time. You having sickness right now?"

She nodded. "Some. And I've felt a little lightheaded lately. Sometimes it's hard for me to catch my breath."

"Had any discomfort in your chest? Pains in your upper arms?"

"No. Maybe a little. I just haven't felt well." She looked up. "Is it my heart? My father and grandfather both had weak hearts."

The doc's features turned somber as a gravedigger's. "I don't know what's happening, hon, but it could be the heat."

Trinity bit back tears. How serious was it? Mae and Tom had only begun their life together. The good Lord couldn't take Mae now, not when everything was falling into place for her. Marriage. Happiness. Mae was too young — too vibrant — too wildly in love with Tom.

"Why don't you all head on out?" said Benjamin. "I want to ask Mrs. Curtis a few questions." He shooed the party out the door.

Tom paced the porch, brooding as they waited. Trinity looked over at Jones, who was standing to the side with a sober expression on his face. He opened his arms and she stepped into them. When his strength closed around her, she sighed. *Heaven must feel like this,* she thought, *only without the worry.* Silence filled the strained void as she trained her eyes on the screen door, willing it to open. Mae's condition couldn't be serious. Just last night she had been laughing and even singing while they transformed Lil.

A sudden cry filled the stilted air. Trinity closed her eyes and pressed her face into Jones's wide chest. The reflex came so naturally that it was several seconds before she realized the impropriety of her actions and stepped back.

Benjamin had discovered her illness. Something so horrid that Mae had cried aloud, unable to hold back her terror.

"It's her heart," said Tom. "I've been afraid of this. It runs in her family . . ." He started for the doorway, but Jones blocked

231

his path.

"He'll be out in a minute."

Fisk excused himself, ramming his hat down on his head. "I best get back to work." He looked at Tom and then at Jones. "You'll let me know . . ."

Jones nodded. "I'll be over as soon as I hear anything."

The screen door swung open and Benjamin stepped out, tears shimmering in his eyes. "Sorry to be so long. Mae and I talked a little more and I think we have this figured out." He motioned for the group to come inside. Gripping Jones's hand, Trinity followed behind Tom.

Tom dropped to his knees in front of the chair and took both of Mae's hands in his. A smile creased her tear-stained face. Her husband turned to meet Benjamin's gaze. "Whatever it is we can fix it. Chicago has some of the best medical care around and the most experienced doctors available. We'll move there."

Mae shook her head, more tears spilling onto her cheeks. "That won't be necessary, darling."

His voice broke. "What is it?"

"It's your son — or daughter. I'm afraid he or she is acting up a bit this morning."

"My son . . ." The words slowly registered,

and a grin spread across the width of his face. "My son?"

She held up a warning finger. "Or daughter. Women can be as temperamental as men on occasion."

Disbelief, pride, and then pure joy erupted in the new papa's features. He lunged to enfold his wife in his arms. Trinity squealed and threw her arms around Jones's neck. His grip tightened around her.

Stepping clear of the mêlée, Benjamin coughed and then removed a large handkerchief from his back pocket and wiped his eyes. Wonder shone on his weathered features. Trinity's thoughts tumbled over and over in her mind. In the darkened bedroom one life was nearly finished — and here a new life was about to begin. Such was the circle of life.

"A baby!" Trinity squealed. And then she was kissing Jones. First it was a short series of ecstatic pecks, and then the kissing slowed and deepened.

Desire flared.

Shock.

Delight. Pure, utter delight.

She pulled back and looked into his dark eyes. Slowly their mouths drew closer and then closed together for another long and thorough embrace.

"Hold it, hold it." Benjamin held up his hand, and Trinity and Jones reluctantly broke apart. "The doc will have to confirm my diagnosis. It's been a long time since I've informed a man and woman they're about to be a mama and papa." His gaze softened. "But I can tell you with firm conviction: This is an hour to celebrate."

The past few weeks had been long and hard, but for the moment Trinity was glad to set despondency aside and celebrate new life.

And even happier to lift her mouth for yet another kiss.

"What was that about?" Jones was holding Trinity's arm as he walked her across the street to the café. The sounds of laughter drifting from the mercantile must have been puzzling the passersby. Of late, nothing but sadness had filled the shop.

"I was purely caught up in the celebration," she said. She'd been hoping he'd taken the spontaneous burst for what it was — pure excitement. But for her — and perhaps for him as well — the kiss had proven more exhilarating than the news that Mae was expecting.

"Do you kiss everyone that way when you're excited?"

"What way?" She shrugged, feeling the blood rising to her cheeks in a way that had nothing to do with the intense heat of the summer day.

They reached the café and he escorted her up the steps. "Remind me to tell you good news more often."

"Why, Mr. Jones!" She affected modesty, not feeling the slightest sense of respectability. "I do believe you're flirting with me."

"And I do believe you're enjoying it."

She grinned. The time for acting coy was past. She was falling for him. Deeply. Did he return the sentiment?

Her footsteps slowed. His roguish grin and curly dark hair loosened her tongue. Why shouldn't he know her scandalous thoughts?

Because he might not reciprocate, common sense argued. But if he didn't share her growing attraction . . . if he rode out . . .

"Are you toying with me?"

"Could be." He flashed a grin. "You're not married."

"Not even spoken for, but there does exist a certain lunacy at the thought of us . . . together. I live in Sioux Falls. You live . . ."

His grin faded to a frustrated squint. "Chicago."

"Come with me." Taking his hand, she pulled him into the café and marched him

to the back wall, where a large map of the
United States was hanging. She pointed at
North Dakota. "Here we are, way up on the
Piedmont Tributary."

His gaze followed her finger. "So?"

"So." Her finger slid to the right and then
down to Illinois. "You live in Chicago.
Would you not agree that it's a long way to
ride to go courting?"

He studied the map and shrugged. "I
haven't said I want to court you."

"No. You haven't. Nor have I indicated I
was fond of the idea. I only mentioned it in
case . . . in case you might be having reckless thoughts." She wasn't going to speak
first. Her reckless thoughts would remain
unspoken until he spoke his.

"Like you are."

"I didn't say that."

"Your kiss did."

She blushed and caught the café owner's
attention. "Belle, I'll need my room for
another few days."

The woman nodded as she cleared a table.
"Already put you down. Is Pauline . . . ?"

Why was everyone so afraid to say *dead*?
Pauline was dying, after all. "She's still with
us." Trinity closed her eyes and scratched
her arm. She was coated in trail grime and
every inch of her itched. "I need a hot bath

and shampoo as soon as possible."

"I'll draw your water." Belle disappeared, and Trinity suddenly found herself caught in a pair of strong arms. She met Jones's dancing eyes straight on. "Is there something you'd like to say to me?" Dare she hope he would be so bold as to steal another kiss?

He dared.

Lowering his head, Jones bent Trinity back and kissed her within an inch of her life. It was an intense kiss, almost challenging, and it made her head spin. When he released her she reached for the top of a chair for support. "What was *that*?" she said finally.

Settling his hat on his head, he grinned. "Rebuttal."

Her hand lifted to cover her trembling lips as she watched the door close behind him.

Was this a tribunal? If so, she was on his side.

It was late in the afternoon when Jones wandered across the street to the mercantile. He'd meant to sleep a while, but he kept being wakened by images of Trinity. Was she actually suggesting that anything permanent could come of their unlikely friendship? A few days ago the answer would have been obvious — *no.* He wasn't looking for a woman. But she had him thinking thoughts he didn't want to think.

A pale-faced Mae stood behind the postal cage, sipping what looked to be soda water.

"Still feeling poorly?"

Nodding, she lifted sick-looking eyes to him. "Still a bit under the weather."

"Do you feel up to sending a telegraph?"

"Of course." She stepped to the machine and picked up a pad. "To whom?"

"Piedmont Bank."

She arched an eyebrow.

Leaning on the counter, he removed his hat. "I've been thinking. Pauline was wrong the first time about the deed's location. It's possible she's mistaken again."

"Do you really think so?"

He grinned. "Seems a reasonable assumption. She's got a heart of gold, but you have to admit she can be confused sometimes."

"Often. She gets perplexed . . ."

"It won't hurt to send a message and ask if there's an old lockbox lying in the vault with Pauline's name on it. Who knows? The deed might be there."

Mae wrote the message, nodding as she did so. "It can't hurt to try." She ripped off the sheet, then stepped to the machine and clicked out a series of dots and dashes.

Jones's eyes traveled around the empty

238

store. "Tom around?"

"He's working on the nursing home. He needs to keep busy." She paused, thoughtful. "Pauline has become very dear to him. He'll miss her."

"I suspect you all will." He stopped by the root beer barrel and snagged a cold bottle. He fished in his pocket and dropped a coin on the counter on his way out. "Let me know when you hear back about that wire."

Nodding absently, she completed the message and then reached for the glass of soda water.

Construction on the Pauline Wilson Rest Home was well underway. The fifteen-room building stretched along the waterfront. The racket of hammers and saws filled the air as Jones approached.

Tom looked up with a grin when Jones found him framing in a hallway. "Here — hold this for me," he said.

Jones steadied the board as Tom nailed it in place. "How does it feel to be a new pa?" he asked.

Pride broke out on Tom's rugged features. "Can't even explain it. It's like comfortable shoes and Christmas morning all tied in a bundle."

Jones chuckled as Tom drove a nail into

place. "I recall a time when you were more interested in wild oats than cradles."

"That was a long time ago. What do you think about the name Stephen?"

"Sounds manly enough."

"Thomas Stephen." He drove in another nail.

"Might be a daughter."

"Could be . . . but it won't be." He flashed another smile. "I should head up and check on Mae."

"She's fine. I just left her."

"Thought you were resting."

"Couldn't, but I did some thinking."

"About what?"

"About how Pauline means well, but we shouldn't take her recollections seriously. She could be mistaken about the deed having been in Dwadlo's bank. I took the liberty of sending a telegraph to the bank in Piedmont. Could be there's something there that belongs to Pauline."

"Ah." Tom's hammer paused. "Trinity's a good woman."

"She is." He wasn't going to elaborate. Good women were hard to come by. Most were controlling or nagging or just mean-spirited. He should stop letting his stepmother sour his views on womankind . . . but the thought of her had a way of making

240

him pull back whenever a relationship got too intense.

"You were lucky to find Mae."

"I've been blessed indeed, and maybe the good Lord thinks it's your time." Tom reached for a nail. "What are the chances you'd be stopping by Dwadlo and find Trinity here?" He didn't answer, and then Tom whistled, long and low. "What are the chances she'd stop by just as we're talking about her?"

Jones turned to see Trinity striding toward him, breathless. He walked over to meet her. "Is everything all right? Is Pauline . . . Is it time?"

He met her dancing eyes, and for a moment he felt like a moth drawn to a flame. She handed him a scrap of paper. "It's time. We hit pay dirt."

EIGHTEEN

Jones scanned the message, satisfaction spreading across his tanned features. "So Pauline does have a box in Piedmont."

Trinity couldn't contain her excitement. "I say we leave right now."

Jones folded the message and frowned. "We can't go now. Your aunt is near death."

Her smile faded. For a moment she had forgotten Aunt Pauline. "But we'll go soon, after the . . . ?" She didn't want to say the word *funeral.*

"Shouldn't be much longer." Tom reached for a handful of nails. "The train's due in Sunday. By then, I imagine Pauline will be in the Lord's presence."

True. And taking the train would be a lot easier than riding horseback. And if the deed was in the lockbox after all, their problems would be solved. She glanced at Jones. Well . . . one of their problems.

She had to admit it — she wasn't looking

forward to leaving Dwadlo. The delay was almost welcome. She was enjoying Mae and Tom's company, and Jeremy could fry the most delicious chicken she'd ever eaten, and even Lil had a certain bizarre fascination about her. Trinity had a hunch that if she stayed here much longer, that outrageous pig farmer might become one of her closest confidantes. Except she would never, under any circumstances, get on the back of that motorcycle again.

Jones took her gently by the shoulders. "Don't worry. The delay won't be long."

Her eyes drank him in. He was becoming far too important to her, and still neither one had confessed their feelings. "I understand. I wasn't thinking." She forced a smile. Once she'd thought her lovely little room in Sioux Falls was a little slice of heaven, but maybe heaven wasn't in Sioux Falls after all. She shook the silly notion aside. Once she had the money from the land she could live anywhere she wanted. Heaven on earth could be anywhere she chose to make it.

Trouble was, she didn't have the slightest idea where that might be.

Only a sneaky idea of who she'd like to share it with.

■ ■ ■ ■

"This is going to take months." Jones groaned, and then bent and sifted through the top layer of rubble, stepping back when the stench hit him. Fisk had been right: It would be impossible to find anything in this jumble, but it was worth looking before making the long trip to Piedmont. And besides, he had a feeling that if he didn't finish his business here soon, he was going to get caught in a trap of his own building. Settling down was starting to sound nice.

His gaze strayed to the post office porch, where Trinity and Mae sat talking. Too nice.

Jones lifted a few boards and peered inside deep holes filled with mounds of wet papers, bank boxes, and broken sticks of furniture. He was searching for a miracle in a haystack.

A pile of boards slid to the ground and he turned to see that Trinity had joined him.

"I thought you were visiting with Mae."

"I was, but you don't think I'd let you look through this alone, do you?"

"Maybe I'm looking for something of mine."

"I think you're looking for something of mine."

"Well, we can both forget the hunt. It's

impossible to find anything in this heap. You might as well go back and keep Mae company."

"She's not doing anything but drinking soda water. The doctor told her this morning that she might feel better in a few months, but she could be queasy her whole term. Benjamin won't let anyone near Pauline now that she's awake, so other than watching the mercantile and post office, her duties are pretty slow. Seems Benjamin intends to use up all the allotted time he and Pauline have left together. They're sweet, aren't they?" She loosened a board and tossed it aside. "To think that he's loved her all these years and they're only now seeing that love bloom."

"I don't recall Pauline saying that she's open to any long-lost suitor."

"She's a woman. She's open . . . for the right person." A grin hovered at the corners of her mouth. She was a romantic at heart, Jones realized. And maybe he was too. Seeing the old couple together did bring a lump to his throat.

Working in silence, they absently sifted through the debris. What papers they found were wrinkled and water-stained beyond recognition. Anything that survived was far from legible. Jones finally acknowledged the obvious. "We're not going to find it, Trinity."

"How long would it take to get a new deed — once Pauline is willing to sign?"

"It depends, but it won't be quick." He straightened. "What about you?"

"What about me?"

"You have a job. How long can you stick around Dwadlo?"

"No longer than this week." She sighed. "I can get a few more days, but my boss is going to have to replace me if I'm not back by Monday." She glanced up. "What about you?"

"I have to leave now, or give the railroad a good reason why I'm still in Dwadlo." He reached for her hand and helped her over a pile of rubble. They walked to the rain barrel and washed up. He wasn't going to kid himself. Leaving her — and this town — was going to be rough. In the short time he'd been here this place had turned his life upside-down. He studied Trinity out of the corner of his eye. Was it the place that had changed him? Or the woman?

He shook the water out of his hair. "Want a cold drink?"

She cupped her hands full of water and doused him. "I'd love one."

In a few short minutes he'd gone to the mercantile for two cold bottles of soda and returned. They planted themselves in the grassy patch beneath the oak tree behind the store.

"The shade feels good," said Jones.

Nodding, Trinity took a sip from the bottle. Her eyes darkened. "Can I tell you something?"

"Shoot."

"I'm going to miss you."

The simplicity of her confession surprised him. The admission had to come hard for an independent woman like her.

"Miss me? What's that supposed to mean? Are you asking me to stay?"

She tipped the soda bottle, her eyes meeting his. Then, lowering it, she whispered, "And if I did?"

What could he say? He looked long and hard at her. "I'm going to miss you too."

A soft breath escaped her. "And what's that supposed to mean?"

Emotions played through his mind, feelings he'd never had before. He would miss her. He would miss the way her brows knitted together when she was thoughtful, the way her mouth lifted into corners and her cheeks pinked when she was teasing. But there was going to be a powerful lot of distance between them, and the likelihood of anything lasting happening between them

247

seemed as remote as Pauline's deed.

"It means it doesn't sound like either of us is in a hurry to go."

Draining their sodas, they shared a companionable silence. Birds sang overhead, and a thin layer of clouds lessened the afternoon heat. He should make a move. Do something. Leave, if he knew what was good for him. Stay, if he was a gambling man.

Kiss her. Would she welcome the advance? No doubt she was warming to him in an unsettling way — which could be good or bad. Their kiss earlier had been due to the excitement of the day. Chances were she wouldn't let him do it again.

But more to the point, did he even want to get seriously involved — heart involved — with this woman? Two weeks ago he would have laughed at the notion. Marriage wasn't for him — the regret and misery he'd seen in his pa's eyes was testimony enough to that.

And yet . . . she looked mighty kissable at the moment, with flushed cheeks and the sunburned tip of her nose. He could easily take her into his arms. Wouldn't mean anything but a warm summer afternoon dalliance. He wouldn't be admitting to anything but being a red-blooded male.

One harmless kiss.

Little more than a peck.

While he hesitated, she reached out and covered his mouth with hers. He instinctively pulled her closer, marveling at how right it felt to hold her. Her kisses were sweet and warm, and her hair was soft under his hand.

"Well, lookee here!" cried a voice from the store. Jones and Trinity sprang apart, eyes wide.

"Didn't no one ever tell you it was rude to kiss in public?" said Lil, her mouth broken into a wide grin.

Early Saturday morning, Pauline sat up and announced, "I'm hungry! Are you trying to starve a body?"

Trinity, Mae, and Benjamin stumbled over one another to reach the kitchen and prepare a bowl of broth and hot tea. It was the first morsel the patient had eaten in days.

It wasn't long later that the doctor was straightening and shaking his head. "Fit as a fine-tuned fiddle."

A grin broke across Benjamin's weathered features. "I told you she was hard to put down."

Not exactly a flattering term, but Trinity didn't argue. She spooned warm broth into her aunt's mouth, swiping at the tears that persisted in springing to her eyes. *Thank You for allowing me more time with her.*

Pauline couldn't live forever, but Trinity welcomed whatever weeks or months they were given.

She made up her mind. She would quit her job in Sioux Falls and move to Dwadlo to be near her aunt. They'd become close — like real family. Trinity had told herself that family didn't matter. After all, the Lord had taken her ma and pa home that day, so He must have known she didn't need anyone but herself to get by. And she had gotten by. Although, if she was honest with herself, it had been an empty life until Jones had come along and stuffed her in that barrel. She'd thought it was the end of the world, but it had proven to be the start of a brand new future. A future with a family she'd never known she had.

The Lord knew Pauline's time, and it wasn't here yet.

Sunday morning, just as the sun was climbing in the sky, Jones and Trinity boarded the train to Piedmont. Pauline had rallied and there was nothing preventing them from making the short journey and settling the matter of the deed once and for all. Doc couldn't say whether or not her aunt's rally was a permanent one, but they'd agreed to take it one day at a time.

There were few travelers this morning, and they had their choice of seats. It felt, oddly, as if they were a couple. Trinity rather liked the feeling. She relished the sense of Jones's warmth, though they kept a proper distance from each other. He was the missing ingredient in her life, and the knowledge thumped her. The touch of a mother's hand or a father's voice — folks took those things for granted, but both had been missing from her life. Until now, she hadn't realized how much she wanted what others took for granted. Rob had been a fine big brother but he couldn't take the place of her parents. He dried her tears and cooked her meals when he hadn't been much more than a boy himself. Had he too felt the need of a pa's hand? A man's wisdom? A ma's apple pie? She'd heard him cry once, shortly after her parents failed to return. When she'd caught him he'd told her he had something in his eyes, but today she understood that that "something" had been a boy's fear. A boy's uncertainty at becoming a man long before his time.

Trinity glanced at Jones as he removed his hat and rested it on his knee. Having this strong, handsome man at her side filled her with comfort and pride. She could make it on her own, but did she want to? She'd never depended on anyone but herself and Rob. She was a bit independent and head-strong and didn't always take well to orders, and Jones would certainly be prone to boss-ing her around, but she could hold her own with any man. She sighed. There was much to consider, but now the thrill of anticipa-tion overrode her growing confusion regard-ing her personal life. The deed was almost in her hands — she was sure of it. She settled on the seat and waited for the train to start chugging forward.

Outside movement caught her eye, and she watched an attendant lead Sue to a back railcar. She turned to Jones, aware that her jaw had dropped. "You're taking Sue?"

"Calm down," he said quietly. "I was go-ing to tell you earlier, but we got . . . distracted. When we conclude our business in Piedmont I'm leaving. I'm long overdue to meet a prospective seller."

Disappointment crushed her. "But we have to meet with the banker, and you need to see the land . . ."

His gaze softened. "I'm sorry. I should have told you earlier, but we'll have time for both. I won't leave until I see your land and what that box contains."

"And if the deed isn't there?"

He shook his head. "Then you convince Pauline to sign that lawyer's paper and apply for a new one. We can't spend day after day chasing after a piece of paper. In a few weeks — or months — we can make the transaction."

She turned to stare out the window.

"I'll give you the money to get back home."

"I don't want your charity and I'm not going back to Sioux Falls. I've decided to move here to be with Pauline."

"I'd say you've made a wise choice."

"Mae and Tom will help me get settled."

"I'm sure they will. You'll be in good hands."

He refused to meet her eyes. He was not obliged to her, and he didn't owe her an explanation about his plans. He didn't.

And yet he did. He was walking away with her heart and he knew it. She fumbled for a hanky as a second passenger boarded the car. Wearing a large hat that sported a huge peacock quill, the young woman reminded Trinity of a proud bird. Her daringly low-cut ruby-red dress and matching hair color was intended to capture a man's eye. She glanced at Jones, who discreetly avoided an overlong perusal. The newcomer flashed a white smile and took the seat directly in front of them.

Trinity shifted. Why, when there were at least a dozen empty benches, did she have to sit so close? She'd hoped to have the time alone with Jones.

A whistle sounded, and then, with a series of groans and clanks, the train started to roll. Trinity settled back, watching her companion. He wasn't exactly staring at the woman, but he wasn't avoiding her either.

The woman turned in her seat. "Good morning!"

He nodded, and Trinity returned a soft hello. She reached for Jones's hand as the locomotive picked up speed. He gave her an inscrutable look, then let go. Farms flashed by. Cattle stood in the fields, heads held high as they watched the big steam engine pass.

The young lady extended her hand. "I'm Melissa — Missy. I'm on my way to visit my daddy. He lives in Farlene. I'm an only child, so I'm rather a daddy's girl — or I was until I left home two years ago. Papa didn't want me to go but I can be a bit strong-willed, or so he says. I adore your dress. Do you sew?"

Trinity nodded. "A bit."

"Oh, I knew it! I can always tell a fellow fashion aficionada. Did you purchase those darling shoes in Dwadlo?"

Jones's gaze shifted to Trinity's boots.

Missy sighed. "I haven't been able to find a decent pair since the train wreck did all that damage. The mercantile used to carry simply everything but now they're so limited in their stock. I'm desperately hoping that once the town is back to normal, and Dale assures me it soon will be, the store will carry a better selection of dry goods. Do you like tomatoes?"

Jones stared at her. She was addressing him now. "Pardon?"

"Do you like tomatoes?"

Trinity noted how closely he fixed on the blood-red lips and the carefully enunciated sentence. "I eat them."

"They give me the hives. Isn't that odd? I ate them all the time when I was a child and they had absolutely no effect on me, but lo and behold I ate one a couple of summers ago and broke out in a rash you would not believe." She scooted forward and bared one arm for his inspection. "For a while I thought I'd gotten into poison ivy or something like that but no, the doctor thought I might be allergic to something and then I told him I'd been eating a lot of tomatoes

255

that summer and he said, 'Well, you might think about avoiding tomatoes for a while and see if that rash won't clear up.' So I did and lo and behold my skin improved within a few days — well, maybe it took a week, but soon after I quit eating tomatoes. Isn't that strange? And then . . ."

Wheels clanked against steel as the locomotive chugged across the countryside. Missy's voice droned on and on.

And on.

By midmorning Jones was dozing, and Missy's voice was still filling the near-empty car. The woman chattered like a magpie. "I love prairie flowers. Do you like flowers? I've often thought I should move to the big city and open a florist shop — they're quite popular in the East. Of course, flowers can be very expensive, so I guess before I'd attempt anything that daring I would have to research the prospect more carefully but being around flowers every day would make a person so happy. Don't you agree? I work at the saloon — now before you judge me let me tell you that I don't do anything but sing. Three songs a night, and if a gentleman asks I'll occasionally draw a fresh draught, but none of that funny stuff, you know? Men don't try anything fussy with Missy."

Jones was grunting answers in his sleep. "Hum. Uh huh. Hmmm. Oh?"

Missy bent and whipped out a pistol, aiming it straight at Trinity. Trinity gave a small shriek and clutched at Jones, who sat bolt upright.

"Ain't she a beaut?" Motherly pride shown on Missy's face. "My daddy sent her to me when I first took the saloon job. Said no daughter of his was going to work in a place like that — if you know what I mean — without proper protection. If you know what I mean."

Trinity didn't know what she meant. She hadn't understood half of what she'd said since they boarded.

Jones came to her rescue. "Lady, don't wave that gun in our faces. Someone could get hurt."

She frowned. "It's not loaded." A foxy grin crossed her features. "You thought it was loaded! Shame on you! Do I look that idiotic?"

Trinity was disappointed when he allowed the question to go unanswered.

"Good gravy." Missy slid the pistol back into her ankle holster. "I'm not addled, you silly man."

Shifting, Jones muttered under his breath. "Couldn't prove it by me."

The train wheels screeched, diverting everyone's attention. The locomotive's speed slowed, and then it slowly rolled to a halt. Jones scrubbed at the window pane to try to clear it enough to see out.

Trinity peered over his shoulder "What's happening?"

"Who knows? I'd say there's an animal out there, or some kids have put something on the track."

"Are we about to be killed?" Missy's eyes were as wide as her face.

"Nothing like that."

"I have my gun."

"I know."

It wasn't long before the conductor came through the car. "Everyone can relax. We've got a snake on the track."

Trinity shuddered. "A snake? Why don't they just run over it?"

Jones slid out of his seat and followed the conductor out of the car. The women trailed behind him. Minutes later they were staring at the biggest reptile any of them had ever seen. The long snake was stretched along the rail, sunning himself. The engineer glanced at Jones. "Those things give me the willies. Never saw anything that big — must have fallen off one of those circus trains that come through every so often. It sure ain't native to these parts."

"Is it alive?"

"Don't know. Haven't asked it, and I don't plan to get that close. I'd have hit it but I wasn't sure what the thing was, so I stopped. The railroad's really antsy about this route these days. We're supposed to check everything."

"Two derailments in less than a year. Yeah, they're getting finicky." Jones stooped and squinted at the snake. "What do you want to do?"

"I say just plow ahead and run the thing over."

Jones shook his head. "The females on board would be squcamish about killing a helpless animal."

"I don't care," Missy said.

Trinity eased closer. "It . . . can you move the thing? It looks rather helpless."

"Helpless my foot. That thing looks like it could swallow a body live."

The snake looked like it could swallow more than a body, and it wasn't going to be Jones if he could help it.

The conductor's eyes fixed on the snake. "Looks like one of those freakish things a circus man carries around his neck."

Trinity shivered. She'd never been to a circus, and she couldn't imagine anyone putting something like that around their neck.

The thing lay motionless. Sleeping. Dead. Waiting to pounce.

The conductor pulled out his watch fob and consulted the time. "We need to do something. We're running late."

Jones shifted on one boot. "If we can find a stout limb I might be able to scoop it up and fling it far enough away that the train can move. Can you tell if it's breathing?"

The engineer's color heightened. "I told you, mister. I don't know if it's dead or alive but either it moves off the track or I run it over."

Trinity eased closer. "It's a shame to kill it. Let's try to move it off the track and let it go its way."

"And pity the poor rider who encounters it later," Jones said.

He started as a shot rang out. Trinity muted a scream when she saw the blood draining from his face. Bright red blood was oozing from his thigh.

Missy smiled tranquilly, holding the smoking pistol. Trinity stared at her, aghast, but then her focus was drawn back to Jones. He wavered, turned a shade whiter, and then passed out.

Trinity's ears were still ringing from the

shot and she could barely hear, but she could just make out Missy's elated words.

"All gone. Snake's dead."

NINETEEN

"He looks to be coming around now."

"Jones!" Trinity cupped his ruddy cheek in her hand. "Wake up!" She turned anxiously to the doctor. The remainder of the trip had been a frantic blur. The conductor and engineer had loaded an unconscious Jones into the railroad car, bound his wound tightly, and then set off full-steam for Piedmont. Now the patient lay on a long, straight table in the doctor's office, slowly coming around.

"Sugar?" Missy bent close, speaking loudly in his ear. "I didn't mean to shoot you! I was aiming for the snake and I got it, but goodness, at what cost? Look at you, poor thing! Your thigh's just oozing blood and it'll be mighty sore for a few days, but don't worry your head a minute. I'll take good care of you." She rose and met Trinity's eyes. Her tone cooled. "You did say you weren't married? Or affianced?"

Trinity shoved her back from the table with her shoulder. "I don't recall saying. But married or not, he's not your responsibility. I'll care for him."

A wicked smile that only another woman could read appeared on Missy's lips. "If he's not married, then he's fair game."

Meeting her brazen eyes, Trinity returned the cutting smile. "You step one foot over the fence, and you'll see who he belongs to. Sugar."

"Ladies." The dark-haired young doctor with a handlebar mustache, standing near the head of the table, interrupted the biting exchange. The young doctor didn't look much older than Rob had been when he passed. "I can assure you that your man . . . or traveling companion . . . isn't going to require much care. It's a superficial wound, but he will have to tend the injury well or risk infection. And his hearing should return just fine, though he may experience a ringing in his ears for a while." He opened a glass-front cabinet and removed a tube. "He'll need to apply this salve four times a day after he's thoroughly cleansed the injury." The patient moaned, and the doctor bent over him. "Sir, your injury isn't grave, but you'll not be able to ride for a couple of days."

Both his eyes popped fully open. Trinity offered an encouraging smile. "Are you in much pain?"

Wincing, he tried to sit up. "What happened?"

"Well, the good news is that the snake is gone."

He frowned. "What?"

"Gone. The snake's gone and we're in Piedmont."

He cupped a hand behind his ear. "What? I can barely hear you."

"It's fine. The doc says your hearing will clear." She glanced at Missy. "We hope."

Missy bent close to his face, yelling. "I shot the snake!"

"And you," Trinity felt compelled to add.

Shaking his head, Jones muttered. "Great. My hearing for a snake's life."

Easing Miss Know-It-All aside, Trinity offered Jones a cup of cool water. He pushed it aside. "How did I get here?"

Missy nudged Trinity to the back. "The conductor and engineer carried you here. You fainted."

"I don't faint."

"He doesn't faint," said Trinity. "The sight of blood just makes him slightly . . . light-headed."

The young woman's eyes narrowed. "He

passed out."

Stepping between the two squabbling women, the doctor helped Jones to his feet. "I'm afraid you'll be on crutches for a few days. You'll need to keep weight off the injured leg."

"Can I ride? I'm due fifty miles up north in a couple of days."

The doctor shook his head. "No riding for now. We can't risk reopening the wound. You're fine for now, and I don't anticipate trouble as long as you follow orders."

Jones looked at Trinity. "I'll inform the railroad," she told him. "I'm sure they'll understand."

He grunted. "I'm glad you're sure."

She wasn't certain. Of anything. If he had never run into her, or helped her look for the deed, none of this would have happened. She turned impersonal eyes on Missy. The woman was sorely grating on her nerves with all that chatter, and now she was openly flirting with Jones. And if she didn't stand back and stop hovering over him . . .

Jones lifted himself up and tested his weight on the wounded leg, sucking in a deep breath. The doctor handed him a pair of crutches. "I hope you're planning on sticking around a few days."

"I wasn't. Are there rooms for rent?"

"I'll have my wife arrange for something . . ." His gaze traveled to the two hovering women. "How many?"

"How many what?"

"Rooms." His eyes shifted, indicating his dilemma.

Trinity filled the awkward silence. "Please arrange for two rooms." She fixed her eyes on the other woman. "Missy plans to continue her journey."

Missy bent close to Jones and spoke low. "I could delay . . ."

"No," Trinity interrupted. "You've been too kind. We have mutual business in Piedmont, and I'm certain your father is eagerly anticipating your arrival."

A shrill whistle sounded, its high-pitched tone filling the small room. Taking Missy by the arm, Trinity ushered her to the door. "So kind of you to help. I sincerely hope that the remainder of your trip is uneventful." She didn't. She didn't care what happened to Jabber-Jaws.

"But . . ."

Trinity nudged her out the door and shut it behind her, none too gently. She turned to meet two sets of amused male eyes. Heat crept up her neck. She supposed she was being a bit obvious.

Jones chuckled. "Doc, you were saying something about salve? Four times a day?"

"Yes. And see that you keep that wound clean!"

A blazing ball of sun dipped low in the west as Jones and Trinity emerged from the doctor's office. The crutches were awkward and only inflamed Jones's foul mood. His persistent grumbles and outright blasphemy — twice — brought a flush to her cheeks, but she couldn't fault him. She'd caused him more trouble than a lawsuit. He'd suffered more than a loss of dignity; he was running the serious risk of losing his job. All because she had this insane need to be with him. For the life of her she couldn't imagine where she'd misplaced her independence.

"We should eat something." She looked at the café. Hours had passed since they'd eaten the lunch Mae had packed, and with the constant commentary from Missy they hadn't enjoyed it much. People were coming and going from the café. "Are you hungry?"

"Not really." Jones shifted on the crutch. "But I could use some coffee." When he paused to adjust his hat, a stocky, bald headed man in manure-covered boots hurried toward them. His eyes bulged and he squawked like a blue jay.

"You Jones?"

"I am."

"You own a little red mare?"

He nodded.

"Got bad news. Somebody's stolen your horse. You best head for the livery — the sheriff's over there now."

Pitching the crutches aside, Jones hobbled after the stranger. Trinity gathered the crutches and caught up. Stolen? The word sent a shock through her. How could it be? The mare had been traveling in a rear stock car. The funny-looking man talked so fast, maybe she'd misunderstood.

"Sue was stolen?" she called out, trying to keep up.

"She was, ma'am. Right beneath our noses. Couldn't stop 'em. Tried. Couldn't. Sheriff'll tell you we chased 'em for over an hour, but we lost 'em."

"Lost who? Who stole the stock?"

"Don't know. Shorely don't know. Sheriff can explain."

Sue. Stolen. It was inconceivable, and it was the worst news yet. That mare meant more to Jones than breathing. If he had ridden out this morning for Chicago instead of taking the train with her, Sue would be with him right now.

Entering the livery, Trinity latched onto Jones's arm. "It's going to be all right. This is a mistake."

He was deaf to comfort, and he approached the man wearing a tin star. "What's this about my horse being stolen?"

The man turned with a frown. "Did you own one of those horses in the cattle car?"

"Yes. A little red mare."

"Sorry. We've had a rash of thievery around here. Seems the stock was unloaded and someone took off with the whole lot. Me and a couple of deputies joined the chase but we lost 'em a ways out of town. Ordinarily I'd say not to worry and I'd think I could get the horse back, but I didn't recognize this gang. They must be new to the area." He shook his head. Sweat was trickling down his cheek. "I don't know what this world's coming to. A man has to keep what he owns under lock and key these days."

Tears blinded Trinity. If Sue was really gone, Jones had lost everything he loved. And he would rightly hold her accountable. She reached out to console him, but he averted her touch and refused to look at her. After a moment, he regained his composure and straightened. She steadied him.

Anguish shook him — both physically and mentally. Ten minutes ago she'd assumed things couldn't get any worse, but they had.

Jones stood for a moment staring at the empty stalls. Clearing his throat, he spoke. "I'll leave a name and a place you can wire me if you find her."

"That'd be wise, son." The sheriff laid a hand on his shoulder. "Wouldn't hold out much hope, but I'll do the best I can." Trinity hurried to catch up with him as he hobbled toward the door. Apparently he didn't plan to stick around to see if the sheriff was successful.

In her heart Trinity knew this was one of the darkest moments Jones would ever face. Sue was gone, and he must have felt like he was abandoning his best friend. His family. His devoted companion.

And she knew he wouldn't be able to forgive her.

The evening stars had settled overhead when Trinity entered the livery. Jones had disappeared shortly after the news that Sue had been stolen. She longed to search for him, to comfort him, but she respected his loss and his need for privacy.

She'd taken the time to walk to the bank — that much she could do. From this moment on she was going to take care of herself and lessen his burden. But when she got to the bank, it was only to find that it had closed ten minutes earlier. She'd sat on a bench outside a storefront and waited. When Jones had failed to show up at the café at suppertime, she'd started a search for him.

She found him at the livery, lost in thought and apparently unaware that she stood in the doorway. Her heart sank when she saw him throw Sue's saddle over an unfamiliar stallion.

"Going somewhere?"

He drew the belly cinch tight. "Sorry, Trinity. I can't stay around here. I'm heading out."

"The doctor said you weren't supposed to ride . . ."

"I know what the doctor said." He jerked the flap over the cinch. "I'm leaving."

She stepped into the dim interior and stood for a moment, letting the silence say what she couldn't. Running away was never the answer. He was so withdrawn from her — from the world.

"It will be dark soon."

"Dark never stopped me from riding."

"You've never ridden with a shot leg before." Venturing closer, she paused, allowing ample space between them. "I stopped by the bank earlier."

He moved to the stallion's flank and tightened the straps on his bedroll. Apparently the livery had supplied his needs for the three-day ride.

"It was closed," she continued. "I'll have to return tomorrow morning."

"The doctor's wife arranged for your room at the boardinghouse." He fastened another strap, preoccupied. Her heart ached. He looked like a small boy who'd lost his best friend.

"Jones . . ."

He shook his head. "I know. Thanks."

She could have reminded him that she knew a little about loss. Her parents. Pauline, someday soon . . . but somehow the comparison paled. Sue was closer than kin. And Trinity barely knew Pauline. Until a week ago her aunt had only been a name.

Sue had been his best friend.

His hand paused, and after a moment he said quietly, "I know you expected me to see this through, but I can't."

"I understand."

"No, you don't. There's no explanation. I just need to get out of here. You'll be fine. The banker will give you the box and you can take the next train out of here."

272

"Wednesday. There's a train on Wednesday. I'll be back in Dwadlo that evening. I purchased my ticket earlier." She didn't mention that she'd bought it with the last cent she had. She was no longer going to rely on him. She could take care of herself. "I can do this alone."

Her heart was shedding a bucket of tears, but she refused to burden him further. He'd been good to her — too good. And now he was riding off with an injury that could endanger his life. But she couldn't stop him from leaving. She couldn't stop his pain. She had no say over his life, no matter how much she wanted that privilege.

"Of course you can do this alone." He turned back to the saddle. He was not going to let emotion override his loss.

She stepped closer and rested her hand on his forearm, but he jerked away.

"I understand your need for privacy, but . . ."

"But nothing! If I hadn't stuck around to help you Sue would still be with me!"

His accusations stung, but she continued. "I agree, and I thank you from the bottom of my heart. I know the sacrifice this trip has cost you, but . . . but bad things happen."

"Not to Sue. She's been bitten by snakes,

273

tangled with opossums and wild dogs, and always she managed to pull through. Now she walks down a ramp and a bunch of men steal her and she's gone." He turned angst-ridden eyes on her. "Why? Why Sue?"

"I don't have an answer." Her grip tightened on his arm. "I don't know why my parents left and never came back. I don't know why your stepmother was so hateful. I don't know why Rob had to die so young while Pauline has lived so long. I don't know, Jones. All I know is that the Good Book says each of us has an appointed time."

He didn't answer, and her gaze moved to the saddle. "How are you going to mount?"

"I'll manage."

He'd manage. With an injured thigh and more grit than good sense. He was so blinded by grief that he wanted to die, but she'd fight him on this.

"What about my land? Our transaction?" Now wasn't the ideal time to remind him of her problem, but maybe if she stalled long enough he'd come to his senses.

"I'll ride by the place on my way out. If the property meets my standards the railroad will wire you the sales price. It'll be waiting for you in Dwadlo when you get a clear deed." He looked at her with a hardness in his eye. "You'll get your money."

He was a stubborn, prideful goat. "Why must you take out your hurt on me? I didn't steal Sue."

"If I hadn't spent my time getting you out of hot water every other day, I would be long gone from here. And I'd still have my horse."

She had never seen him so mean-minded and harsh. "You don't know that, and I never asked for your pity."

"No, it's the railroad's money you want."

She knew bitterness drove his hurtful words, but they still stung. "That's not true." She faced him, her anger rising. Heartache made him lash out, but he had no cause to distrust her intentions. She'd grown fond of Sue as well. She'd miss the animal. And she'd miss Jones — and at the moment the thought of him leaving made her envy the stolen horse. He adored Sue. He would move heaven and earth to have the mare safe. But he was willing to ride away from Piedmont, leaving Trinity without a backward glance.

And when he did, it would destroy her. What had she done? Once self-reliant and happy, she was reduced to a simpering, hopeless wreck of a woman who'd fallen in love with a man who loved his horse more than her.

The man has never once indicated that he loved you, Trinity told herself. *He's saved your hide more than once, but never professed any feeling other than the need to leave.*

She stepped back. "I'm sorry you think my feelings for you are so superficial."

He reached for the reins and mounted up. She could tell it took a great effort, and the agonizing image made her turn away until he was seated. Pain flared on his features, but he trained himself to remain stoic. "I hope you find your deed. Tell Tom and Mae I'll stop by the next time I'm in the area."

She swallowed against the tight knot in her throat. And what about her? Would he ride away and pretend they'd never met, never shared the past week?

Reining the horse, he walked the animal out of the livery. She followed to watch his back retreating down the street, his posture slumped on the rented horse. He pulled his hat down low and never looked back. *This is the last time I'll ever see him,* Trinity thought.

Drawing on her last ounce of pride, she prayed. *Let it be so, Lord. Let me learn my lesson. I will never find love — the lasting kind — this side of heaven. I've often accused You of forgetting about me, and now, well . . . If*

276

You truly love me, make him turn around and come back.

She wanted love. She wanted it from God and she wanted it from Jones. From the day her ma and pa had ridden off there had been a missing ingredient in her life. She didn't know much about unconditional love at the tender age of five, but she knew about it now. Tom and Mae gave that love to each other in a way she'd never experienced. Seeing them together, sharing their laughter and happiness, had stirred something inside of her that she wasn't sure she could ever quench.

God was in His heaven. Her faith might be small, but she held onto hope, however faint. The man she adored was riding away from here and there was nothing she could do to stop him. He kept riding slowly away from town until his figure disappeared in the shifting shadows of tumbleweeds and rock formations. She had her answer.

Stiffening her shoulders, she nodded sharply and spun on her heel to walk to the boardinghouse. She'd tried depending on someone else, and it had been a mistake. It was back to managing her life on her own.

Apparently, God wasn't watching.

TWENTY

Trinity took her first step toward regaining her independence the following morning. She sat on the bank steps and listened as the clock tower struck nine. The faint stirring of the clerk's purposeful movements as she flipped the hanging sign from *Closed* to *Open* brought her to her feet. Shaking the folds of her dress, she tidied her hair and prepared to go inside.

Last night had been the worst in her life. Lying awake for endless hours, she'd finally crawled from the sheets and dressed, even though dawn hadn't come yet. Her thoughts no longer centered on the deed. The piece of paper didn't matter unless Pauline needed the funds to live out her last days more comfortably. A blanket of melancholy settled around her shoulders, heavy and nearly smothering. But she was going to see this through to the end.

Her stomach growled. She'd had no

money for breakfast.

"Good morning!" chirped the fashionable clerk dressed in dark calico. "Mr. Price will be right with you. Can I offer you a cup of cold water?"

"Thank you. That would be lovely."

Momentarily the banker appeared, his hand extended. "Miss Franklin. So good to see you again." He led her to his desk, piled high with papers. "I trust all is going well?"

"As well as can be expected." She sat down, fanning her face with her hand. Even with the windows open to the morning the building felt stuffy.

"Of course, of course. I understand that your aunt has rallied?"

"For the time being. She's still very weak."

"But what a fighter!" He smiled. "Well, I suppose you're anxious to retrieve her property."

A gust of refreshing wind fluttered papers on the banker's desk. "My," he said, glancing toward the darkening sky. "It appears we might be in for a bit of rain."

Returning his attention to the desk, he shuffled through a stack of papers and came up with a single sheet. His eyes perused the document. "Box two. My, my. One of the oldest boxes in the establishment." Pushing back in his chair, he motioned for Trinity to follow him. She stood and trailed to a closed door at the back of the room. Inserting a key in the lock, he smiled. "It feels almost like Christmas morning, doesn't it?"

He was always so helpful. So polite. A thought struck her so forcefully that she almost recoiled. The man claimed to have been a close friend of Rob's, but she didn't know that for certain. Rob had never mentioned him in his letters. What if Rob *had* left her more money . . . and he'd kept it for himself?

You're exhausted, Trinity. Your mind is working overtime.

But he could be wicked. He could be planning to harm her. Everyone knew that Wilson's Falls was a prime piece of property.

The water rights alone were worth a fortune, and with her and Pauline out of the way the banker would have a clear path to manipulating the deed for his own use.

What if he was playing her for a fool, keeping her on a wild goose chase when he knew exactly where the deed was located? He could have the missing document in his possession and be slyly biding his time until Pauline passed away.

He could be taking her into a deep, dark cellar from which she'd never return.

Fear was causing these crazy assumptions!

Panic played havoc with her reasoning. The clerk was upstairs and would stop him — if she wasn't in on the treachery herself. But even if her theory was correct, Pauline still legally owned the property. Unless the banker was truly the worst sort and had powerful connections, her imagination was working overtime.

A soft gasp escaped her. Rob could have lost the deed to the banker in a card game. Her brother hadn't been a fool. He'd known the land's worth, but men took foolish chances when they gambled. He could have lost a wager, signed the deed over to the banker immediately, and then waited for Pauline to pass . . . but that would mean Rob had known they still had living kin and not told her. He could have been so ashamed of his actions that he banked on Trinity never finding out about the betrayal.

Hope failed her. The thrill of expectation had ridden away with Jones. Each passing day with him had been like a parlor game — exciting, frustrating, but always full of anticipation that the missing deed would appear. She felt tears welling up and swallowed them back, her mind centering on the day Jones had stuffed her in the barrel. But try as she might, she couldn't conjure up that same seething, righteous anger she'd felt then. All the memory produced was more tears.

The door swung open and a hush fell over her. A set of narrow steps led down into a dark, musty-smelling vault. Fear snatched her breath.

The banker didn't appear to notice. He descended the stairs carefully, wiping cobwebs away with his bare hand. She shuddered. When he was halfway down, he turned and removed a lantern from the wall. A match flared and illuminated the blackness. He glanced up. "Coming?"

"Can you . . . can you just bring the box upstairs?"

A frown creased his features. "There are so many stored down here. It's clean, Miss Franklin — just a bit damp and musty." He extended his right hand, holding the lantern in the left, then looked around her and spoke to the clerk who was peering after them. "Kathleen, would you care to run to the café and get us a cup of coffee? I'll listen for customers."

"Of course, Mr. Price." The clerk left the bank and the door slammed shut.

Swallowing her building hysteria, she went down the first step, and then the second. Lantern rays cast jagged shadows along the dirt walls. She deliberately made her mind blank when her foot touched the third step.

There were twelve steps, but it felt like a thousand.

Eventually her boots found solid ground. The black pit was every bit as horrific as the other cellar she remembered. Her gaze traveled the mud-packed walls lined with rows of shelves. The black boxes were numbered, but they weren't arranged in any kind of order.

"I'm afraid my father wasn't much for keeping order," the banker apologized. "There was no one better with accounting and numbers, but organization wasn't his strong suit." He paused to hold a piece of paper up to the lantern light. "Says here your aunt's box is somewhere in this section of shelves."

She counted the long rows and lost track when she reached thirty. At least the search had been narrowed. She hunted through the first row for a few minutes, looking for a box marked with a 2.

Bang!

She whirled as the cellar door slammed shut. Terror choked her, and her fists clenched so hard that her nails dug into her skin.

The banker continued down the second row, absorbed with his task. "You'd think

Father would have had his clerk organize these on slow days," he said. He brushed away some cobwebs overhead.

Trinity couldn't breathe! Her windpipe closed and she brought both hands to her throat.

"Four. Nineteen," the preoccupied banker read aloud.

It must have been a strong wind that had blown the door closed. A thundershower brought lots of heavy wind bursts. There would be wind — lots of wind. Nothing to be concerned about. Mr. Price was acting perfectly normal. But then, he always did.

He's a harmless banker, Trinity. Not an ax murderer. She was sleep-deprived, hallucinating. She needed to get out of this tight space.

The lantern light was casting eerie rays along the walls. She struggled for a clean breath of air. The numbers on the boxes blurred. She was locked in this dark hole with a man she'd barely met. Her heart hammered so violently in her chest she thought it might break loose. When she took a step back she brushed against a huge web. She gave a little shriek and brushed frantically, trying to knock its occupant free.

"Aha! Number . . . oh, nope. Sorry. It's twelve, not two." The banker moved on.

She had to get out of here! Just as she turned, the door opened and sent a fresh rush of air down the steps. "Sorry," the clerk called. "I just got back with coffee. It's coming up a nice shower."

Weak-kneed, Trinity sank against the shelves and closed her eyes. Moments later, catching her breath, she straightened and continued the search.

Slam!

Whirling, she realized that the door had slammed shut again. The same paralyzing fear seized her. But it was only a moment before the clerk must have opened it again, and she was able to resume breathing.

This time a figure was slowly making its way down the steep staircase, hesitating at every other step. It wasn't the clerk's petite form — the silhouette loomed large and threatening. Where was the clerk?

Options raced through her mind. She was going to be tied up. Murdered. And now the banker's accomplice was slowly making his way down the steps to . . .

Stepping back into the shadows, she pressed herself tightly against the shelves. A pulse throbbed in her neck. Too late she realized how she had played straight into the banker's hand.

The figure kept descending. Each measured step was taken slowly and with care.

"I'm here like you said," spoke a voice. A deep, male voice. The voice of a stranger.

The banker glanced up and spoke to the intruder. "You're a bit early, but no matter."

The figure reached the bottom and stepped off. He could see her. She was in the shadows but he knew where she was.

Worse yet, *she* knew where she was — at the mercy of two corrupt men. Her eyes searched the room for a weapon — anything she could use to defend herself. Could she throw the boxes at them? If she could knock one or the other off balance she could race up the steps and scream for help.

But before her escape plan was fully formed in her mind, a hand reached out and caught her around the waist. Strong. Unyielding.

Wilting, she mentally said goodbye to the world and mercifully lost consciousness.

She knew his scent. Warm. Male. Trinity sleepily drank in Jones's familiar essence.

"Trinity?" A finger lightly tapped her cheek. "Wake up."

She would have liked to oblige, but a fuzzy warmth wrapped her in a soft cocoon and she didn't want to come out.

"Trinity? Wake up!" The sharp command

286

opened her eyes and she focused on the man in front of her. Jones. He'd come back.

"I didn't mean to frighten you," said another voice. The voice that had been in the cellar. She turned to see a man wringing his hat between his hands, a worried look on his face. "I just came to sign some papers, and the clerk said Mr. Price was down in the basement . . ."

"Oh. I . . . I thought . . . never mind." Her mind had been outrageously out of control. Reaching out, she lovingly tracked the outline of Jones's face. "Hello."

"Hi." He gently helped her sit up, pushing a stray lock of hair out of her eyes. "Are you all right?"

"I was scared." She didn't dare admit where her wild thoughts had led. Heat flooded her cheeks.

The grim-faced banker hovered above her. "Should I send for help?" he asked.

"No." Fully aware of her surroundings, she shook the fuzziness away. She was upstairs now, and she could feel the fresh breeze. "I'm — did I faint?"

"You did. Did you hurt your arm again?" Relief and concern filled Jones's voice.

He did care about her!

She made a cursory inspection of her arm. But other than a cobweb on the front of her

287

dress, she appeared to have survived another calamity. The arm was no worse. "I think everything's intact."

She stared up at Jones in happy disbelief. His tired features, his curly hair, the concern in his eyes — it was all so familiar. A slow grin broke across her features. "You came back."

He met her gaze with apologetic tenderness. "I came back."

"But you left," she accused. The man had a most annoying way of coming and going at the most inconvenient times, but she would learn to adjust to that peculiarity.

"Let's just say I was having a bad day. I came to my senses half a mile out of town, but by that time I was in so much pain I had to stop for the night." His eyes held her captive. "I'm sorry."

"Bad day? You call getting shot and losing Sue a *bad* day?" She shook her head, then grinned. "Sissy britches."

Grasping her hand, he pulled her to her feet. Their lips brushed before the banker cleared his throat. "Ahem — ahem! You'll be happy to know that I located the box just moments before you . . . swooned." He handed her the metal container. "Pauline and Priss Wilson. Now, if you'll just give me the key, we'll see what we have here."

288

Trinity glanced at Jones and silently mouthed, *Key?* She'd never once considered that a key wouldn't be available at the bank. "You don't keep the keys here?"

"Oh, goodness no! Once the two Miss Wilsons rented the box they would have been given a key." A frown crowded the man's features. "You do have the key?"

Slumping, Trinity bowed her head over the box. Of course she didn't have a key. That would have been too simple. "No. I don't."

"Oh, dear. Well . . . if I may? You're the second party this week inquiring about the box. Perhaps that person has the key?"

"Second party?" Trinity frowned. "Who was the first?"

"Why . . . there was a gent in earlier this week. He too was interested in the box, but when I informed him that only the next of kin could claim the item, he left."

She turned to meet Jones's puzzled gaze. "Benjamin?"

He shook his head. "Couldn't be. He hasn't left Pauline's side."

"Then who?" She wracked her brains for a suspect. Who, other than she, would have a keen interest in Pauline's lock box? She faced the banker. "What did this person look like?"

"A bit rough around the edges, I fear. At first I thought he might be a drifter, but he rented a place over at the hotel. Seemed to have money — or at least he was able to house and feed himself. Stuck around most of the following day. I'm sure the hotel would have a record of his stay."

"Thank you. I'm free to take the box?"

"Yes. I hate to mention this, but you'll need to know — those boxes are made for keys. I'm afraid that if you can't find the key, whatever is in there will remain so." He handed her the box. "We don't ordinarily give these boxes to customers, but as it's so old, and you're the next of kin, and we have no way of opening it, you're free to have it."

When they were clear of the bank, Jones drew her into the relative privacy of the shadows on the side of the building. Taking her deep into his arms, his whispered, "Forgive me?"

"I forgive you. I don't care what brought you back — just so you're here." Her gaze softened. "I thought I might have to come after you."

"You wouldn't have had to ride far."

"I prayed God would send you back to me."

"When Sue . . ." He shook his head. "I lost myself for a few hours. I shouldn't have taken it out on you."

"What about your job?"

He shrugged. "I have a valid reason to stay put." He looked pointedly at his wounded thigh, and for one selfish moment she was almost glad for the injury that would keep him there.

Jones held the hotel door open and Trinity stepped timidly into the lobby, where a couple of oscillating fans were slowly stirring the air. The day clerk was busy watering some potted plants. "Need a room?"

Color flooded her cheeks, but Jones quickly stepped to the counter. "Just some information."

Setting the watering can aside, the man wiped his hands on a cloth and stepped behind the high counter. His eyes swept the couple. "What can I do for you?"

"Is it possible to see your guest list for the past week?"

Suspicious eyes regarded him. "Why would you ask?"

"Personal business."

"That so?"

Jones reached into his hip pocket and removed a leather wallet. A few bills changed hands, and the register appeared in front of them.

"Looking for anyone in particular?"

"No. Well — sort of — but we don't know his name." Trinity scanned the names. There were only three — apparently business had been slow the past week.

Nadine Withers.

Seth Pentsen.

James Franklin.

She took in her breath sharply. "Someone you know?" asked Jones.

She read the name again. And then again. James Franklin.

It had to be a coincidence. Pure happenstance. James Franklin, her father, had died more than a decade ago.

Jones reached for the register and scanned the list. "Trinity? This James Franklin — any relation?"

Drawing a deep breath, she pressed her lips together and shoved the registry back across the counter. Turning on her heel, she walked out of the hotel. Jones hobbled behind her. When she paused on the porch, he cornered her.

"What's going on? Who's James Franklin? More kin? They're coming out of the woodwork now."

"Perhaps. But it's not possible . . ." The idea churning in her brain was so preposterous and farfetched that she hated to believe what she'd seen written in the book. "James Franklin."

"Okay. Franklin. Any kin?"

Fixing on the buckboard moving slowly down the street, she spoke softly. "I think my father's trying to claim Aunt Pauline's bank box."

He frowned. "Your father's dead."

Swallowing hard, she fought back rising tears. "Apparently he isn't."

TWENTY-ONE

"Calm down. There's bound to be more than one James Franklin in the world." Jones settled back onto the hotel pillow, closing his eyes. Trinity had taken the situation in hand. She had first rented a room for Jones and then ordered him to bed. Amid his objections, she checked his bandaged thigh and noted fresh bleeding. Not a good sign.

"It doesn't matter if the man is my father. I want nothing to do with him." She had only a vague recollection of James Franklin, and none of it was endearing. A dark scowl, a raised voice, ruddy, angry features.

The idea that he was the man who'd walked away and left her years ago was too implausible to accept, but why else would this stranger be prying into Pauline's business? How would he even know that she had a bank box in Piedmont unless . . .

Mother would have known. She had to

accept that this man could be her father. They'd never found his body. There was no gravesite at which to mourn.

Yet nothing but Jones's health concerned her now. "While you rest, I'll change my train ticket to Sunday and purchase yours. By then you should be able to make the trip back to Dwadlo." The ticket agent would think she'd lost her mind — this would make the second time today she'd changed her reservation — but it wasn't his place to judge.

"I'm not an invalid."

"Your wound says the opposite." She pulled the light sheet up under his chin and fluffed his pillow. His pallor worried her. He'd lost a lot of blood. "I pray you haven't aggravated the wound further. Have you been applying the salve?"

"Twice. Maybe once." Even his tone sounded dog-tired.

"You were supposed to apply it every four hours."

"I wasn't keeping time." He slowly drifted off. She gazed at him, bending to lightly stroke the dark stubble on his cheek.

"Thank you for coming back, Jones," she whispered. He might try to run from his feelings, but he was more man than James Franklin had ever been.

He stirred, rolling to his side.

She softly closed the door behind her and descended the stairway with the bank box under her arm. He'd sleep for a while. Meanwhile, the curiosity was gnawing at her. There must be a way to get the box open without a key.

Thank goodness the blacksmith was close. The box was cumbersome to walk with.

The blacksmith was at his forge when she walked in. "Excuse me!" she called out.

He turned. "Ma'am?"

"Can I borrow a tool — perhaps a crowbar?"

His features furrowed, and then he bent and spat on the ground. "Can I do something for you?"

"No. I need to open a bank box."

"Use a key."

"Don't have one."

He studied her for a moment and then turned and walked into the shed. She followed, trying not to let herself get overly excited. What treasures had Pauline and Priss hidden in the box? Nothing about her eccentric aunts would surprise her, but the anticipation of hidden treasure in addition to the deed heightened her enthusiasm.

The smithy returned carrying a heavy pry bar. "I'll be glad to open it for you."

"Thank you, no." She was rather looking forward to the challenge. "Care if I work in front of your business?"

"No, ma'am." He spat a straight stream, wiping tobacco juice onto his sweaty sleeve. His eyes fixed on the box, curiosity etched on his roughhewn features. He spat another stream. "I can shore help iff'n you need me to."

"Thank you, but I'll manage." She set the box down on the ground. Standing back, she perused the situation and admitted that the iron box looked pretty well impenetrable. She took a step back, lifted the bar, and brought it down across the box with a swift and powerful *whack!* The box jumped off the ground. Stepping closer, she saw a big, ugly dent in the middle of the lid. But it remained locked.

Getting a tighter grip on the rod, she dug her heels into the ground and swung with all of her might.

The box shot straight up. Then fell to the ground. A sizable dent creased the lid sideways.

But the closure was still locked tight as a vault.

Three more whacks and she'd made no progress. The smithy stood in the doorway, mopping away sweat and chuckling as he watched her failed efforts.

"Do you have anything bigger?" she called.

"Yeah, got a pickax but I'd have to swing it. Want me to give'er a whack?"

"Would you?" By now her arms were shaking like a three-dollar horse.

He approached with the ax. His hairy, beefy arms reminded her of a gorilla. There was enough power in those limbs to break Gibraltar in half. He eyed the box, took in a breath, and let fly.

The ax caught the side of the box and sent it spiraling into the air. Chickens squawked and raced for cover under business porches. A crowd started to gather, gazes focused on the work in progress.

Another powerful swing of the ax and the box nearly bent double, but still the latch stayed closed.

Shaking her head, Trinity had to admit that the banker had been right. That box was made of something too strong to break into.

"Ma'am? If I might offer a suggestion — why not try prying it open?"

Trinity sighed. Prying. Of course. And here she was trying to beat the thing to death. "Yes. Try that."

Nodding, the blacksmith braced the crow-bar under the lid and pulled upwards. His biceps bulged and sweat pooled on his forehead. Shaking his head, he muttered something and then yanked so hard that a blue vein stood out in his neck. Pausing, he caught his breath, inserted the tip of the bar under the locked lid, and jerked. Laboring, he pulled. And pulled. After a bit he let go, his face red as a cherry. "I ain't never seen anythin' like it. I got a stick of dynamite . . ."

Trinity bit her lip. "No. That would defeat the purpose." A stick of dynamite might open the box, but in the process it would blow the deed to smithereens — if it was in there at all.

"Try shooting it open," a man called from the sidelines.

She glanced at the smithy. "What do you think?"

He disappeared into the building and returned with a shotgun. "You best let me do this."

"I can shoot."

"No, this here's got a hair trigger. I'll do it." His gaze swept the crowd. "You all stand back, now!"

The crowd retreated to safety. Two women plugged their ears with their forefingers.

Boom!

The first shot rocked the ground. The box was knocked back and kicked up a puff of dust. A finger-sized bullet hole appeared in the largest dent.

The blacksmith lifted the rifle, took aim, and fired again.

Boom!

Windows rattled, and dogs set to howling and scattered. Another hole appeared in the box, but the lock still held firm. Across the street a woman appeared on a balcony. Trinity glanced toward the hotel. Had Jones heard the racket?

A lone man who'd been watching from the crowd slowly approached. She assessed the dirty bandana tied around his neck, denims, and feed-sack shirt. A drifter — or someone who lived on the trail. "I don't think you want to lose the contents of that box, ma'am," he said.

Trinity nodded. She couldn't risk losing Pauline's personal effects, especially if there was a deed in there.

She opened her mouth to speak and then stopped, looking at the man more closely. He was the spitting image of Rob. Same sandy red hair, hazel eyes, and fair complexion. Freckles dotted the stranger's forearms. And he was about the right age . . .

He met her eyes. "You're Trinity, aren't you?"

He knew her name. She faced the man.

James Franklin. She barely remembered her father, but there was no doubt in her mind that this was the man who had ridden away one day and never come back. The man who'd locked her in the cellar to punish her. The man who'd made her terrified of water. The man who'd helped to give her life.

"What did you do with Ma?" Her words held more accusation than question.

"She died that day." He didn't need to clarify which day he was speaking of. "Can we talk somewhere?"

The crowd was starting to disperse, evidently sensing that the spectacle was over. The dented, bullet-ridden box lay upended on the ground, still unopened. The smithy bent and picked up his crowbar and pickax before he disappeared into the livery.

"You and I have nothing to discuss."

"You may not want to hear what I have to say, and I'll understand if that's your choice. But you deserve to know what happened that day. Will you spare me ten minutes?" Her father held out a chapped hand. "That's all I ask."

Ten minutes. That was all the time he needed to explain the last fourteen years? Ten minutes? She and Rob had longed for a ma and pa. Childhood. Proper food on the table. Proper clothing and schooling.

What could possibly make a father leave his two children and never return?

If he could clarify that in ten minutes, she would grant his request.

TWENTY-TWO

"Why were you searching for Pauline's bank box?" Trinity settled onto a patch of grass behind the smithy and set the box beside her.

Her father stood awkwardly in front of her. He seemed hesitant about sitting down. She nodded. "Sit. I have a few minutes."

He took his place beside her. His discomfort was evident. "I'm working in this area and I remembered that the deed to the property was kept here. I wasn't sure if she was dead or alive or if anyone had claimed the land, but I rode through there a few days back, looking around. The place seemed deserted."

"I was staying there until recently. The place was robbed and I had to leave."

"But the grounds were . . ."

"Desolate? Grasshoppers took care of what the thieves didn't." Though she hardly cared, she felt obliged to ask. "Do you work with the railroad?"

"In a way."

"What way?"

"Mostly track work." There was a long pause. "My boy?" he asked.

"Rob? You saw him if you rode through the place."

"I saw no one."

"You did. He's buried fifty feet from the cabin."

Pain crossed the man's features. "My boy's dead?"

"Your *boy*?" Turn the other cheek, the Good Book said, but that was mighty hard to do when the man who'd slapped hers raw was sitting in front of her. "How dare you call him that? We meant nothing to you."

He nodded. "Fair enough. I deserve that."

"Where's my mother? What did you do with her?"

"She was swept downstream that day. I heard her body was found later."

That much Trinity knew to be true. The unnamed woman had been buried in a pauper's grave. "What happened to you? Why didn't you save her?"

"I can't swim." His eyes teared up. "I never learned — though I tried. I'm plain scared of water. I couldn't do anything but watch your ma being swept away, calling my name, pleading with me to come save her."

The horror of the story swept over Trinity. How terrified her mother must have been. How hurt that her husband could do nothing to save her.

"I got to the next bank and just started walking. Walked for days, weeks, trying to get the sound of your mother's cries out of my head. After a while, I came out of my stupor and tried to deaden the pain with liquor. Every day I drank to forget her — and you kids. It was five years before I came to my senses. By then I figured you were better off without a drunk in your life, so I didn't try to find you. I'm not a good man, Trinity. You were far better off without me. You'll have to take my word on that."

Bitterness made her want to strike out. She longed to mock him, to call him a liar, to ask what sort of man would abandon innocent children — but the sincerity and regret in his tone stopped her. Anything she might say, any accusations she might make, he had already made to himself long ago.

"So you came here to claim Pauline's inheritance."

"No. I came here to find the box and see that it was delivered safely into Rob's hands. I'd known of the deed's existence since I married your mother, and I knew that you didn't. You were too young. I had no knowledge of Pauline's whereabouts, and I suspected she was gone. She must be close on a hundred now."

"Ninety-four."

He whistled. "She always was a tough old bird."

Benjamin's opinion exactly.

James slowly lifted his eyes to meet Trinity's. Heartache swam in their depths. "I would ask you to forgive me, but I know I have no right to ask it."

Her lingering resentment melted. Forgiveness. She'd never considered the word in light of her parents. They were dead, and there was nothing to forgive — or so she'd thought.

"Where's your home?"

"Here. There." He closed his eyes. "I'm dying, girl."

She recoiled.

"All those years of drinking and carousing caught up with me. Pain goes away but memories don't. The doc says my liver's gone. Seems you can't do what you want in life and not pay a heavy price."

"I'm sorry." And for the briefest moment she really was. He had deprived his children of much, but he'd denied himself more.

He shrugged. "I've asked the Lord's

forgiveness. Don't know how He'll stand on the matter until it's my time to face Him in person. I have no answers for the actions I will be held accountable for."

"Grace is free."

He looked up, a mist shimmering in his eyes. "Thank you. It's good to be reminded. I believe and have accepted His Word, but I'm still a bad person."

Seemed to her she could use a good dose of remembrance herself right now. She had no particular feelings — good or bad — about this man, this stranger. Rob had told her he'd been a heavy-handed pa, but she didn't associate the term *father* with anything other than dark cellars and a fear of water.

She lifted her chin. "I forgive you."

The tears rolled from the corners of his eyes. "Much obliged." His words struggled past the gravel in his throat.

"And . . . Pa? When you stand before the Lord you will simply say that you are covered in His blood." She smiled. "But then, He'll already know that."

Shaking his head, he stood up. "I have something I want to give you."

"You don't . . ."

"Yes. I do." He reached for her hand and helped her to her feet.

307

"Is it something of Ma's?" A locket? A piece of her hair? Maybe a tintype? She had nothing to remind her of the woman who had given her life.

"No, nothing of your ma's."

They walked side-by-side around the building and she followed him a short distance down the road. Her interest grew with each hurried step.

"Hold up here."

She paused and watched him disappear into the heavy thicket. Overhead, nuthatches chirped and flew in and out of branches. For the second time that day, the thrill of anticipation rendered Trinity heady with expectation.

James reappeared leading a small red mare. Disbelief triggered a scream that shattered the peaceful silence. The mare shied, shaking her heavy mane.

"Sue!" Lunging, Trinity wrapped her arms around the animal and held on tight. "Sue! We thought we'd lost you forever!"

"I saw you comin' off the train," her father said. "You look just like your ma. No mistakin' that red hair. And no mistakin' the look in your eye when you looked at the fella you were with. I've seen that look in your ma's eyes a million times . . . back when I was a better person. I heard he was pretty attached to a little red mare, and I thought he'd like to have her back."

"Back? But where did you find her? She was stolen from the train . . ."

Her father calmly handed her the reins. "I told you I sorta worked with the railroad."

"Sort of? I assumed you meant you were with the company."

"I spend a lot of time on the rail," he said.

Trinity turned back to the horse, happiness bubbling up inside her. For the moment her father's life of crime didn't matter. Jones. She had to get Sue back to Jones.

Clearing his throat, her father reached out his hand. "Thanks for hearing me out."

They shook. "Thank you," said Trinity. "You don't know it, but you've given me a gift without measure."

"I sorta figured this little mare would please you. Didn't know she was your friend's." He glanced at the animal. "One missing horse ain't going to hurt anyone. The boss won't ever know."

"Pa?"

He looked her way.

"Is it true? Are you really dying?"

He nodded. "Everything I told you was true."

Her heart softened. As bad as his failings were, they could not justify her turning him away at his darkest hour. "Do you have anywhere to go?"

He shook his head. "No. One night I'll lay my head down under God's sky and I won't wake up."

"How long?"

He shrugged. "Soon."

She took a hesitant step toward him, and then lunged into his arms. "I'm sorry."

"I'm sorry too, baby girl. You got a bad break in life, but I never stopped loving you. Or Rob." The embrace tightened. He smelled dirty and unkempt, but she hardly cared.

The moment passed and she pulled away. "If you don't . . . If God decides to leave you here a little while longer, come to Dwadlo. They're building a new place there for . . . well, for folks like you."

His features broke. "You would want me there?"

Want him there? She couldn't go that far, but she knew she would take care of him for the remainder of his life, if he asked.

"Thank you for telling me what happened."

He chucked her under the chin, smiled, and then turned and walked away. She followed him with her eyes until he disappeared into the thicket, and then said softly, "Goodbye, Pa."

The tears started halfway back down the road. The whole emotional exchange with her father had left her dry-eyed and drained. Now, leading Sue and picturing the joy this offering would bring Jones, the emotion swallowed her. Hot tears rolled from the corners of her eyes and dripped off the tip of her nose. The long-sought answer to her parents' disappearance was solved. How she wished Rob was alive to know. She no longer had to worry why they'd never come home. She and Rob had struggled, but perhaps God's plan for her was greater than the life she would have had if her father had returned after all. Her life would have been so different if her parents hadn't crossed the river that morning. But then, God had a way of turning tragedy into blessings.

She reached the café and secured Sue to the post, and then ran up to Jones's room and burst through the doorway, sobbing. The day had been too much. She couldn't stem her vacillating emotions.

Jones sat straight up, torn from a sound sleep. "What?"

"Guess what I found." She caught back a shuddering sob.

He wilted back to the bed and pulled a

pillow over his face. "New hat?"

"No. Get up."

He lifted the pillow and stared at her. "I'm resting."

"No, really. You have to see this. Just come to the doorway."

He frowned. "Why are you crying?"

"God is so faithful."

"Agreed, but why the waterworks?"

"Come to the door and you'll see." She crossed the room and helped to ease him into a sitting position.

"I was sleeping," he griped.

"You won't be sorry."

"This had better not be something girlish, like a dress or sweet-smelling soap."

"Have I ever asked you to do anything frivolous?"

"You've asked me to do plenty . . ."

"Stop."

He hauled himself out of bed, wincing. Leaning on Trinity for support, he allowed her to lead him down the stairs and to the door of the hotel. She gently eased him in front of her. The bright sunlight was blinding, and his arm came up to shield him from the assault. It took a moment to focus.

The mare stood at the hitching rail, swishing flies with her tail.

Skepticism and disbelief played on Jones's

face. His eyes were fixed on that little red mare. "Sue?"

"My father gave her to me!"

Breaking away, he made his way to the rail as quickly as he could. Sue looked up and whinnied. Approaching the animal, Jones wrapped his arms around her and buried his face in her mane.

Trinity leaned against the door, the tears flowing harder. A man and his horse.

Twenty-Three

Late that evening, Trinity and Jones sat on the bottom steps of the hotel and fed Sue handfuls of hay. The moon was bright overhead, even with the town lanterns burning.

Leaning back, she drew a deep breath. "This has been one fine day."

Chuckling, Jones shifted and stretched out his injured leg. "It's one I won't soon forget."

She'd told him about her father, the brief meeting, and how she held no bitterness. Oh, she regretted the family life she could have had, but it was mingled with relief at having an answer to the long mystery and a recognition that life had turned out just fine in spite of her father's desertion.

"I wonder how long he has to live," she mused.

"Only God knows the answer to that, but it was good of you to invite him to Dwadlo.

Sounds like you've decided to stay there."

"Yes." She leaned back, studying the twinkling canopy overhead. "I think I have. I like it there. I love Mae and Tom, and I'll enjoy whatever time I have left with Pauline."

"What about that guy at the diner?"

"Who?"

"The fellow in Sioux Falls — the one with the kids."

"Oh. Him. He comes in pretty often and we've had some lively conversations over pie and pot roast but . . ." She glanced over.

"But what?"

"But I don't have any real interest in him."

"When you told me about him before it sure sounded friendlier than pie and pot roast."

"About as serious as that woman you've been trying to court in Chicago. She must be getting pretty tired of waiting on you."

He shrugged. "She won't regret the wait."

She leaned over and poked him.

He fought off the attack. "Feeling feisty tonight, Miss Franklin?"

"Feeling good," she said. "And you?" He'd seemed to perk up once Sue had been safely returned.

"Better." His gaze strayed to Sue. "Actually, much better."

"Do you feel well enough to go for a short ride?"

"At this hour?"

"It must be all of eight o'clock."

"Dead of night," he teased. "Sure. Where do you want to take me?"

"You'll see. Stay here." She stood and brushed the hay off her shirt, and then started across to the livery. Within half an hour she was pulling to the front of the café in a two-man spring wagon.

Jones struggled to his feet, his eyes fixed on the box-like contraption. "That's an Amish rig, isn't it?"

She nodded, grinning. "The only thing they had available." She motioned to the seat beside her. "Climb aboard."

He stored his crutches in the back of the rig and heaved his frame aboard.

"You seem to be moving better this evening," she noted pleasantly.

"I am. It seems I may live after all."

"That would be nice."

The buggy took off with Trinity behind the reins. The wheels bounced along the rutted road, following the moonlit path. Tonight she felt free, free and unencumbered. Black-eyed Susans, tick wood, and meadow roses filled the fields as they headed out of town. The short ride was not without purpose. There remained one last piece of business before she and Jones said their goodbyes and she returned to Dwadlo. Watching Jones ride away again would be the hardest thing she'd ever faced, but God had a plan for her life. She was absolutely certain.

Pulling up half an hour later, she sat silently, staring at the scene before her. The reason Pauline, Priss, and their father had stopped here that day so many long years ago was evident tonight. Her family's land lay bathed in moonlight, which illuminated the gentle hills, tall cedars, ashes, and maples — still noble although stripped bare of leaves. It wasn't hard to understand why they'd picked this particular spot to lay down roots.

Jones's voice broke into her thoughts. "I gather this is your land?"

"You don't remember riding through here earlier?"

He shifted. "I remember water. A screaming lady." The moonlight caught his naughty grin. "Something about someone who couldn't swim."

She allowed his cheekiness to play out. He was a sick man. Her mouth curved into a smile. "Do you remember anything other than your bad behavior that day?"

"Let's see." He thought for a moment. "Seems to me the screaming woman was pretty. Rowdy, but the prettiest thing I'd seen in a while. A barrel — yes, I'm remembering now — and rapids?"

She elbowed him.

"Ouch — watch the leg."

"Let's get out and walk."

"I can't walk."

"A bit of exercise will limber you up." Setting the brake, she looped the reins around the handle and stepped out. Coming around the carriage, she came to Jones's side.

"I'm not an invalid," he reminded her.

"That's not what you said a minute ago."

He grinned and heaved himself out of the buggy, leaning on Trinity for support. He tested his weight on the injured leg and then straightened.

"Better?"

"Not too bad."

Looping her arm through his, she supported him along the uneven ground. "I want to show you something," she said. She took it slow, matching his stilted gait.

The fields had been stripped and the grasshoppers' destruction was still evident, but the land was going to come to life again. Tonight the property had a calming feel, as though she'd come home. Rob had loved the land, poured his sweat and blood into the plowed fields and once-waving cornstalks. Tightening her hold on Jones's arm, she followed the sound of water. Approaching the bank, she stopped. "It was right about" — she moved a couple of steps to the right — "here that we met."

His gaze roamed the area. "So this is where it changed."

"What changed?"

"Life."

Laughing, she located a grassy spot. "Want to sit?" They sat down, surrounded by the night sounds. An owl hooted from a branch nearby. Frogs croaked. The rapids burbled in the distance, not so terrifying from this distance.

"Well, your kin was right about one thing. It's real peaceful here." Jones lay back, resting his head on a root.

"Doesn't that hurt?"

"What?"

"Using a root for a pillow."

"Yes."

"Then why are you lying there?"

"I like to look at the sky."

Wiggling closer, she stretched out full-length and gazed at the stars with him. "This reminds me of another night."

"Which one was that?"

"The night we were on the way here — for the first time. When Lil came and told us Pauline had collapsed."

"I remember."

It seemed like all her memories included him of late. They lay in companionable silence, staring at the heavens.

"Did you ever really recover from that motorcycle ride?"

She shrugged. "It took two bottles of Hostletter's Celebrated Stomach Bitters, but my stomach finally returned to normal." She rolled over and propped herself up on an elbow. "What do you think of the place? Still want to buy it?"

"Haven't seen anything but a path and this riverbank."

"Well, there's a house — not in the best condition at the moment, but the railroad will tear it down anyway. Nothing fancy. Just a cabin. Two-story. Very old. It's seen a lot of summer nights like this one."

"How many outbuildings?"

"Four. For cattle and horses."

"Won't it be hard to sell the land you grew up on?"

"I didn't live here. I was eleven when I was hired by a wealthy family to be a nursemaid to their two children. The mother was ill and didn't live long. The father moved the children to California but I remained in Sioux Falls, where they'd lived. There was a wonderful woman there — Emma Lee — who lost her husband a few years back. They owned a small café, and she invited me to wait tables there. She's been like family to me, but I fear she's been overwhelmed with work. I've been gone much longer than I'd anticipated."

"Does she know you plan to stay in Dwadlo?"

"After today she does. Before I went to the bank I sent her a wire informing her that my plans had changed and I wouldn't be coming back."

He sat up slowly. "Are you sure about that? That's a big decision to make overnight."

"Positive." She sighed. "God's taught me a few things lately." She glanced over. "Things I should have known all along, but He managed to get my attention."

"Things like what?"

"Like the fact that there are more important things than jobs or clothing. That family is one of the best things in life. I always thought I was happy, but I was only content."

"Nothing wrong with being content," said Jones. " 'Not that I speak in respect of want:

for I have learned, in whatsoever state I am, therewith to be content. I know both how to be abased, and I know how to abound: every where and in all things I am instructed both to be full and to be hungry, both to abound and to suffer need.' "

"Philippians."

He met her gaze. "You know your Bible."

"I remember Rob reading me that verse. We knew we were in bad shape, but he said there were folks who were worse off and we needed to be mindful of that fact. Content is good, but there's a whole big world out there. Had I not come here, I wouldn't have found the missing ingredient in my life. I thought I was perfectly happy in Sioux Falls. I thought I'd stay there until my hair turned silver and I was stooped with age. But then Rob died and I had to come here and from that moment on my life changed bit by bit, every day, until I woke up one morning and decided that everything I wanted was in Dwadlo, not Sioux Falls. Friends. Family. Love."

"You been running low on love lately?"

"Empty. But I didn't realize it until I came to Dwadlo."

"I guess finding your father was a gift."

"Well, it certainly answered some questions. Pauline was the real gift. Wrapped in crinkly paper and a bit worse for wear, but she brought real family into my life."

"Cut your father some slack. He can't be all bad. He didn't have to return Sue."

"He stole her." Lifting her face to the breeze, she spoke softly. "A father isn't born. He's shaped. He earns his children's love and devotion. I just met a man who helped to give me life."

"Still, he is your father, and Sue's a good horse. She'd have brought a handsome price." His gaze met Trinity's in the moonlight. "A man like James doesn't ordinarily go around returning what he's stolen."

"Apparently he knew what you mean to me."

Shaking his head, he spoke softly. "I wish you'd stop doing that."

"Doing what?"

"Talking like you and I have a future. I'm not marriage material. I've been on my own so long and I'd make a selfish, self-centered husband, Trinity. Good Lord knows you deserve better than that."

"Sounds like you've considered the prospect."

"Sure, I've considered it. Long and hard. Tied down to a wife and family . . . that wouldn't work for someone like me."

"Tied down? How flattering. And I happen to disagree with your prediction of what you'd be like as a husband, but that's for you to decide." She decided it would be safer to switch topics. "So what about the property? Are you ready to buy?"

His gaze traveled along the riverbank, roaming the moon-drenched river. "You don't want to sell. This is a family home. It needs kids, laughter, people running through it — not rails. What I'm offering is a pittance for your heritage."

"Pauline has needs. And eventually I'll require more than I have to survive. I've spoken with Belle and she might have a position open in the fall, but I can't depend on that income." Her gaze traveled to the river. "A while back I would have said I didn't want this land and I couldn't wait to get back to Sioux Falls, but I could learn to love this place. I just can't afford to."

"I think you love it already. I won't steal it from you." He sat up and adjusted his hat brim. "If you want to sell to another railroad I can't stop you, but I can't in good conscience buy this property."

"I thought you represented the railroad."

He shook his head. "I thought so too."

Sighing, she lifted her eyes and fixed them on the North Star. "It doesn't matter. I have everything I want. Almost. Perhaps I'll keep the land, perhaps not. At the moment, I am content."

"Love seemed to be real important to you a few minutes ago."

"I have love."

"You're looking at me that way again."

"I am not. I'm looking at the sky."

"You were thinking of me. And if you take my advice, you won't sell this property. The railroad will come through and rip out the fields and lay track. They'll destroy what your kin found to be good and meant for future generations."

She turned to face him. "Don't you think that love — real love — has been missing from your life too?"

"We were talking about the land, not our feelings. A man doesn't go around speculating on 'real' love."

"You don't long to have somebody who finds you special? Someone who thinks that spending her life with you would be a blessing too big to contain?"

"Until a few weeks ago I didn't know you existed. And you wouldn't have given a wooden nickel for me the day we met."

"You wouldn't have either," she countered. "You didn't know I existed, but time changes things."

He reached for a flat river stone and threw

it out, skipping it across the water. "Don't sell, Trinity. One day that love you're so dead set on will show up, and you'll want this home."

Sitting upright, she tugged her bodice into place. "Then perhaps you might want to personally purchase the land."

"Me?"

"You. No matter what you say, someday the right woman will come along and you just said this would be the ideal place to raise a family. A whole brood of little Joneses." She giggled. "What is your given name, anyway?"

"Does it matter?"

It did to her. If she was going to marry the man — though he was yet to be convinced — she'd earned the right to know his name. "It matters a great deal. We've known each other all this time and I'm certain you have more than one name."

"Maybe not."

"What's your name, Jones?"

"Marcel."

"Oh." Her tone dropped. "Marcel?" She floundered, struggling to keep a straight face. She shouldn't laugh. She cleared her throat, but a grin escaped. "Well? Do you want the land or not?"

"I don't want it. Not without . . ."

"Me?"

"Stop twisting my words." Grumbling, he struggled to his feet and hobbled off toward the buggy.

"I'm going back to Dwadlo tomorrow!" she called. "You have time to reconsider!"

"Not a chance! I have work to do."

"Your leg is still hurt. You don't have to leave tomorrow."

"Yes." He paused. Apparently she'd struck a nerve. "Yes, I do, Trinity."

His voice was tired and beaten. She understood his meaning. Either he left tomorrow, or he let his feelings overshadow grave doubts.

She wanted Jones. Marcel. She shook the name aside. Jones. She wanted Jones, and she wanted all of him.

Given a few days, he'd see that contentment wasn't all it was cracked up to be.

The station agent glanced up the next morning. Seeing the young woman standing at his counter, his brows shot up to his hairline. "You're not going to change your ticket again."

"No." Trinity grinned. "I'm traveling alone this morning."

Jones stood on the platform with her bag and the battered bank box. She was going

327

home — to Dwadlo. She still owned her land, she didn't have the deed, and she didn't care. Life was good. And as soon as the train left, he would ride out in the opposite direction.

Trinity could hardly take her eyes off him. Yes, they were parting, but he would be back. She couldn't feel this way about him and not have him return any of the affection. God wouldn't be so cruel. Jones was stubborn, but he would recognize that they both supplied what the other was looking for. Love. And he would come to claim it from her.

They'd spent years building up solid walls around them. They depended on no one but themselves, feeding the empty holes festering deep in their hearts on foolish thoughts. Telling themselves that love and family didn't matter.

They did. Life was never lived to its fullest without those gifts.

The sound of the train whistle brought her back and she left the counter. Jones waited beside the bag and bank box, resting on his good leg. He was in pain — she could tell.

"Are you sure you can make the trip?"

"I promise to take it easy." He grinned and took her arm to escort her to the waiting coach. "You'll let me know if you get the deed out of that box."

"If you don't want to buy the land, why should I tell you?"

"Because I want to know."

"I dutifully promise to inform you the moment I find the deed."

Pausing beside the rail car, he drew her into his arms. "If I kiss you goodbye are you going to read lifetime commitment into the gesture?"

"No, sir." She lifted her face. "I promise to react with as much cold indifference as I can muster."

"I bet."

"Just kiss me."

Their mouths drew close — so close — and she wanted him to hurry up but he took his sweet time. His gaze locked with hers. "I will admit that I'm going to miss you, Trinity Franklin."

"You could marry me right now, Jones, and save yourself a heap of trouble."

"I'll marry you when — and if — I feel that would be best for your life."

"Who gave you permission to make that decision?"

The final whistle sounded. His mouth closed over hers, warm and hungry. Snuggling closer, she wrapped her arms around his neck and held on tight. The world blurred, and for a moment she lingered in her own little piece of heaven.

All too soon the conductor cried, "All aboard!" They broke apart. Leaving his arms was the hardest thing she'd ever done. He put a hand to her cheek, and she smiled. He would come to his senses. He would admit that what they'd found in each other was a new beginning.

He had to.

TWENTY-FOUR

Nothing in Dwadlo had changed.

The train eased to a rolling stop a hundred feet from the platform to allow Esau safe passage across the track. The elephant slowly lifted one foot and then the other, lumbering across the rails as he crossed to the open field beyond the tracks.

A plume of steam shot up and the engineer eased the cars the final distance to the station.

Trinity was off and running, dodging Pauline's dogs and cats, the moment the big engine stopped. She was headed for the mercantile, carrying her bag and the dented box.

Mae stepped out to meet her, waving. "Where's Jones?" she called from the porch.

"Trying his best to outrun me!" She approached the store, breathless. "Pauline?"

Mae opened her mouth to respond just as a solemn Benjamin opened the screen and focused on Trinity. She caught her breath and slowly lowered her bag to the ground. The air turned thick enough to slice with a knife.

"She's gone, hon."

"Gone?" Shaken to the core, Trinity blinked back hot tears. That couldn't be. Everything had been going so well! Jones had left, but he would be back. She had the deed — probably. God couldn't — *wouldn't* — let Pauline die now.

"When?" she managed.

"Thirty minutes ago. She's over to the church setting up weddin' plans. I told her I'd go with her but she had Fisk push her in one of those newfangled things on wheels. Wanted to plan the whole shebang without me."

Trinity clasped her hand to her heart. "Oh my goodness, Benjamin, don't ever say that Pauline's gone without saying where!"

He looked sheepish. "Sorry if I alarmed you."

Alarmed her? He'd scared the stuffing out of her! She hefted up the battered box. "I got it," she announced. She grinned when she heard Mae's appreciative squeal.

"You found the deed!"

"Not exactly. Maybe. I'm not certain. I haven't been able to open the box, but I will. We just need a key."

Mae nodded, then looked quizzically at the twisted metal box. "What happened? Did a train run over it?"

"No. I tried to break the lock." She shook her head. "There's always the remote chance that Pauline will know where the key is located." She shrugged. Even Trinity had to admit that wasn't likely. "I'm going to the church to see her. Care to come along?"

"Of course," said Mae. "This should be good."

Pauline was fast becoming the town entertainment.

They covered the ground between the store and the chapel that sat east of it. Trinity's excitement grew. "So it's true? Pauline's agreed to marry Benjamin?"

"It's true! I wish you'd been here — it was so sweet. He got down on one knee and asked her to please marry him and she accepted. Said there was nothing to gain by playing hard to get any longer. She didn't have the time or energy."

"Did she know what she was saying?"

"She said she did."

A giggle bubbled up in Trinity's throat. Soon — very soon, she prayed — Jones would reach the same conclusion. He had to. He would realize that once love struck there was little he could do but embrace it. Already she missed him like a warm coat on a cold night, but would it take him as long to come to his senses and welcome love as it had for Pauline? She didn't want to wait seventy years for him to come back.

The women matched steps up the church stairs, and Pauline lifted her head when the two burst into the sanctuary. Slowly she labored to her feet. "Is someone robbing the bank?"

"No." Trinity was appalled to see that she was dressed in the same stained pink housecoat she favored. "Tom should never have bought that for her," she said out of the corner of her mouth.

"I know. But she takes such pride in owning it. It was lovely once — before she butchered a bull in it."

"I hope she doesn't plan to wear it for bridal attire."

"Oh, surely she wouldn't." Mae frowned. "I must speak to her about the possibility."

As the women approached the altar Pauline focused and broke into a smile as she recognized them. "Well, it's my kin! Hello!"

"Hello, Aunt Pauline." Trinity planted a kiss on her forehead. "I understand a great deal has happened since I left."

"You been gone?"

"Yes, for a few days."

"Where'd you go? Hawaii?"

"Hawaii?" She glanced at Mae. "No, I went to Wilson's Falls."

"Wilson's Falls. Believe I've heard of the place. It's overseas, ain't it?"

Mae took her arm and smiled at the waiting reverend. "We hated to interrupt, but we need to ask Pauline a question."

Releasing a breath, the man nodded. "Good luck."

"Pauline," said Trinity, carefully guiding her aunt back to the pew, "I need for you to think real hard. Your recollection about the bank box being in Piedmont was correct . . ."

The elderly woman broke into a grin. "It was!"

"It was, and I brought it back with me." She held it up for inspection.

Pauline eyed the box warily. "It's beat all to thunder."

"Yes. I've had . . . a bit of difficulty opening it, and I need to know what it contains."

Pauline nodded. "What's in there?"

"I don't know, but we'll both have an answer soon." Trinity took both wrinkled hands in hers and gazed into her eyes. "Where is the key to the box?"

335

Pauline took back a hand and reached into the pocket of her housecoat. "This key?" The object flashed in the sunlight streaming through the glass windowpane.

Burying her face in her hands, Trinity nearly wilted with relief. The chase was over — she'd found the key, and perhaps the deed! *Jones — we've found it!*

"Have you always carried that key in your pocket?" exclaimed Mae.

"Only since Tom gave me the housecoat." She rubbed the worn fabric and preened. "It's my favorite dress." Glancing up, she lifted a brow. "Say, where's that nice feller that's been keeping you company?"

Trinity took the key and reached for the box. "He's off on business, Aunt Pauline. He'll be back soon." She prayed.

"Well, he's a fine man. Like my Benjamin. Helpful. Solid. Real good to me. You ought not to let him get away, young'un."

"I'm doing my best," Trinity murmured, though she could easily be feeding false hope. For the first time in days her faith slipped a notch. Jones was gone, and maybe she just had to accept what she couldn't change. She'd been so certain he wouldn't leave, so convinced that what they shared was mutual and lasting. She wanted to hold on to hope, to pray for his love, but right now she had a sinking feeling that he wouldn't be back. Everyone she loved left her.

She slipped the key into the lock and heard a soft click. Slowly opening the lid, she blinked and stared. And blinked again. Reaching out, she picked up the box's lone object and held it up between her fingers for inspection.

The reverend cleared his throat. "A mustard seed?"

Pauline nodded happily. "Priss gave it to me when we were little. Said to keep it safe because if I had the faith of a mustard seed, I'd be pleasing to the Lord." She lifted her eyes to meet Trinity's. "It's yours now."

A lump formed in Trinity's throat. All the journeys, all the angst, all the tears, all the time spent chasing the deed had been in vain. *But not entirely,* she thought. In the pursuit of the deed, she had found family and gained love — and wisdom, in the form of a tiny seed. Instead of a financial windfall, the good Lord had given everyone present a good dose of humility — one she sorely needed.

No doubt about it, the box contained treasure in its purest form — the kind greed couldn't erode.

The evening found Mae and Trinity sitting on the Curtises' porch drinking lemonade. "It's been quite a day," Mae was saying. "Quite a year, actually."

"Are you feeling better tonight?" Trinity had noticed that she'd barely eaten two bites of her dinner.

"Still a little queasy, but the doctor says it could pass in time."

"Tom could talk of nothing but the baby tonight. He's so certain it's a boy."

A smile lit Mae's face. "He's so excited about this child. I've never seen the like. Maybe it's because we're a little older than most newlyweds and we know what happiness children can bring into a person's life."

"Sounds to me like this little one will have lots of brothers and sisters."

"If Tom has his say, I guess you'd be about right."

Trinity smiled and fixed her eyes on the soft summer sky. Where was Jones tonight? Riding further away from her? Struggling with his emotions? She prayed it was the latter, but she knew the man too well. He was afraid of love. He was terrified of handing his feelings over to another person, and she couldn't imagine how he'd feel about having children. But folks didn't get to make their own decisions about life.

"Do you think he'll come back?" Trinity whispered in the silence of the porch. She knew full well that Mae would encourage her, not wanting to take away her new friend's last hope. But she didn't.

"I don't know," Mae said. "Tom said Jones has always been a loner, a hard man to figure out, but Trinity — if he doesn't come back he isn't the man God intends for you."

She knew Mae was sincere, but sitting in a sinking boat with no life jacket was different from standing on the shore and watching the boat go down.

"Maybe God doesn't intend any man for me." She fixed her eyes on the North Star, wondering if Jones was looking at it too. Thinking of her? Or stubbornly intent on running away from the things Trinity threatened — love, stability, and family?

"Perhaps not, but if He does He'll make that man quite evident in your life."

Silence settled over the two women. It was a long while before Trinity spoke. "I wonder if there ever was a deed."

"We'll get the lawyer back and convince Pauline to sign."

"I don't know if we should. I don't want

her more confused or distracted. I pray the time she has left will be nothing but happy ones with Benjamin."

"That's my prayer as well. They both waited a long time to find true happiness."

"Perhaps that's what it takes. Time."

"To find happiness?"

"Yes."

"I was beginning to think I would never find the right man when Tom happened along."

"But the Lord is good."

"And faithful."

"Ever faithful."

Trinity had to cling to that hope tonight, no matter how small it seemed.

TWENTY-FIVE

"Ms. Wilson, I do declare. You look as pretty as a young widow with her wood cut."

Pauline grunted. "Are you gonna wash up before you come to my weddin'?"

Lil curtsied. "Yes, ma'am, I shore am. Gonna take care of that right now. Gonna comb my hair, spitwash my face, and put on my finest dress." The pig farmer stuck out her tongue at Fisk as she swept around him. He returned the gesture.

The hour had come, and Pauline and Benjamin were about to pledge their eternal love to each other along the beautiful banks of the river. The half-finished home for the elderly stretched along the placid water, a reminder of new things to come.

If Trinity had handpicked this day, she couldn't have imagined anything more perfect than the one provided. The temperatures were beginning to cool and the first hint of fall filled the air. An azure sky provided a canopy, nature offered fields of goldenrod, and the good earth had supplied the contents of the dishes steaming on the long rows of tables bedecked in white tablecloths. Cakes, apple pies, and ginger-bread waited to be consumed. It seemed that all of Dwadlo had turned out to witness Benjamin and Pauline's vows.

Trinity reached out to smooth Pauline's white hair, placing a pearl comb just so. She had carefully dressed in a lovely, soft, honey-colored gown that fell in graceful folds to her feet. Trinity was dressed in a darker shade of warm gold with a large, wide-brimmed hat. She carried the Wilson family Bible. Everything just seemed so . . . family.

The nursing home wouldn't be finished to accept the new bride and groom, but Fisk had graciously offered to bunk in with Dale at the post office so the newlyweds could enjoy private quarters.

"Don't know why we'd need privacy," Pauline told the assembled guests.

"Hush." Trinity reached for her hand and the guitars struck the first cord, a melodic warning that the bridal procession was about to begin.

Pauline clung feebly to Trinity's arm. "Where are we goin'?"

Smiling for the congregation, Trinity

342

whispered from the corner of her mouth. "We're getting married, Aunt Pauline. Smile."

She gave her a strange look.

"Not *we*," Trinity corrected, her smile fixed in place. "You. You are marrying Benjamin."

"That young whippersnapper? I thought I told him to stop comin' around."

"Now Pauline, you know you're in love with him."

"Well. I suppose I might have feelin's for him, but Ma told me that a real lady shouldn't be overly forward."

"I believe it's perfectly acceptable for you to show your feelings for Benjamin. He's a good man, and he loves you deeply."

If only Jones would pursue her half as fervently as Benjamin had pursued his bride. She'd watched out the mercantile window for the past two days for Jones to appear, but there'd been no sign of him or Sue. *The faith of a mustard seed.* Tiny — and so difficult to hold onto. *God, forgive me. I'm looking to Jones to strengthen my faith when I realize that it's You I need to look to. Give me the wisdom to accept with gratitude whatever You have planned for my life.*

"How far are we goin'? My bunion's actin' up today."

"Not much further." Before the ceremony Benjamin had asked that they keep the festivities brief. His gout was giving him fits.

"I have a surprise for you," Pauline said.

"That's nice. We're almost there, now," Trinity urged.

"You'll like it."

"I'm sure I will, but today is *your* special day."

"My surprise is really going to be a surprise."

"Hush. People are staring." Trinity smiled at the assembled onlookers.

As they approached the altar the music swelled. Trinity caught sight of Benjamin accompanied by two men dressed in their Sunday best. The older gentleman looked spry and happy clothed in dark trousers and a waistcoat, and she'd never seen Tom looking more handsome. The crowd was blocking the second man for the moment. Lil, Mae, and Jeremy waved, wreathed in smiles, from where they stood in the shade. True to her word, Lil had cleaned up. The light rose dress and pink hair ribbon softened her features and she looked downright comely. If it weren't for her boots, still covered in muck, Fisk just might recognize what he was missing.

The crowd shifted and the second man came into full view. Harry Strauss — a young farmer who came into the post office frequently. He and Benjamin must have taken to each other.

Pauline steadied her arm. "Did you expect to see your feller? You got to play hard to get, girl. Your feelin's show on your face. Hey, don't swoon on me. I ain't got the strength to keep us both on our feet."

"I'm sorry, Aunt Pauline. I just love him so much." She couldn't cry now, not in front of all these people! This was Pauline's day.

"And he loves you."

She whirled when she heard the familiar baritone. Jones was trailing her down the aisle, looking better than any man had a right to look in his wedding finery. "Jones?" Were her eyes playing tricks on her? Did she want him so badly that she'd begun to hallucinate?

He took her hand. "Since folks are gathered here for Pauline and Benjamin, we need to keep this brief. I love you, Trinity Franklin. I'm sorry I caused you pain, but sometimes a man has to convince himself of what he knows to be the truth." He smiled at her aunt. "You did well keeping a secret, Pauline."

"Shucks. Weren't hard for me. I didn't remember you were comin' until a minute ago."

Stunned, Trinity whispered, praying his answer would be the one she desperately needed to hear, "And that truth is?"

"That I am awfully in love with you."

"Awfully?"

His eyes devoured her. "Knee-deep and getting more so every moment."

"Me too," she said softly.

The gathered guests sat transfixed, smiling. Waiting.

"Take your time," Benjamin offered from up front. "Just finish up in time for me to get a nap in before the party."

"If it's all right with the reverend" — Jones looked at the preacher — "and Benjamin doesn't object, I wonder if you'd join me in holy matrimony? I've been doing a lot of thinking about what you said the other night. Wilson's Falls would make a good home for our children. I gave Pauline a voucher for the land last night. It's mine. Ours. Now what I need for you to say is that you love me, and you forgive me for being a little slow, and more importantly that you're willing to spend the rest of your life with me. What do you think?"

She caught her breath. "I think you're being pretty arrogant. You think you can just keep riding off, telling me you won't be back, and then showing up and asking me to marry you? Do you take me for a complete fool?"

"No, ma'am." He took a step closer. "But if you take a chance on me, I'll make you the best husband this side of the Mississippi. And" — he continued as she held up a finger to interrupt — "I can sincerely promise that there will be no more riding off, and no more wondering if I'll be back." His gaze locked with hers. "I'm back. No reservations, no qualms. I'm a man deeply in love and I don't reckon fifty or sixty years is overstating my intentions."

It was the grin that got her. That cocky, self-assured grin. He was always so sure of himself, but now he was publicly handing his life, his hopes, and his dreams over to her — not an easy concession for a man called Jones.

Sniffling, she broke into a slow smile, tears blurring her vision. "You're impossible. Do you know that?"

He nodded, his gaze locked with hers. "Why don't you marry me and change my ways?"

"Right now? Right this moment? In the middle of Benjamin and Pauline's vows?"

"We're not getting any younger."

"True." Trinity glanced at Pauline, a question in her eyes.

Her aunt smiled. "Go get him, girl. Ain't nobody but the whole town lookin'."

Stepping into Jones's arms, she drank in his essence. He smelled so good today, clean and soapy. Oh, how she had missed him! Loved him with all her heart! Fifty or sixty years together wouldn't be nearly enough. Never had she been so glad that God had allowed her time to find this man — this one special man.

"I take this to mean you accept my proposal?" He kissed her softly along her hairline. "I love you, Trinity. And I've missed you like the dickens." He squeezed her so hard the breath almost left her.

"I accept your rather hasty proposal. Completely and forever," she confessed. Their mouths came together and remained for a long, uninterrupted kiss. The gathered guests broke into applause.

The minister cleared his throat. "Shall we begin? Seems we have a full agenda this afternoon."

Pauline covered the remaining distance to the altar. She met Benjamin, and the four blue-veined hands joined together. Trinity and Jones stood together, waiting. What had started out as a beautiful day had turned into a magnificent one.

"Wait!" Mae held up a hand. Slipping from her bench she came to stand beside Trinity. Squeezing her arm, she whispered, "A girl can't get married without a matron of honor."

Smiling, Trinity gazed up at her groom. She didn't need anything. She had all that she wanted, forevermore and amen.

DISCUSSION QUESTIONS

1. Trinity and Jones both had difficult child-
hoods, and their youthful struggles influenced the types of people they became.
Do you still struggle with childhood fears?
How has your past influenced the person
you've become?

2. Trinity is initially very hostile toward
Jones. When have you judged someone
based on a first impression? Was your
initial judgment correct? If not, what happened to change your opinion?

3. Trinity didn't come to Dwadlo expecting
to care for an aging aunt, but she turns
her life around in order to do just that. If
you had a distant relative who needed
care, how would you respond?

4. Benjamin and Pauline find love together
after decades apart. Describe a time when

you saw love blossom over time.

5. Jones is reluctant to get married because of his experience with his stepmother. Have you ever hesitated to take a risk out of the fear that you'll make a mistake?

6. Trinity says that she'd thought Jones stuffing her into a barrel was "the end of the world, but it had proven to be the start of a brand new future." Have you ever experienced a setback only to find that God was leading you down a new path?

7. When circumstances aren't going her way, Trinity begins to doubt God's providence. Have you ever doubted that God was looking out for you? How did He show that He was there all along?

8. When Trinity's father returns, her first instinct is to lash out in anger. After she hears his story, though, she is ready to forgive him. If you were in Trinity's place, would you have forgiven him? Why or why not?

9. Trinity and Jones both feel that there's a "missing ingredient" in their lives — love. Is there a missing ingredient in your life?

If so, what is it?

10. If you could glean one specific personal or spiritual lesson from this story, what would it be?

ABOUT THE AUTHOR

Lori Copeland is the author of more than 90 titles, both historical and contemporary fiction. With more than 3 million copies of her books in print, she has developed a loyal following among her rapidly growing fans in the inspirational market. She has been honored with the *Romantic Times* Reviewer's Choice Award, The Holt Medallion, and Walden Books' Best Seller award. In 2000, Lori was inducted into the Missouri Writers Hall of Fame.

She lives in the beautiful Ozarks with her husband, Lance, and their three children and five grandchildren.

The employees of Thorndike Press hope you have enjoyed this Large Print book. All our Thorndike, Wheeler, and Kennebec Large Print titles are designed for easy reading, and all our books are made to last. Other Thorndike Press Large Print books are available at your library, through selected bookstores, or directly from us.

For information about titles, please call:
  (800) 223-1244

or visit our Web site at:
  http://gale.cengage.com/thorndike

To share your comments, please write:
  Publisher
  Thorndike Press
  10 Water St., Suite 310
  Waterville, ME 04901